# NOTH
# SINCE THE GREAT FLOOD!

*World War III had arrived! This is an epic story of America under siege—the dark days when she fought for her very survival and a chance at a new beginning. Because of atomic bombs, The United States and much of the world were flooded with waters from the melting polar ice caps. But here and there were a few people who refused to be the world's pallbearers.*

*Rog Phillips was one of the most prolific sci-fi writers from the golden age of pulp magazines. Here he spins a grim tale of Cold War science fiction…*

**FOR A SECOND COMPLETE NOVEL, TURN TO PAGE 85**

# CAST OF CHARACTERS

## NEAL LOOMIS

*He was a simple air force pilot before he became the key man in the government's plan for ending World War Three.*

## EINAR THARNSEN

*The war had caused him to lose everything—including his wife and children. Being thrown into prison didn't help matters either.*

## GEORGE LORD

*He was a revolutionary fighting for the downtrodden men of America, but was that all he was fighting for?*

## MARVIN SWANK

*He was just trying to reunite a broken family, but the timing of it might be crucial to the future of the country.*

## HARRY DRAKE

*He was a prisoner with a BIG mouth. Unfortunately it got him into BIG trouble.*

## CHARLIE ADAMS

*He was a hospital patient who had fallen for his beautiful nurse. Naturally he tried to set her up with the guy in the next bed!*

## FRANCES

*She was torn between her love for a helpless paraplegic and a happily married man.*

# WHO SOWS THE WIND

By
ROG PHILLIPS

ARMCHAIR FICTION & MUSIC
PO Box 4369, Medford, Oregon 97504

*The original text of this novel was first published by Ziff-Davis Publishing*



*For more information about Armchair Books and products, visit our website at…*

**www.armchairfiction.com**

*Or email us at…*

**armchairfiction@yahoo.com**

# CHAPTER ONE

NEAL LOOMIS had the uncanny feeling that he was a disembodied spirit hovering over the snake-like, slowly moving streams of humanity far below. The feeling didn't leave even when he manipulated the controls that sent him plummeting straight down, to halt abruptly five hundred feet above the trouble spot he had discovered, looking down upon individual dots that were men, while those dots glanced upward at the plasti-nosed jetcoptor carrying him.

Automatically he flicked on the radio and called base. "Loomis," he identified himself. "Slide twenty miles south of point seventy-one point four. Route seven. Ambulances and excavating equipment needed. Terrain—mud."

He listened to the playback, grunted his "Okay," and flicked the mike over to the P.A. speakers.

"Help is on the way," he said into the mike; and outside the coptor his voice boomed thunderously. "Ambulances and excavating equipment will be here by freightcoptor within an hour."

He grinned mirthlessly as he saw microscopic arms far below wave their gratitude for his prompt action. Touching the controls, he dropped still lower.

Most of the dots down there were men. Men walking from Duluth, too impatient to wait their turn on the busses, or anxious to get to the Arctic and find a place for their families before the women and children arrived by bus.

The slide, Neal saw, was a bad one. An embankment of the gorge, which the ribbon of humanity had been flowing through, had given way, washing down over the trail for a distance of two hundred yards and engulfing a hundred or more.

But now a new danger threatened. With those in back along

the route still coming forward, in another hour there would be thousands at this spot. Such a weight would probably cause more cave-ins.

He whirled his jetcoptor about and sped down the line with his P.A. system on, ordering the column to stop its march because of trouble ahead. He followed the line back this way for five miles until he reached a broad flat where there would be no possibility of cave-in. On his way back he saw with satisfaction that most had complied with his order. The few who pushed on out of curiosity to see what had happened, dropped back into line as he explained briefly there had been a cave-in.

The first of the freightcoptors was settling gently. There was a bold white cross on it. It would have doctors, nurses and a complete emergency setup on board.

"Calling three-seven-seven," the radio said. Neal flicked the radio over.

"Three-seven-seven," he said, "Go ahead."

"Go to aid of two-four-three on route six, at point seventy-one point two. Fighting going on."

Neal climbed to five thousand, shut off and retracted the lift blades, and—taking a deep breath—turned on the jets. The air speed indicator rose rapidly to five-fifty and held there. The barren landscape below slid underneath unrealistically. Abruptly there was another column of human ants ahead, then underneath as he banked northward. Ahead he saw the island of milling men. He shot upward in a steep climb and shut off the jets. When air speed dropped to a hundred, he extended the lift blades and pressed the button that activated the coptor motor.

Then he was dropping almost in free fall to where he could see another jetcoptor hovering.

"Two-four-three," an excited voice erupted from the radio, "Carl Adams. What shall I do?"

"I'll do it," Neal said, "Stay where you are and report my arrival." While he said this he dropped below the other coptor and brought up fifty feet above the melee of struggling men. He flicked on his P.A. and said, "I'll give you all five seconds to stop your fighting and get moving. Then I'll gas you." His voice boomed out underneath the coptor. "One! Two! Three! Four! Five!"

While he spoke, he broke out his binoculars and studied the men below. One man, standing apart from the others and surrounded by a compact group of half a dozen men, had been evidently shouting at the fighting mob. He now was looking upward, shaking his fist and shouting something. Abruptly he whipped out something dark. A flash of flame erupted; A second later there was a plunk from somewhere behind Neal, followed by the sharp report from below.

Neal opened the tear gas cocks and gyrated over the mob, the lift blades sending the stuff downward. He did this with one hand while he broke out his gas mask with the other, constantly keeping his eyes on the man who had fired at him.

The gas was taking effect quickly. The fighting mob was now milling about in confusion as men became blinded and struck out wildly at friend and foe alike.

Neal used both hands to bring the jetcoptor over the leader. In a maneuver that had been drilled into him he opened the bottom hatch and dropped a rope about the man, jerking it taut. Seeing that it had landed just right, he started a gentle climb while pulling the man upward through the trap.

"Stop moving so much and let me handcuff you," Neal said calmly, "or I'll use a sap on you."

The man's reply was unprintable invective.

"Sorry," Neal murmured. He brought the leather-cased blackjack sharply against the man's scalp, and saw the flailing arms go limp.

THE NAME tattooed on the unconscious man's chest was Einar Tharnsen. Neal handcuffed him to the frame of the plastidome, then slid a second pair of handcuffs around the pipe support of the seat and locked Einar's ankles.

With that done, he steadied the coptor and radioed his report. He was being told to bring the prisoner to base when Einar opened his eyes and shook his head groggily.

He tried to lift a hand to his eyes. Suddenly he became wide-awake. He took in the handcuffs—the bleak landscape far below.

"You're in for it now," Neal growled. "Why'd you do such a fool thing as to incite trouble? You should have known—"

"Sure," Einar said bitterly. "I should have known. You try walking for two weeks in stinking mud instead of sitting upstairs in your chrome-ornamented observation jetcoptor with its air-conditioning and thermos of hot coffee—"

"Where'd you get the gun?" Neal said. "You were searched before—"

"Wouldn't you like to know…" Einar taunted.

"Just curious," Neal murmured, "I don't know what they're going to do with you at base when I turn you over, but they can shoot you if they wish."

"And probably will," Einar said. "They're just that stupid. They've been nothing but stupid all along. I have a wife and four kids. What happens? They give my wife and kids passes on the bus and expect them to go up without me!"

"Why not?" Neal said, "The seat you wanted probably has some woman or child in it. You're lucky they let you start the trail. Maybe they'll send you back down to the States and let you die with the ones there won't be room for up north."

"Yes," Einar said. "While you ride around in your nice plane and have your bed at base made up by an orderly."

"According to you," Neal said, "we should all he riding around in jetcoptors or all be walking the trail together. If you were in my shoes I doubt if you'd land your coptor and join those going northward on foot."

"The whole thing's stupid," Einar said, "You soldiers don't deserve to be in the driver's seat while we citizens are herded like sheep. I know a lot more about it than a lot of people. I know, for instance, that the big brass knew they were wrecking the world when they dropped those bombs all over Europe. Plenty of people knew that DeVree tried to tell the Government what would happen, and was told that they knew what would happen, but had to make a choice between wrecking the world or submitting to world conquest."

"What choice would you have made?" Neal asked idly.

"Surrender," Einar said, "Slavery for a generation or two, then revolt. It would have worked. And Europe and the Mississippi Valley would still be livable."

"Me," Neal said, "I was drafted. I do what I'm told." He gave Einar a sidelong smile and said, "Maybe you'll learn to do the same."

Far below, the trail of human ants formed a narrow ribbon stretching from the southern horizon over the desolate lifeless terrain to the northern horizon. Neal retracted the suddenly stilled coptor blades. In the unnatural silence the wind could be heard whistling past the falling ship. Then, with a coughing snarl, the jets came to life, pressing both men firmly against the backs of their seats.

Neither spoke as the air speed indicator crept up to five-fifty and held there. The plastic-and-metal ship hurtled northward across landscape that—until two short years before—had not seen the light of day since before the dawn of known history, buried eternally, it was thought, under the ice and snow that was the arctic wasteland of the world before World War III.

EINAR THARNSEN paced the small cell impatiently. In spite of his frustration and anger he found himself curious about his surroundings. The walls and floor seemed made of mud blocks, yet when he rapped on them with his knuckles they gave off a solid sound like the best of concrete. And when he scraped against them with his fingernails surprisingly little scraped away. The only thing wrong with them from the structural standpoint was their exceeding ugliness of color.

There was no window, barred or otherwise. The door was of solid metal with a small square up at eye level with heavy wire mesh apparently welded in. Light in the cell came from a single neon tube, unprotected. Einar's heart had leaped when he first noticed this, then dropped as he realized that the reason it was unprotected was that if the prisoner in the cell wanted to monkey with it he would be left in darkness.

Footsteps had been going up and down outside the door all the time, so that Einar paid no attention to them. Now, suddenly, there was a scraping sound against his door. He whirled toward it, a mixture of emotions on his face.

A man fully as big as he was outside as the door swung open. Behind him were others, all in army uniform.

"All right, you," the big one said. "It's your turn in court. Get moving. The lieutenant will be mad if you keep him waiting."

"No breakfast before court?" Einar asked.

"Breakfast?" the sergeant said incredulously. He shook his head and then said, "The only prisoners that eat around here are those that art sentenced to be shot. Come on! Get moving."

The corridors and courtroom were of mud block construction—the same as the cell had been. As Einar entered and glanced quickly around he saw there were only three people in the room: Neal Loomis, a WAAC who was obviously a secretary, and a lieutenant, short and slight of frame but with an unusually high forehead and calm expressionless features.

As Einar paused, the sergeant wrapped a beefy hand around his arm and guided him forward to a spot directly in front of the lieutenant's desk.

"Your name?" the lieutenant asked.

"Einar Tharnsen."

"The charges against you have already been presented. Have you anything to say about them?"

"How do I know what they are?" Einar said defiantly. "I haven't heard them."

"They were factual," the lieutenant said coldly, "Where did you get the automatic you used to fire on an army plane?"

Einar gulped, suddenly nervous. The way that had been

stated made it sound bad, "Firing on an army plane!"

"I owned it," he said. "I brought it along with me because I didn't knew what I would be running into on the long trip up here."

The WAAC was writing rapidly in shorthand.

"Lieutenant Loomis reports that you seemed from the air to be inciting a riot. You were surrounded by what seemed to be bodyguards. You were shouting what may have been instructions to one faction of the rioters. Those are the appearances. Have you anything to add in the way of explanation?"

"I most certainly have," Einar said. "I am not going to name any names, but there was a tough punk with a half a dozen lizards in the group. The first week they won all our money—from all the rest of us. After that they made us take second place in everything. At night they took the pick of bunks in the rest camps. If they didn't have as much as they wanted to eat out of the rations doled out, they went around and made the rest of us fork over part of ours. We had to organize. I did the organizing. That riot was the showdown."

"That doesn't check with your actions. If that were true, why didn't you welcome the intervention of Lieutenant Loomis rather than try to shoot him down?"

"I didn't try to shoot him down," Einar said uncomfortably. "I thought he would shoot back up again and give us time to really clean up on those hoods before it was stopped. Instead—" he turned accusing eyes on Neal, "—he used tear gas."

The lieutenant turned to the WAAC secretary, "He is to be transferred to labor camp twenty-three for a minimum of six months," he dictated. "A report on his conduct must be filed with this court every Monday."

"But my wife and kids—" Einar said, dismayed.

"Will be taken care of by the machinery set up," the lieutenant snapped, suddenly showing irritation. "Lieutenant Loomis was of the opinion that you think we should run things for your special benefit. I can see why he was of that opinion." He leaned forward, placing his elbows on his desk and said, "I want to warn you, Mr. Tharnsen, that your sentence has a minimum, but no maximum. If you are mildly intractable you will never be free. If you are more than mildly intractable you will wind up before the firing squad. You should be grateful that you are being given a chance to survive, and your children and their children. Only a very small percentage of mankind gets this chance. But you—you criticize the conduct of the war, show continued defiance of authority, and seem unable to appreciate your privileged position and treatment. It is only the mercy of this court that prevents you from being sentenced to be shot—and the fact that we have a serious labor shortage in the mud block manufacturing industry."

His look at the beefy sergeant was an order to take the prisoner away.

## CHAPTER TWO

"GOOD MORNING, Lieutenant."

Neal snapped out of his reverie and glanced at the speaker. "Oh, hello, Marv," he said.

"Thinking about home?" Marvin Swank asked, grinning good-naturedly down from his height of well over six feet.

"As a matter of fact, no," Neal said. "I was thinking of a poor devil that just got sentenced to the labor camps."

"He's lucky," Marv said, "How about dropping into the canteen for a cup of coffee with me—or are you in a hurry?"

Neal glanced at his watch. "I guess I can take half an hour without getting court-martialed. How've you been, Marv?"

They fell into step and started down the street together.

"I'm in mourning," Marv said. "The last of the Texas Panhandle is under water since about twelve hours ago. In a way though I guess it's poetic justice."

"What do you mean?" Neal asked.

"I owned a thousand acres of Panhandle," Marv said. "I made the money I bought it with by selling underwater Florida real estate. Now my thousand acres are under water."

"Oh," Neal said, his mouth quirking into a half smile.

"The most interesting development though," Marv said, "is that the Atlantic and Pacific have gouged a channel through Honduras and Guatemala. They tried to delay it by blowing up a couple of mountains, but no soap."

"Well, that was inevitable," Neal said. "The mean level of the oceans in the tropics was eight feet above prewar normal six months ago and still rising."

"It'll be bad if the peninsula breakthrough washes a wide channel in a hurry," Marv said, pushing open the canteen door for Neal. "The Atlantic wash up the Mississippi Valley will become a tidal wave then, and probably extend the rest of the way up to the Canadian border. Funny about that, too. Maps of the United States are beginning to look quite a bit like prehistoric America."

The two men got in line with trays. Ten minutes later they were settled beside a window that looked out on the drab blocks of buildings and the equally drab street, all the color of mud.

"Things compensate though," Marvin Swank said, stirring his coffee. "The last of Texas goes under—and another thousand square miles of northern Greenland is dried out enough now for habitation. They're sowing it with wheat right now, in the hopes that enough of it will grow to hold the land in place. All this soil has been under ice so long there isn't any body to it to keep it from being washed away."

"Heard from your family?" Neal asked.

An expression of pain crossed Marvin Swank's lean features and was gone. He shrugged. "No news," he said, "But then, no news is good news. They're probably quite happy without me. How about your family?"

"No news yet," Neal said.

"Your wife, Annette, was in St. Louis wasn't she?" Marvin asked.

"Up until a week before the first tidal wave rolled over it," Neal said tonelessly, "That's the last letter I got from her. She told me about the bombing. It got our house. She was living with some friends just off Lindell Boulevard near Forest Park. Poor kid…she was trying to cheer me up by telling me all about how Joan and Frank ran wild over the zoo."

"She had the car, didn't she?" Marv said. "In all probability she got away safely to the high ground of the Ozarks."

"But—damn it—that was six months ago!" Neal said. He took a deep breath and got hold of himself. "Let's change the subject," he growled, "Sometimes I can almost feel the way Einar Tharnsen feels."

"Who's he?" Marv asked.

"The prisoner in court this morning," Neal said, "He sort of felt the army should move heaven and earth for him so he could be with his family. Maybe I should have told him the reason my own wife isn't safely up here is because the army feels it must lean over backward not to show discrimination toward families of its personnel." He looked at his watch. "Got to get going," he said, shoving his chair back and rising.

"Me, too," Marvin said, "We'll check in about ten thousand new arrivals today, according to estimates."

NEAL SENT his jetcoptor straight up to five thousand feet. Below, the growing mass of base sprawled out over several square miles, a geometric pattern in the dark mud. To the north there was a different kind of pattern where tiers of cement-impregnated mud blocks were stacked up to dry, with portable wind generators lined up beside them. It was labor camp twenty-three—the one where Einar Tharnsen had been sent.

The feeling of being disembodied and suspended in thin air began to be felt. With a feather touch on the controls Neal swung the jetcoptor slowly around, carefully surveying the landscape below and the far-flung horizon.

Several miles to the south the head of the main ribbon of migrants on foot was slowly approaching, giving the impression of being the forward end of some gigantic worm slowly slithering along.

To the west there was the occasional glint of sunlight

reflecting from patrol craft. Idly Neal wondered if the Russians from their bases in Alaska were planning an attack. Probably not. Reports were that they were too preoccupied with survival there as the last of the ancient ice floes sent vicious torrents down through the newly naked valleys. And two thousand miles was too great a distance for heckling operations. That was one of the reasons why base had been established three hundred miles north of Chesterfield in a large plane of what had once been Hudson Bay. That, and the fact that the spot was the ideal radiating point for the vast lands opening up by the melting of the arctic snow and glaciers and the emptying of the thousands of square miles of inland seas.

Still, why were there so many fighter patrol craft out and about at this time? Neal shrugged off the question uneasily as he stopped the motor and retracted the lift blades while the jetcoptor plummeted in free fall. A moment later and the jets were blasting in full thrust, the air speed indicator reaching toward the five-fifty point.

Below, the ribbon of human ants branched into three narrower ones. Five hundred miles to the southward they would further branch, until they were divided into perhaps fifty separate streams originating from as many points of the Canadian-American border.

From ahead came the glint of another patrol jetcoptor, and lower down, to the east, a huge freightcoptor moved along like an overgrown bumble bee, "Maybe it's from that slide I reported yesterday," Neal thought.

"Calling three-seven-seven," the radio said suddenly.

Neal flicked the radio over, "Three-seven-seven," he said, "Come in."

"Base hospital reports your wife has a baby," the radio said, "I hope you thought to buy cigars for the event."

"A boy or girl?" Neal asked, suddenly tense.

"No definite report on that yet. Several of the babies are girls, but which is yours, I don't know. Anyway, congratulations, I'll be seeing you—I hope."

Neal looked anxiously to the west. There wasn't a sign of anything yet. Throwing in the autopilot, he got out of his seat and climbed out of the plastinose into the center-of-gravity section.

He had known his armament would be in order, but he wanted to make certain. The *cigars* glistened dully, target-seeking rocket missiles in racks where they would feed automatically into the firing tubes.

With a grunt of satisfaction, Neal returned to his seat at the controls. A hasty glance to the westward reassured him. The sky was still empty. He fastened his seat harness. Now if his plane were hit he could press the seat ejector stud and be free of the plane.

He glanced toward the west again, tensely. What would he get? A "girl" —a relatively slow duster-type plane? Or a "boy"—one of the jet fighters? Neither, he hoped. But one might get through the fighter net and try to run along several miles of the rivers of men, spreading radioactive dust or virus dust.

Or they might have an entirely new weapon to try out. That would be more likely. The radioactives and virus dusts were pretty much a waste of time now with the G.I. germicide masks and the new plasma technique.

With startling abruptness Neal found himself staring at a plane with the same feeling he would have staring into the barrel of a gun. And it was remarkably similar in shape!

HE DID two things simultaneously. He pressed the firing stud on the control panel. He pressed the stud that would bring out the lift blades.

There was a still-photograph memory of his target-seeking rocket exploding near the enemy plane. It hung stationary in his vision as he felt himself thrown violently forward.

The violence of his forward motion jerked his hand from the stud. There was a long moment of utterly dizzy flight before the lift blades retracted from their partial extension and the autopilot sought and found a steady course.

There was another long second while he got used to the idea of still being alive. As he looked around outside for some sign of the enemy plane a strange calm took possession of him. He welcomed it. He had possessed it before in air combat. Sometimes he had wondered at it, wondered if it were something new or the same as the calm that may have possessed all men fighting for their lives under the constant presence of death, even in the days when such fighting took place on horseback or on foot.

There was no sign of a burning plane streaking toward the ground. That meant the attacking plane hadn't been hit mortally. Below, the ribbon of men was flowing out into a wide, indistinguishable blot as the migrants recognized their danger and spread out to minimize it.

From the north a plane appeared, following the line of the migrants' trail. Behind it a widening cloud of white streamed. In split seconds Neal turned his plane in its direction and fired. This time there could be no miss. The target-seeking rocket would have an appreciable fraction of a second to get its bearings and locate its target.

The "girl" saw its danger and pointed upward to escape at the last instant, then disrupted into flying bits of metal.

"Gawd…it's quick!" Neal muttered, "I'll never get used to it. Never!"

Another plane appeared. His heart stopped. Then he recognized the familiar lines of an American fighter. There were others now. The sky was full of them.

Neal sent his plane into a steep climb and shut off the jets. The airspeed dropped. At a hundred he sent out the lift blades and started the motor. His role now would be that of decoy if any enemy pilot were inexperienced enough to want to make him a target.

The danger was far from over, but the fight was out of his hands now. He deliberately forced himself to ignore it and concentrate on what lay below.

The streamer of cloud the enemy plane had laid out was resolving itself into individual parts now. Parts that fluttered and fell slowly.

"Papers!" Neal grunted.

He dropped his jetcoptor toward the mass of fluttering slips of paper. They shied away from him as he sank into them. He had to drop all the way down and get out of the plane to get one.

"Huh?" he grunted as he read it.

*Comrades of America. Revolt against your warlord slave-masters who have brought ruin to the world. Unite with us for peace and brotherhood. There is room for us all. Destroy this note and bide your time until we come to help you liberate yourselves.*

It was signed, *The People's Army.*

Neal contacted base and read it.

"Turn it in at the end of your day," came the instructions. "We can find out all sorts of things from it."

"Right," Neal said.

He folded it carefully and put it in his billfold, then lifted the jetcoptor and began his patrol. Half an hour later he passed over the landslide of the day before. The ribbon of men had been routed around it. Huge machinery was clearing it away in a futile search for victims that might still, by some miracle, be alive.

It was nearly four hours before his hands began to itch a little and he looked down and saw the green blotches on them.

## CHAPTER THREE

"SUCH AN old trick," Dr. Green said sadly. "But maybe that's why it succeeded. The first thing I would have thought of with those pamphlets was disease or chemicals."

Neal made no answer.

"And such an interesting new disease," Dr. Green went on. "Gangrene in healthy tissue…"

"Gangrene?" Neal said.

"Yes, that's right. Gangrene…and we're going to have to act fast. I think it works only by contact and by spreading from cell to cell. We'll save enough of the infected areas of your skin to study it. You will undress now. Be careful you touch no other parts of your skin with your fingers. Your face?" The doctor became suddenly concerned. "I hope you haven't touched your face!"

"I—I don't think so," Neal said.

"After I saw the blotches I didn't anything, naturally. Before that I'm not sure."

"There seems to be no infection on your face," Dr. Green said. "If you haven't touched it there won't be…perhaps. Here, Dr. Ohrman," he said to the intern beside him. "Help him undress. Put some rubber gloves on so you won't catch it. Take him to the surgery and put him under anesthetic, then cauterize a narrow band around each infected area back far enough into the healthy flesh to make sure it's confined. I'll be up shortly after I've informed base and given them instructions for dealing with the migrants and destroying the pamphlets. This may be more serious than we think. We must act quickly."

He left the room, taking his calmness with him.

"Sit down and hold your hands out away from you," Dr. Ohrman said, going to a drawer and taking out a pair of red rubber gloves.

Neal took in the paleness of the intern's features and sensed the man's panic. A little of it spread to him.

"What's making you so frightened?" he asked as he sat down. "After all, gangrene is an old ailment. Surely you doctors can handle it?"

"Of course. Of course," Dr. Ohrman said, giving Neal a smile that was meant to be reassuring, "We'll find out all about it and learn to handle it effectively."

"It's just the same old disease stepped up in virulency, isn't it?" Neal persisted as the intern unlaced his shoes and pulled them off.

"Of course," Dr. Ohrman said, not looking up from his task.

"Now we will slip off your trousers…"

"NOW WE will slip off your trousers."

Neal came fully awake at the words. It took a moment to place them, then memory flooded into his mind. He opened his eyes and looked up at the ceiling. It was white enamel. Some reason for that. Oh yes, he was in the hospital!

"My hands!" he thought. He lifted his head to look at them. They stretched beside his body, but on top of the sheets. He studied the bandages anxiously until he was sure they outlined un-amputated hands and arms.

"I must have dreamed they chopped them off!" he thought, his head sinking back onto the pillow in the weakness of relief.

The door opened. A pretty brunette came in.

"He's awake now," a voice sounded to the right.

Neal looked from the nurse to the owner of the voice. For the first time he became aware that there were others around him. He was in a large ward.

He looked back toward the door but the nurse was gone.

"How do you feel?" the man in the next bed said cheerfully, "Brother, you've sure been through hell this past week. Kept me awake darn near every night."

Neal jerked back to look at the man, saw the unnatural flatness of the sheets below the man's hips.

"Yeah, lost my legs. Both of them," the man said. "A cave-in on route seven."

"I saw that," Neal said, "I was the patrol that reported it."

"Thanks," the man said. "Guess I owe my life to you. The doc said if he'd gotten there fifteen minutes later I'd have been dead. By the way, my name's Adams…Charlie Adams. Yours?"

"Neal Loomis," Neal said.

"Glad to know you, Neal," Charlie Adams said gravely, "I'm sorry I said that about you keeping me awake nights. You sort of have a right to since I owe my life to you. Anyway, I guess maybe it was the itching on my stubs that kept me…" His voice trailed off as the door opened again and the doctor came in, followed by the nurse and the intern.

"SO YOU'RE awake?" Dr. Green said cheerfully. "That's fine. We've had a lot of trouble with you. Remember any of it?"

"A little," Neal said. "Not much. And most of what I seem to remember seems more like dreams."

"It'll straighten out," Dr. Green said, "You were luckier than most of the others that picked up those pamphlets. That was because we got you hours earlier."

"How long have I been here?" Neal asked, "It seems like only hours, but this man next to me—Charlie Adams—he—"

"Yes?" Dr. Green said.

"Well—he seems to have been here quite some time, and I know he must have been brought here less than twenty-four hours before I was."

"I've been here three weeks," Charlie Adams spoke up.

Dr. Green frowned at the man, then nodded. "Yes, you've been here three weeks, Loomis. It took time to find anything that would touch the disease. It was in your bloodstream, of course. We cut off all the infected skin, but it didn't do any good. Still, with that skin we finally found the counteragent and saved you. Wish I could say the same for the other victims."

"How—how many were there?" Neal asked.

"More than there should have been," Dr. Green said. "But we're ready for any new attacks."

"How many?" Neal repeated. He had shouted it, and now was surprised and a little alarmed at himself because he had had no intention of shouting. He wasn't even angry, but his voice had been hoarse with anger.

"Quick, Dr. Ohrman," Dr. Green said.

Neal saw the two doctors spring toward him, one on each side of the bed.

"Get the hypo, Miss Phelps," Dr. Green said jerkily.

Neal's mind was numbed by the utterly fantastic contradictions it was observing. He was quite calm—but he could feel the muscles of his face contorting with rage. He was giving no orders to his muscles, but it took both doctors to hold his shoulders and arms pinned down.

Everything about him seemed to have developed a will and mind of its own.

A slow lassitude seeped into the flesh of his left shoulder. It spread rapidly. He felt the lingering withdrawal of the doctor's fingers from his shoulder.

"At least it's an improvement," he heard Dr. Green say, "I tend to think that's the first time true consciousness has manifested itself. Dissociation was showing in his expression. That's something…"

Neal waited a long time for Dr. Green to finish his thought before he realized he had been asleep.

"Are you awake?" a voice sounded. "They told me to watch your eyelids. When they show your eyes moving underneath you're awake."

It was Charlie Adams, "Yes, I'm awake," Neal said. He opened his eyes and smiled ashamedly at him. "I guess I made an ass of myself."

"You couldn't help it," Charlie said.

"I don't know what hit me," Neal said. "I wasn't mad—"

"The doctor said something about your subconscious going wild," Charlie explained helpfully. "He says it's a little loose or something. He sort of forgot anyone was around to hear him, and was talking to Ohrman about some of the others that have got what you've got. Raging wild beasts while they cry for someone to stop them."

"That'll be enough, Charlie," a feminine voice said.

Neal turned his head. The brunette nurse had come in. She smiled at him and walked up to stand beside his bed. He smiled back, a part of him wondering why she hadn't called the doctor in case he had another attack.

"We have you nicely secured so your body can't act up," she said, reading his thoughts.

He glanced down and saw the straps around his chest and

arms.

"Oh," he said. He glanced up at her, "What came over me? I can't understand it..."

"It's a nerve virus," she said, "Something quite new. *They* found it first. The gangrene was only a symptom caused by its giving the skin cells a bad case of the jitters. But don't worry, you're quite definitely going to be all right again."

"Her name's Francis," Charlie Adams said eagerly. "And if you ask me, she's fallen for you, Neal. You ought to see the way she stands and watches you."

A slow flush spread over the nurse's face. Her eyes withstood Neal's stare for a moment, then lowered.

"Shut up, Charlie," Neal said.

Sometime later Marvin Swank came by.

"Hi, goldbricker," Marvin said as he fidgeted with his cap and smiled down at Neal.

"Hey, Marv," Neal said. "Take a load off your feet and tell me what's going on. By the way, this eager eyed pup in the next bed is Charlie Adams. He was walking up, got tired of walking, and stuck his legs under a landslide."

"Smart lad," Marvin said, nodding cheerfully at Charlie, "They'd have been worn down to the hips by the time you got here anyway. This way you got a ride. By the way, where are you from?"

"California, Bakersfield."

"Oh," Marvin said, disappointed, "Ever been to Amarillo?"

"Yeah," Charlie said, "I was working there for about six months before I started up here."

"Yeah?" Marv said, hope dawning in his eyes, "You didn't by any chance ever hear of Thelma Swank did you? She had a dress shop on Polk Street..."

"No," Charlie said, "A relative of yours?"

"My wife," Marvin said, "I haven't heard from her."

Charlie looked at Marvin thoughtfully. "I wouldn't worry about her," he said. "I was there when the water came in. There was plenty of warning, and nobody got hurt as far as I know."

"Thanks," Marvin said. He turned back to Neal. "They tell me you picked up one of those Russian pamphlets with the nerve virus on it."

"I did," Neal said. "Stupid, but I can't think of everything. They've been dropping pamphlets about every third time they've come over here, and none of them had anything like that before."

"It seems we'll never learn they always have a reason for everything they do," Marvin said sadly, "They do something stupid like dropping pamphlets saying, *Workers arise!* And we laugh at how stupid they are. Then we wake up too late to the fact that they were leading up to something. They got almost fifteen thousand with that nerve virus before we found the cure."

"Fifteen thousand dead?" Neal asked, dismayed.

Marvin nodded,

"Then why didn't I die? I was among the first to get it!"

"They kept you doped," Marvin said, "I've been calling almost every day, Dr. Green explained it to me. The nerve virus works by getting into nerve cells and triggering them. They had to keep you alive because you were their guinea pig. Pretty ticklish there for a while. Your heart started acting up. Jumping around. They finally had to bypass it with a mechanical heart. Then they found the counteragent and tried it on you. It worked."

"So that's why I was unconscious so long," Neal breathed.

"That's the way most of them died," Marvin went on. "The virus got to the heart nerves and started working them. The heart would pump about ten times as fast as it should and build up pressure that ruptured blood vessels right and left. There's no more danger from that though. Everybody's inoculated. Gad! I've had inoculations against so many things now my blood's nine-tenths vaccines!"

He sat down and slumped out so that his legs stretched out an unbelievable distance from the chair.

"You kept up on the war news?" he asked,

Neal shook his head.

"The Ruskies laid a hundred mile deep belt of radioactive dust all along the fifty-fourth parallel so that anyone in the lower half of Europe and Asia who tried to get north to safety would die before they got across the belt. Not only that, they had over three million of their own troops below it. They're still there, raising hell. Think they're going to be pulled back across by troop transport when the war's over."

"Maybe they will be," Neal said, "Russia's going to need all her manpower to rebuild with the snow and ice gone."

"Nah," Marvin said, "She's got too many, same as us. By the way—another scientist came out with a theory about why the Earth speeded up seven minutes a day in its rotation after the Polar ice melted."

"Can you get a copy for me?" Neal asked, "I'd like to study it while I'm lying here. That problem intrigues me. Everything we know says that if anything, it should have slowed down a bit."

"I think I can," Marvin said.

A pleasant feminine voice sounded from the doorway, "You'll have to go now. Visiting hour's up."

Marvin glanced around quickly. "Okay," he said. He kept his eyes on her as she came into the room and passed the tips of her fingers against Neal's temple to count his pulse. He grinned at Neal. "I think I'll pick up that nerve virus myself," he said.

"You don't stand a chance," Charlie spoke up. "Frances is going to marry Neal when he gets out. I've already got it fixed."

"Yeah?" Marvin said. He opened his mouth to say something and saw the expression on Neal's face. His grin came back. "Well, far be it from me to take her away from him, better man though I undoubtedly am."

He went to the door. "So long," he said. "I'll see if I can find that paper, Neal. Don't go taking any long walks on short piers, Charlie."

A look passed between Frances and Neal. She followed

Marvin out into the hall. He dallied, looking at her expectantly.

"I wanted to tell you," she said, "that I know Neal's married. It's just that—well, I don't know how to explain, but we feel that Charlie Adams shouldn't be told that. His interest in the supposed budding romance between me and Neal helps keep him cheered up."

"Yeah?" Marvin said. "Want to know what I think? I think you should stop kidding yourself and admit you love—Charlie!"

He walked down the hall, conscious of her startled eyes on his back.

## CHAPTER FOUR

"WHAT'S your name, punk?"

Einar Tharnsen doubled his fists and glared. "It's on that card in your hand, squirt."

"Wise guy, huh?" the guard said, his lips pulling back in a mirthless smile. Without warning his hand shot out and slapped viciously against Einar's cheek. "What's your name?"

Einar blinked from the blow, then instinctively went into a fighting crouch. From somewhere in the depths of his mind a voice spoke. It was that of the judge, *"If you are intractable you will never be free."*

The mad glaze in his eyes slowly softened. He straightened and relaxed while the guard watched him, mocking contempt in his expression.

"Einar Tharnsen."

"That's better," the guard said. "Ever run a shovel?"

"No."

"You're going to run one. Follow me." He turned his back on Einar and started across the yard.

Einar hesitated, then followed him. They got into a jeep. The guard drove it at a mad pace across rough ground toward a point a quarter of a mile distant where men and giant machines were at work.

"You'll have someone with you the first couple of days," the guard said. "This is your only chance for a soft job. If you don't make good as a shovel man you'll be emptying cement sacks."

"You mean one of *those* big things?" Einar said in dismay, pointing at the giant shovel scooping up two yards of semi-solid mud at a time and dropping it expertly into a waiting truck.

"What did you think I meant?" the guard sneered. "One you spade a garden with?"

He brought the jeep to a skidding stop near the behemoth of intelligent steel, stood up, and waved for the operator to come over.

The man leaped lightly from the cab and came over, grinning at the guard and looking curiously at Einar.

"New prisoner," the guard explained, "Show him how to run the shovel."

"Sure thing," the man said, "Come on, fella. Can't hold up the trucks." He gave Einar a welcoming grin and started back to the shovel.

Einar glanced at the guard, then leaped from the jeep and followed, catching up with him.

"Name's Jeff," the man said. "Yours?"

"Einar."

"Einar, huh," Jeff said, "Used to know a guy by that name. What's your last name?"

"Tharnsen. I'm from Cincinnati."

"Nope," Jeff said, reaching for a handhold and pulling himself up to the first step to the cab of the shovel. "That guy's last name was Pederson. Mine's Smith. Portland Oregon." He pointed at a rivet-studded box. "Sit there and watch. No use telling you anything until you get used to the feel of a shovel."

During the next half-hour Einar watched with absorbed interest as Jeff casually put the tons of coordinated machine through its paces.

"Uncovered something a week ago," Jeff shouted, glancing at him. "Some bones...big ones. I sort of watch every shovel load. Never can tell. I heard a rumor that they uncovered some sort of ruins further up north not long ago. Supposed to be strictly hush-hush, but it leaked out before they clamped the lid."

"I wouldn't be surprised," Einar shouted above the noise. "The theory's been advanced several times that the Arctic was the cradle of mankind."

Jeff looked at Einar and lifted his eyebrows in surprise. Einar didn't notice this. His eyes were on the shovel, studying the black earth it was forcing its way into for another load.

THREE MORNINGS later the sun shone brilliantly.

Einar grabbed the handhold and leaped lightly up into the cab of the shovel. "G'morning, Jeff," he said cheerfully.

"Hi, Einar," Jeff said. "Today you get to you run the shovel and I watch."

"Good," Einar said. "You know, I have to laugh. This is supposed to be punishment or something, and instead I'm learning a job I think I might actually learn to enjoy. The worst punishment they could dish out to me right now would be to take me off this job."

"Don't get too cheerful," Jeff warned. "They can't use any more shovels on this project. I think as soon as you can handle her they're going to send you up north farther."

"That doesn't make any difference," Einar said, "It's the job. I never knew before the thrill of handling a few tons of metal with a personality."

"Wake her up," Jeff said, smiling.

Einar got into the operator's seat and stepped on the starter. The motor came to life at once with a throaty roar that settled into a contented rumbling purr.

"Just take everything calm," Jeff warned, "Don't go getting excited about anything. If you do you'll pull on the wrong levers and maybe bash in the cab of one of the trucks."

"Did you hear about that nerve virus the Russians used?" Einar said, conversationally.

"Yes," Jeff said. "I heard. Only was it the Russians?"

"Of course it was the Russians!" Einar said, looking at Jeff in surprise. Jeff stared back at him. Einar frowned. "What do you mean, was it the Russians? That flying saucer stuff has been pretty well exploded. Don't tell me you think it was men from Mars?"

"No," Jeff said. "Did you ever stop to think how silly it would be, the Ruskies going to all that trouble to give away the secret of a weapon like the nerve virus? Why didn't they make an all-out attack and give the germ to the whole lot of us. We'd all have died, doctors and all, before a cure was found. The war'd be over." He shook his head thoughtfully. "No, I don't think it was the Russians."

"Who, then?" Einar demanded.

"Us," Jeff said, "That's the only thing that makes sense. It wouldn't matter if a few thousands of those coming up died. There won't be room for all of them anyway." He spread his arms in a gesture. It's killing two birds with one stone. Getting rid of a few thousand undesirables and testing a new bacteriological weapon at the same time. Only they'd never dare make *that* public."

"But those planes!" Einar said. "This guy that came into our block last night said he saw the Russian planes overhead. They didn't drop any of the pamphlets along his route, but he saw them fly over."

"We're capturing Russian planes all the time," Jeff said. "What's to prevent us using them for a thing like that?"

"I don't believe it," Einar said, shocked.

"According to what they tell us," Jeff said, "the Russians are all bad and we're the fair haired boys. I'm of the opinion we don't know the half of it."

Einar frowned uncomfortably. "I've never thought much about it," he said. "What *are* we fighting about?"

"You tell me," Jeff said, grinning.

"What are you driving at?" Einar asked.

Jeff puffed studiously on his brown paper cigarette. "Just this," he said. "There's a lot of us in these concentration camps up here. When the time is right we could take over, join with the Russians, and the war would be ended."

"Hey there!" a voice shouted. "Get that shovel goin'!"

## CHAPTER FIVE

"NO, I DIDN'T forget it," Marvin Swank said. He reached into a pocket and brought out a folded sheet of newspaper. "This fellow—a Ph.D. by the name of Mason—has his theory pretty well worked out. He's got the math there, too. All it needs is some new surveys to check his results."

"Thanks, Marv," Neal said, laying it on the stand beside his bed, "I'll read it later."

"What's it say?" Charlie asked.

"This fellow, Mason," Marvin said, "claims that starting about five miles down, the Earth is semi-molten in state…due to the tremendous pressure…and that even iron and granite that far down begin to act like syrup in some ways. When the billions of tons of ice and snow at both poles started to melt and flow toward the equator it took some of the weight off the pales. As a result, the balance on the fluid center shifted, and that center shifted its shape to compensate for it, causing the diameter at the equator to become a little less, and the diameter at the poles to become a little greater. That made the ocean level at the equator go up and raised a lot of land up here and in the Antarctic. But the angular momentum of the entire mass had to remain the same, and the only way it could was for the Earth to speed up its rotation. He's got the figures predicting just what they'll find the measurements to be now."

"But why weren't there earthquakes and things like that?" Charlie asked.

"Mason says the reason there weren't was that the solid crust could stand the little stretching and compressing that took place without shifting appreciably. One thing that checks already is the amount the oceans have risen in the tropics. Even the most fantastic estimates of the amount of water contained in the snow and ice at the poles couldn't account for all of it."

"I still can't see how all that would speed up the Earth though," Charlie said.

"Look at it this way," Marvin said. "At the equator it was travelling a thousand miles an hour, roughly. Let's say a thousand to keep it simple. Twenty-four thousand miles around the world, and any spot goes all the way around in twenty-four hours."

"Okay," Charlie agreed.

"So then it shrinks down to twenty-three thousand miles around," Marvin said, "but it still goes a thousand miles an hour because there's nothing to slow it down. So the spot gets all the way around in less than twenty-four hours."

"Yes," Charlie said, "I see it now. I think he's right."

Neal and Marvin looked at each other and smiled imperceptibly.

"Were you awake during the earthquake last night, Neal?" Marvin asked.

"No," Neal said, "Charlie was, though."

"The radio says it was pretty bad in the United States," Marvin went on, "The breakthrough at the Isthmus expanded too fast. The few feet of difference in the level of the Atlantic and Pacific down there built up a momentum of several billion tons once it got started. Blowing up a couple of mountains with buried hydrogen bombs did more harm than good by weakening the bedrock Barrier, too."

"Gawd!" Neal muttered, his eyes very wide. "It seems that anything we do lately takes on world proportions. Those atom bombs in Europe—how could we have known?"

"What about that scientist that tried to tell them at the Pentagon?" Charlie asked.

"I don't believe that," Neal said quickly, "They have stories like that about every war. They had one about the British sinking the ocean liner with their own submarines, bringing us into World War I, instead of the Kaiser's U-boats. They had the one about Roosevelt knowing Pearl Harbor was going to happen, but let it, to incite the American public to enter World War II. You'll always find stories like that."

"But *somebody* must have known," Charlie said gravely. "Why even I heard stories about atom bomb weather."

"The point is," Neal said, "nobody did know. At least I don't think they did."

"I guess I don't either—now," Charlie said.

"How're your legs coming, Charlie?" Marvin asked quickly to get the subject changed.

"Pretty bad sometimes," Charlie said, "I get the feeling that they're itching, or cold, or wet, or moving around by themselves." He shook his head. "But of course they aren't. And Dr. Ohrman gives me a shot when it gets too bad."

Marvin looked at his watch, "Got to run," he said. "I'm late now. I just ran in during my lunch hour instead of waiting until Saturday to bring you that article, Neal. Take care of yourself. You too, Charlie."

MARVIN LOOKED speculatively at the mud spattered bus with its pile of worn-out tires and new tires still in their wrappings on the top, and the weary faced women and children still disembarking and huddling in a compact group, waiting to be told where to go.

Skirting the tired group, he entered the station, nodding to the driver, though he had never seen him before. Driver and bus had made a one-way trip. From now on they would remain in the northland, transporting people to the various new centers as they opened up. Ten thousand of them in a year and a half, and each loaded with people.

"You're in charge?" the driver asked, Marvin. "Here's the passenger list."

"Thanks," Marvin said. "That girl over there behind the desk will tell you where you're to go. A mechanic will take your bus to the garage. Have a nice trip?"

"Nice?" the driver echoed. "Ha! But we didn't have much trouble. They could get something better for a road though.

That metal grill stuff tears the tires, and once they start to go…"

"I know," Marvin said. "I've made the recommendation. Every driver says the same thing. The big trouble, they inform me, is that they have to shift the road so much due to slides. Can't pave it with anything permanent."

"Well, it ain't my headache any more," the driver dismissed the subject. "One of the women died on the way up. She's in the back seat wrapped in a blanket."

"Her name?" Marvin asked quickly.

"It was just last night," the driver said. "You can find out when you check them off." He started toward the desk Marvin had pointed to, then turned back. "She was—kinda nice. Somebody's grandmother, I guess," He turned again, quickly as though ashamed of this display of sentiment.

Marvin went slowly over to his own desk, his eye skimming the passenger list. They stopped at a name, frowning.

"Damn," he muttered. "That name's familiar…Mrs. Einar Tharnsen. Where have I heard it?" He picked up the hand mike lying on his desk and pressed the button at its base. "Will Mrs. Einar Tharnsen please step inside?"

He laid the mike down and watched the street door expectantly. The woman who came in was rather pleasant looking, with straw colored hair done up in a thick braid nesting on top of her head. Two boys and a girl came with her—the boys, quiet and brave; the girl, about six, holding her mother's hand, eyes wide with fear.

Marvin watched them approach his desk. He knew at once he had never seen them before. Suddenly memory struck him. He sucked in his breath.

Mrs. Tharnsen stopped, her eyes mildly curious. "I'm Hilda Tharnsen," she said quietly.

"Would you have your children wait outside please?" Marvin said politely.

"Is it something about Einar?" she asked numbly, "You can tell me in front of them, please."

Marvin hesitated, looking searchingly at the three child faces waiting stoically for him to speak. He realized suddenly that they were wailing for him to tell them Einar was dead.

"Oh! It isn't that bad!" he said, chuckling. "Mr. Tharnsen got into a little trouble on the way up and was arrested. He's safe enough—in one of the labor camps. And maybe now that you're here you'll get to see him. Go over and sit on that bench and I'll have one of the girls make a few calls to see if we can fix it."

"He—he wasn't killed by the nerve virus?" Hilda Tharnsen asked. She stood there for a moment looking at Marvin.

"Pop's alive!" the older boy shouted. "See, mom? I told you they couldn't kill him!"

Hilda was weeping quietly. "Come, children," she said. "The man told us to go over and sit on the bench. Waiting won't be hard now. Come on, and stop jumping, Hannes—or you'll be in jail too!" She flashed Marvin a tear-brightened smile; then, alternately weeping and chuckling, she led her brood over to the bench against the drab mud block wall.

"See if you can get the court's okay for—" Marvin said to the girl at the desk nearest his.

"I know what to do, Marv," she said.

"And get them over to take care of the dead woman, too," Marvin added. He picked up the mike. "All of you form a line beginning at the door and as close to the building as you can…" And through the window he saw the tired bus passengers move to comply.

EINAR WAS overjoyed when his wife and children were allowed to visit him over the next few days. Knowing that his family was safe gave him an overwhelming sense of relief that made life in camp far more bearable.

Jeff approached him one afternoon, shortly after one of his family visits.

"They're transferring you to Camp Fifty," Jeff said as he entered the cab of the shovel and dropped down onto the rivet-studded toolbox. "So—tonight you meet the big boy and you get your instructions."

"Good," Einar said without turning as he brought the loaded shovel over a waiting truck and dropped two yards of black wet dirt into it, then swung the shovel back for another bite at the embankment.

"How's it going with your wife and kids?" Jeff asked. "I heard they came to see you again today."

"They're sending them to the Repulse Bay settlement," Einar said.

"They'll be okay there," Jeff said. "Nice place. You won't have to worry about your family."

"Well, I can be with them in four months," Einar said.

"Four months?" Jeff said. "Look, Einar, I thought you were taking this seriously…"

"I am," Einar said.

"Well, you don't think this is coming off in four months, do you?" Jeff said. "It'll take maybe six months more. Maybe not, but we can't be sure. You're going to have to pop a guard when you get to Camp Fifty. Not anything to get you a punishment job, but enough to keep from getting out on the minimum."

"Why?" Einar asked. "Can't I be just as good—even better—if I'm outside where I can get hold of things?" He glanced at Jeff questioningly.

Jeff shook his head. "The whole thing's being kept in the labor camps," he said. "When the time comes we've got to know where each man is, so he can get his orders and act. We can't risk setting up communications and organizations where there's a lot of smart intelligence officers with big eyes and ears. They're not looking inside the labor camps. Not for revolution."

"How many men have we got now?" Einar asked, bringing a full shovel over the roadway and holding it stationary while an empty truck drove up.

"Maybe only you and me," Jeff said. "None of us had better learn too much. If they got wind of this thing they'd torture everything out of you. There's a war on, you know." He stood up and hung on as the cab swung ponderously around, carrying the shovel to the embankment again. "I'll hop off now," he said. "I'll see you after chow tonight in the recreation yard."

JEFF WAS leaning against the mud block wall beside the entrance to the yard as Einar came out. He looked at Einar meaningfully, then started to stroll leisurely through the scattered crowd of two hundred prisoners, hands in pockets, nodding to this and that man as he passed them.

Einar stood watching until Jeff had gone about fifteen feet, then slowly followed. The guards on the wall would notice nothing. They watched for only two things: rapid movement such as running or fighting, and the collecting of small groups.

Never directing his face toward Jeff, Einar kept his eyes on him. After a while he saw Jeff pause beside a heavy shouldered man with jet-black hair, turn slowly, and stare in his direction.

The black haired man looked at Einar briefly, made an imperceptible gesture with his head that indicated he wanted him to follow, then started strolling in the general direction of a relatively deserted corner of the yard.

Einar looked at Jeff, who nodded slightly and looked meaningfully at the black haired man's back. Einar dipped his head, stretched as though tired, and slowly moved after the man.

The black haired man finally stopped against the wall. Einar looked doubtfully up at the guard stationed in a small wooden shack a few feet overhead. The black haired man glanced casually up at the wooden faced guard.

"Come on over here," he said to Einar. "You don't have to worry. He's one of us." He smiled at Einar as he approached, "So you're the new recruit," he said softly, "Good boy. You won't regret it. We're going to succeed. Got to, or this war will go on forever. I'm Don Welles. You're Einar Tharnsen. I'm not the big boy in spite of what Jeff said. Nobody will know who the big boy is. Maybe he's that guard up there," He grinned. Suddenly he held out his hand. When Einar took it he shook hands warmly. "For peace," he said. "May she come soon."

"For peace," Einar repeated clumsily.

"Now listen carefully," Don Welles said. "The way we identify one another is by rubbing your eyes with your middle finger on your right hand. Do that occasionally at Camp Fifty where you're going, and watch the others. In a week or so you'll know which are with us. Two of the guards up there are. One of them is as big as you. He's the one you're to sock after you've been there a few days. He has orders to give you the excuse. Unless you get instructions, you're to do nothing except wait. Got it?"

"I guess so," Einar said.

"Good," Don Welles said, "And from now on you don't know me. And—when the revolution succeeds you won't have to worry—you'll be on top." As he said this he laid a hand on Einar's shoulder and looked at him sternly.

Then he was walking away, strolling as though going nowhere in particular. Einar stood where he was, watching him depart.

## CHAPTER SIX

"HOW YOU feeling this morning, Neal?" Dr. Ohrman asked, placing his fingertips against Neal's temple and frowning at his wristwatch.

"Never better, Fred," Neal said. "When are they going to let me out of here?"

Dr. Ohrman didn't answer. After a moment he took his fingers away from Neal's temple and went around to the foot of the bed and took the chart off its hooks.

"Hmm," he said. "No attacks for seven days now. How about relapses of consciousness, Neal? Any more of those mysterious jumps of fifteen minutes to a couple of hours?"

"Nope," Neal said. "I doze off several times a day, but it's just sleep. No blinking my eyes at four o'clock and finding it suddenly eight-thirty."

Dr. Ohrman went around to the side of the bed again and touched the back of Neal's right hand gently, bending over to look closely at the spiral pattern of white and pink skin.

"Skin graft is doing OK," he said to himself.

"A little numb," Neal said, "and here—" He touched a spot on his wrist. "When I touch here I'd swear I'm touching my arm up above the elbow."

Dr. Ohrman smiled. "That's probably where that section of skin came from." He traced with one finger. "We sliced thin strips of skin along the arm and spiraled them over the areas we took the infected skin from, leaving them attached at one end. That way there was just a narrow gap between each strip for scar tissue to fill in. Eventually your mind will relocate the sources so that you'll lose the sensation of being touched where the skin came from."

He turned Neal's hand over and looked at the fingertips.

"We'll have to take your fingerprints before you leave, so that you can be identified from the new ones. Are you able to feel anything with your fingers?"

"Just pressures," Neal said. "I do all right when I'm watching what I touch, but when I close my eyes…"

"That may be permanent," Dr. Ohrman said. "It won't bother you to speak of, and your new—" He stopped abruptly, biting his lip.

"New what?" Neal asked.

"I suppose I may as well tell you," the doctor said. "Those tests we've been running you through—fatigue and reflex tests—show that for some unaccountable reason your reaction time has speeded up about fifty percent and your fatigue time has lengthened to something fantastic. We don't know if it will be permanent, of course."

"You mean those tests where I wiggled a finger until it was too tired to move any more, and pressed a button when a light flashed on?"

"Yes," Dr. Ohrman said. "There's some slight physiological change in your nerve fluid brought about by the virus or the antitoxin, we don't know which. It's made you just about the fastest thing alive."

"I've noticed it a little," Neal said. "I just thought I was still nervous. Jerky."

"I might as well tell you the rest of it while I'm at it," the doctor said, "The Government wants to use this new faculty of yours as soon as we release you."

"How?"

"I don't know that," the doctor said. "They didn't tell us. All I know is that they're very interested in you all of a sudden and want us to release you for active duty as soon as possible." He straightened up and stood looking down at Neal. "So I guess we'll have to let you go—tomorrow. I hate to. I'd like to keep you here and study you another month." He turned abruptly and left the room.

"Golly…" Charlie said, wide eyed. "Maybe they want to transfer you to U.S.O. and make you into a boxer!" A concerned look appeared. "And what about Frances?"

"Why don't you get wise to yourself, Charlie?" Neal snapped, suddenly irritated. "Everybody but you knows she's in love with you."

"You're wrong!" Charlie said quickly. "I haven't got any legs. Why—"

"Yeah, you haven't got any legs," Neal snapped. "You're a coward. You want to give up and be a cripple. You don't want to get a couple of mechanical ones and spend hours learning to walk, and then dance, and work. You feel sorry for yourself or you wouldn't try to marry off the girl you love. You'd fight for her if you weren't yellow. You'd—" He stopped, brought up short by the expression on Charlie's face.

"You shouldn't have said that, Neal," Charlie said.

"This is a man's world—what there is left of it," Neal said. His lips worked soundlessly. Suddenly he plopped over with his back turned to Charlie.

It was much later that Charlie's voice came, quiet and sort of wondering. "You know, Neal, the world now is something like that. A man who's lost his legs. And—and—"

"Sure, Charlie," Neal said, his voice muffled.

It rained all that night and Neal had trouble sleeping, twisting and turning in bed, regretful of what he'd said.

THE FOLLOWING morning after his release, Neal dropped in on Marvin Swank.

Marvin looked up as Neal entered. Shoving his chair back he leaped to his feet, a pleased look on his face.

"Why you son of a gun!" he said. "How the devil did you get out of the hospital? And why did you keep it as a surprise?"

"I didn't," Neal said as Marvin took him by the shoulders and held him out at arm's length, "Dr. Ohrman just told me yesterday evening."

"Well," Marvin said, releasing him, "back in harness for you again, I suppose. Sitting on high and watching the poor wretches down below."

"Got time to have coffee with me?" Neal asked.

"I'll take time," Marvin said, "You girls hold things down while I'm gone."

He put an arm over Neal's shoulders and forced him toward the door while the WAAC personnel looked on, smiling broadly.

When they reached the sidewalk he sobered, "What's up, Neal?" he asked. "You got out awfully sudden—and you wouldn't have dropped in on me at the job unless you're going away. You'd wait and surprise me at the officers' club tonight."

"Any other clues, Mr. Holmes?" Neal asked, a smile playing on his lips.

"As a matter of fact, yes," Marvin said, "You changed the subject without comment when I said you were going back to the old patrol job."

"You should be in M.I.," Neal said, smiling broadly. "You've missed your calling."

Marvin looked around secretively and brought his finger to his lips dramatically. "Maybe I am!" he said in a hoarse whisper.

"Soviet or U. S.?" Neal asked.

"Both," Marvin said brightly. "And am I making money…A savings account in three Kansas City banks—"

"They're under water," Neal said.

"Verkhoyansk?" Marvin tried.

"I believe you," Neal said. Grinning, he grabbed the arm of a passing M.P. and stopped him. "Arrest this man," he said with his tongue in his cheek, pointing at Marvin, "He's a Russian spy."

"Nyet nyet…" Marvin said. "I'm on vacation yet. By the way—" He sidled up to the now grinning M.P. "Are you a Comrade? Nyet? Too pad. Ve could drink wodka ofer old times."

"He has a savings account in Verkhoyansk," Neal said.

"Money?" the M.P. said, still playing along. "That makes you a capitalist. On your way before I report you to the I.R.B."

"Comes the revolution, Comrade!" Marvin said, glowering at the M.P. and pushing Neal ahead of him down the street.

The M.P. watched them, the smile on his face just a bit nervous. Superior officers didn't usually behave that friendly toward enlisted men.

"Know where you're going?" Marvin asked, his face suddenly serious.

"Officially no," Neal said.

"Unofficially?" Marvin looked at him questioningly.

"If we hadn't been kids together back in Spokane I wouldn't tell even you," Neal said. He waited until there was no one walking within earshot. "I'm being sent to New Mexico."

"Patrol duty?" Marvin asked. When Neal shook his head Marvin uttered a soft low whistle of amazement. He turned to Neal, suddenly unbelieving, "But you're just out of the hospital! What's the matter with them?"

"My reflex and fatigue indices were changed by the nerve virus or the cure, they don't know which," Neal said, "They don't know how long it will last so they want to use me while it's there."

"Then that's it," Marvin said, his face filled with wonder and hope. "They're ready to use men."

"I guess it means that," Neal said. "It's been a public secret that they've been all out for space travel since right after the outbreak of the war. A year ago there were reports of an atom explosion on the Moon, but the Government announced officially that no American rockets were yet advanced enough for that, and if it had happened it must be the Russians."

"It could have been, too," Marvin said. "Watch out when you get up there."

"*If* I get up there," Neal smiled. "My assignment may be a desk job, for all I know."

"How's Charlie taking it?" Marvin asked.

Neal frowned. He started to speak several times. Finally he said, "I feel terrible about him. I—shot off my mouth at him. Go up and see him, will you? I feel like hell about it..."

"Of course I will," Marvin said, pushing open the door to the canteen.

"AND," MARVIN said when they were comfortably seated by a window, "if you get a chance, take a look at Amarillo and write me what it looks like. You might even keep your eyes peeled for Thelma. She's a tall blonde, kind of—"

"I know," Neal said, "Statuesque. You showed me her picture, too," He smiled, "If I find her I'll tell her how you died bravely, and on your death bed you made me promise to find her and give her a good time. And *will*..." His voice trailed off as his eyes widened with, surprise.

Marvin turned to follow his gaze. Frances, the nurse, was standing in the doorway across the room, searching over the crowded room. Her gaze jerked in his direction almost psychically. Her face lit up with recognition, then settled into grimness as she started over.

"Trouble, Neal," Marvin muttered, "she's looking right at you. What the hell did you say to Charlie?"

"I told him she was in love with him and if he wasn't a

coward he'd face life and marry her," Neal said under his breath. He looked at the approaching nurse then quickly looked away. "This is the first time in my life that I feel an irresistible urge to find a hole and crawl into it," he said to Marvin under his breath "Charlie just struck me wrong with the things he was saying... worrying about me and Frances after I left. I just got tired of hearing about it over and over again."

"Well, you've got it coming so take it," Marvin muttered out of the corner of his mouth as Frances came up to their table. Then he perked up and said, "Hi, Frances. Come to say goodbye to the girded warrior?" He grinned at Neal.

Frances's eyes were on Neal, wide and staring. Abruptly she leaned forward, gripping the edge of the table, "What did you say to Charlie Adams before you left the hospital, Neal?" she demanded.

Neal watched his finger making small circles on the tabletop. "Why nothing much," he said, "I just—"

"Go on," Frances said, her voice seething with controlled fury.

Neal looked up at her helplessly, then dropped his gaze back to his wandering finger.

"—told him that I wished him luck, and—and sort of hinted, indirectly, that you were in love with him and he should..."

"He should what?" Frances demanded.

"Well, sort of try real hard to master mechanical legs and—" Neal's finger stopped tracing. He looked up, "I'm sorry, Frances. I made an ass of myself...an utter stupid ass. If there's anything I could do to undo it I would. I wish I could blame it on the nerve virus, but it was just a plain stupid reaction without thinking. He was worrying about what would become of the 'romance' he imagined was budding between you and me. I couldn't leave with him thinking like that...you know...being a martyr to love and all that." A bit of anger and defiance crept into his eyes.

She continued to stare at him, her expression unchanging. Something in her eyes alarmed Neal.

"What's happened?" he asked. He could see now there was more than just irritation in her expression. "For cryin' out loud...don't tell me he did something crazy. He didn't try to kill himself did he?" He half rose from his chair, trepidation on his face.

The answer was on her face. She nodded affirmatively, tears welling up in her eyes.

"Good Lord," Marvin muttered somberly.

"Is he alive?" Neal blurted out.

She nodded again. "He's probably going to be fine...no thanks to you, though."

Marvin was suddenly up out of his chair. He wrapped his arm around Frances's shoulders. Neal sat there with a stupefied expression on his face.

"Come on, Neal. We're going to the hospital," Marvin said gruffly. Then he looked at Frances and said, "and I think you should come along with us. We need to find out exactly what's going on and how and we're going to straighten this whole thing out."

The trio headed for the door.

Out on the sidewalk Marvin asked, "How did it happen, Frances? Or do you even know?"

She swallowed hard and said, "I wasn't there when it happened. They told me Charlie c—crawled out of b—bed and dragged himself—to the window..." she bit her lip and couldn't go any further.

Marvin was hurrying her almost at a run to avoid the curious stares of passers-by. Neal was keeping pace, an expression of distress etched into his features.

When they entered the hospital Frances shrugged off Marvin's hold and dried her eyes, holding her head erect with a semblance of her old professional calm.

She led them to the ward Neal and Charlie had occupied. The door was closed. She opened it. Marvin and Neal saw that Neal's bed was made up and empty. Screens were around Charlie's bed.

Neal's face cramped queerly at the sight of doctors' feet under the bottom part of the screen.

Noiselessly, her face infinitely sad, Frances went to the screens and pulled them aside enough to peek in, with Neal and Marvin crowding behind her, holding their breath.

A SHEET covered Charlie up to his chest. He was flat on his back, his head turned sideways with his face against the pillow. Beads of perspiration dotted his forehead. His eyes were closed and his lower lip sucked in between his teeth.

Dr. Green was taping Charlie's arm against his chest while Dr. Ohrman held it rigid. In a moment they finished.

"That should hold it until we can get him through X-ray," Dr. Green said, his voice cheery. "Come in and give him another two C.C.s of the same sedative in an hour. And get a nurse in here!" The last was politely exasperated.

He half turned, then noticed Frances.

"Oh there you are, nurse," he said. "Where have you…" He stopped talking when he saw Frances wasn't even hearing him.

Charlie had opened his eyes and jerked his head around to look. His eyes rested on Frances for a moment, then went past her to Neal. He turned his face against the pillow again and closed his eyes, his expression agonized. After a moment he forced his eyes open again and turned his head with slow deliberateness to face them.

"Hello, Neal," he said weakly. "Come on in."

Neal looked at Dr. Green for permission. Dr. Green dipped his head in unwilling acquiescence and pushed the screen back to make more room. He whispered into Neal's ear, "that big bushy hedge below his window broke his fall. Some scratches and bruises—maybe a broken bone—but he'll be all right."

Neal looked down at the pitiful figure in the bed. "Hello, Charlie—" he began. He stopped, with a feeling that anything he might say would be worse than saying nothing. He went very slowly past Frances and stood beside the head of the bed while Charlie kept watching him.

"I guess they told you, Neal," Charlie said. "I'm sorry. I had wanted to wait until you were gone long enough and far enough away that you wouldn't ever hear about it…but I couldn't."

"You shouldn't have done this, Charlie," Neal said softly but firmly. "You have everything to live for." He turned his head and looked at Frances, a grim light in his eyes. "You still do."

"No, Neal," Charlie said. "Remember I said the world was like a man who's lost his legs? After you left this morning I realized it was. Only it's just an unthinking jumble of humanity and doesn't comprehend what's happened to it. *I* know what's happened to me. I won't let Frances tie herself to a cripple who will have to walk around on metal legs and smile and be proud of being able to walk." He was speaking too loudly.

Neal was twisting in mental torment.

"You should all probably go. He needs his rest," Dr. Green said, but no one was listening.

"And you just think she loves me," Charlie went on. "*I* know. You think she loves me, and you wanted to get out of the picture so you wouldn't be taking a woman away from a helpless crip—"

"Damn it, Charlie," Neal cut in. Don't you know I'm married? I don't love Frances. She doesn't love me. She loves you, and you'd better get the courage to face it. Running out on your life will only break her heart. What the hell do you think love is, anyway? La-de-da with perfumed lace?" He glared down at Charlie, his fists clenched with cold sweat and his face contorted into a mask of self-torture, regret for what he couldn't stop before it was out.

Suddenly, to everyone's surprise, Frances pushed past the screen and sank to her knees by the bed.

"He's right, Charlie," she said. "You poor deluded darling." Her eyes were brimming with tears as they locked with his, and his were looking up out of the depths of a death wish to the first rays of the sun, rising above the horizon of life. She took his hand and kissed it gently.

Neal backed away with a reaction of weakness and relief.

Marvin gripped his arm, "Let's go," he muttered against Neal's ear. He led Neal unresistingly toward the door.

## CHAPTER SEVEN

THE SOUND of the truck became different. Einar awakened with a strong impression that it had stopped, but it hadn't. It was going faster. The tires were humming. There wasn't any slow upheaval as bumps were taken. Instead there was the rhythmic thud of tires thumping over regularly spaced tar expansion joints in concrete.

He stood up so as to see over the body of the truck through the heavy wire mesh that kept him and the other twenty assorted prisoners from escaping. What he saw made him oblivious of the man who had sat next to him slumping down and occupying his seat.

He might have been in California or the Delta country of prediluvian Texas. Mathematically exact rows of young trees whizzed past, stretching back from the highway to be lost in the distance. Verdant alfalfa grew to luxurious depths in between the row of trees. And the highway itself seemed to be of real concrete—not steel grill or packed mud.

Einar stumbled over sprawled feet of sleeping men to where he could look alongside the driver's cabin.

"It is concrete!" he muttered incredulously.

What" had happened? Had it all been a vivid dream? A mile ahead he could see signs of a city of some kind. A billboard flashed by. It was gone as he noticed it, so he couldn't catch what it said. He watched anxiously for another one to appear. In a moment it did.

*One mile to New Fernando, the capital of Foxe Basin,* it read, *Pop. 13,487.*

There was more on the sign but it was gone before he could read on.

"Looks just like home, doesn't it," a quiet voice at his shoulder said.

"Yes," Einar said. He stared in fascination at a service station they were passing. No cars were at the gas pumps, but near the grease rack was a glistening black sedan with its hood raised and the coveralled posterior of a service station attendant bent over a fender. When it was gone he turned to the man who had spoken, "How'd this get here?" he asked, "I thought there was nothing but mud and people up here yet."

"This was put in last year by private capital," the man said, "I remember reading about it. It was when everybody was thinking this upset of things wouldn't be as bad as it is. Foxe Basin is Canadian though. None of us get to come here and stay."

"Oh," Einar said, disappointed. "I thought maybe…"

"Ours will be just as good when they get going," the man said, "Give us another year…or even more. Personally, I want to settle somewhere in Baffin Bay. The soil is really rich there. Plant alfalfa and soybeans there as thick as they'll grow for five years to get all the salt out of the ground, and then you have something besides a small fortune from the alfalfa and soybeans."

"I guess this is on the way to Camp Fifty," Einar said, "I wonder where it is?"

"It must be on Baffin Island," the man said, "I studied the geography up here pretty well. Base is just west of the southern tip of Southampton Island and we're headed northeast right now."

"I'm glad we passed through this," Einar said. He rubbed his eye with the middle finger of his right hand slowly as though it were an absentminded habit. "It shows me what can be done up here. Maybe things won't be so bad after all up here."

"Heck no," the man said. "It's a new frontier. Just like Oklahoma and Kansas were at one time. In ten years there won't be no difference. Concrete highways, roadhouses, railroads."

"But farther south," Einar said. "Why don't they fix that up too instead of making us walk through it all?"

"Some kind of treaty with Canada maybe," the man said. He watched Einar rub his eye again with his middle finger. "Something in your eye?"

"Yeah," Einar said, "I think it's out now," He lowered his hand, "What about this treaty with Canada?"

"I think the United States and Canada must have made some kind of a treaty to allow us to come up here," he said, "I don't think the U.S. would let a few million of its citizens become Canadians without a struggle."

"I thought it was just part of the war setup," Einar said. "Canadian and U.S. defenses were combined, and industry, too. When everything's settled down they'll straighten it out."

"Oh," the man said. "Maybe that's it." He was studiously silent for a minute. Suddenly he chuckled. "I was just thinking," he explained, "Suppose Canada insisted that we become citizens. There's only about eleven or twelve million Canadians, and there'll be a lot more than that of us. Then we could vote Canada into the U. S. and they couldn't stop it!"

"Could be," Einar said. "I wonder how things *will* be when it's all over? Somebody told me before I started up here that I was a fool to come. When this atom bomb weather tapers off and things gets back to normal it'll freeze all year round up here again."

"Naw," the man said. "That won't happen. Maybe in a few centuries but not in our lifetime. It's going to be just the other way around. They'll have icebergs at the equator and summer all the time at the poles."

"How do you figure?" Einar asked.

"Things are going back to the way they were during the ice age," the man said, looking at Einar owlishly. "They've found plenty of evidence that at one time the human race lived in the north. *I* think the Garden of Eden was at the North Pole, and mankind spread from there."

"What's your name?" Einar asked, suddenly interested in the man.

"Harry Drake. I'm from Kansas City."

"I'm Einar Tharnsen. I came from Cincinnati."

"Oh! Just like me!" Harry said, "Your home town's under the ocean."

"Yeah," Einar said. "Tell me, Harry, if the birthplace of man was at the North Pole and there was an ice age, how do you tie them together? When the glaciers extended all the way down to the United States—"

"There weren't any in the Arctic then," Harry said. "They were piled up in the Temperate Zone and maybe even on the equator. The air currents were reversed then just like the atom bombs reversed them. Ever see a whirlpool form in a washbasin? You get it started and it keeps going by itself. Stick your finger in and stir the other way. It makes things boil around for a minute, then presto! You have a nice stable whirlpool going in the opposite direction."

"But that isn't what hap—" Einar began.

"Yes it was," Harry said, "I read all about it and that's exactly what took place. The way things were before they exploded the atom bombs in Europe, starting about a hundred miles up off the surface there was a steady wind from the equator toward the North Pole all the time. There the air went upward, and about five hundred to a thousand miles up it went the other way, toward the equator. When it got there it came down and started back toward the pole. The atom bombs blasting in Europe hit down hard enough to blast everything. But what they didn't stop to think was that it hit up as well. And every time one of them hit up it raised hell with the upper air currents. Finally it split the big whirlpool into two smaller ones."

"It did that all right," Einar said, "but you've got the rest wrong. It went the other way. A hundred miles up it went south, and a thousand miles up it was going north."

"No, you got it wrong," Harry said, "Anyway it doesn't make much difference. The idea is the same, and the end result is the same. Don't you see? Now the same upper air currents exist in the temperate zones as did exist at the North Pole! And before long there won't be anything at the equator except ocean, so the only place there'll be for people will be the Arctic. That's why I'm going to settle as far north as they'll let me. Watch and see, Einar. In ten years they'll be having arctic weather all over the U.S."

"What about the southern half of the world?" Einar asked. "The atom bombs in Europe couldn't have upset the air currents down there."

"Who cares what goes on down there?" Harry said, "All I care about is what's going on up here. And anyway," he added triumphantly, "there never was an ice age in the Southern Hemisphere."

"Are you sure?" Einar asked.

"Sure I'm sure," Harry said, "or they would have mentioned it along with the ice age in the Northern Hemisphere. So it doesn't make any difference."

"What do you mean, it doesn't make any difference? We should have gone south instead of north?"

"Not enough land," Harry said, shaking his head. "Have you looked at the maps? The eastern half of South America is going under water. So is two thirds of Africa and nine tenths of Australia. And half of China and nearly all of India are already so far under you can sail an ocean liner to Tibet."

EINAR TURNED and watched the trim orchards of Foxe Basin whiz by. A frown settled on his face. How much of what Harry Drake had said was true? Probably almost none of it. But if it were? He wished he'd read more, kept up more. But—

The question rose into full clarity in his thoughts. Was what was going on a mere repetition of the history of the Earth a few hundred thousand years ago? Was there, in that remote era, an atomic war that drove fleeing remnants of a global civilization to the north through a thousand miles of mud, to later migrate southward and build up modern civilization?

His eyes went toward the low-lying hills far ahead on the highway. Baffin Island, according to Harry. Maybe he'd uncover something interesting with his shovel."

Then, abruptly, he remembered something more important to him than prehistoric civilizations. He turned around and studied the faces of the men in the truck with him. One of them looked at him sideways, then with apparent absentmindedness brought his hand up to rub his eyes with the middle finger of his right hand. Einar moved to join him and get acquainted.

"Hi," he said as he sat down on the floor of the truck beside the man, "Wonder how much longer we'll be cooped up in here?"

"So long as they give us chow regular I don't care," the man said cheerfully.

Einar studied him openly. The man was barrel-chested, and with the silkiest jet-black hair he had ever seen on anyone. His face was round, with a smooth flawless skin.

He was studying Einar just as frankly.

"I'm George Lord," he said.

"I'm Einar Tharnsen," Einar said. "Why don't you take a look outside? They've got nice orchards started here. In a couple of years they'll be supplying all the fruits the northland will need."

"It doesn't interest me," George Lord said. "I'm just interested in mud."

Einar frowned. George Lord seemed to be laughing at him down underneath, though on the surface he seemed just friendly. He looked away and slowly rubbed his eye with the middle finger of his right hand, then looked back casually. George's deep brown eyes were twinkling.

"I was watching you up front with Gabby," George said.

"Oh," Einar said, getting the hidden meaning. He smiled ruefully, "His name's Drake. He's from Kansas City. Harry Drake. He has a theory that in ten years there will be glaciers down around the fortieth to the fiftieth parallel like there were in the ice age."

"That's right," Harry's voice intruded. Harry squatted down in front of Einar and George. "There'll be a ring of ice in that band, all around the world. South of it will be nothing much but ocean…"

Einar closed his eyes. After a while Harry's voice put him to sleep. When he awakened, the truck was in the jouncing rolling rhythm once more, and moving slowly. He found he was draped against George Lord's side.

With a muttered apology he straightened. George looked at him with the same twinkle in his eyes that he had had before.

"Have a good sleep?" he asked, "We'll be there pretty soon now. The guard up with the driver passed the word back about five minutes ago."

Einar struggled to his feet, gripping the wire mesh covering of the truck to steady himself. Outside the truck was nothing but dark mud and occasional rock outcroppings. Here and there were ridges of round pebbles where the mud had washed away with the melting of the eternal ice.

Ahead and drawing nearer was a high steel mesh fence that stretched to the right and to the left to disappear over nearby hills. The truck was headed toward a large double gate and a Quonset hut.

The gates were even now being swung open by two men in military uniform. Two jeeps were parked beside the Quonset.

Einar kept his eyes on the soldiers as the truck he was in passed through the gates and headed toward a distant low line of dark bulk which, though the same color as the mud, was obviously the collection of buildings that made up Labor Camp Number Fifty.

A few minutes later the buildings had resolved themselves into distinct structures. The prison block with its three story buildings and long high wall interrupted with small shacks for the guards along its upper rim. The neat office building set apart from the prison. The mud block mills. The garages and repair shops with road equipment parked, waiting to be repaired or ready to be returned to the job.

The truck was heading for the prison block. The solid metal gates in the wall were pulled aside. Guards were standing in the yard waiting to handle the newcomers.

Einar kept his eyes on the guards as the truck passed through the gates. There were four of them. Would one of them be the guard he was supposed to sock? He found himself swallowing loudly.

"Let's try to stick together, Einar," George Lord said in a voice that wouldn't carry; "We'd be better off as cellmates."

"Okay," Einar said without turning. He was studying the guards, waiting for one of them to give the secret signal.

The gates slid shut. One of the guards unlocked the tailgate of the truck so the prisoners could slide out to the ground. And still none of the guards had rubbed his eyes with the middle finger of his right hand.

"Tough looking guards," George commented.

Einar turned and looked at him. His eyes were still twinkling.

"Yeah," Einar agreed. "Tough."

He got down on hands and knees and slid out of the truck.

## CHAPTER EIGHT

"SO LONG, Neal," Marvin said, gripping his hand, "Don't forget, if you have a chance to look for that woman of mine and find her, tell her to write. Give her my P.O. address."

"Sure," Neal said. He smiled, but after the situation with Charlie and Frances, he couldn't bring himself to do any kidding. "And I'll write you. I'll tell you everything. If the censor cuts the pages to ribbons it won't be my fault you don't know what's happening."

They released hands. Neal climbed into the cockpit of the jetfighter. Five minutes later from the control tower, Marvin watched it take off, its booster rockets throwing off mammoth twin trails of smoke that suddenly terminated high in the clear blue sky as they exhausted their charge and were discarded.

In the jet Neal looked down at the bleak monotony of the drab landscape with a feeling of nostalgia. To the left he could see the trail of human ants—ants whose hill had become flooded and were moving to a new site for their colony. Almost directly underneath was a caravan of busses plodding along—or were they stopped? There was no way of knowing. The jet with its eight hundred and fifty miles of airspeed left them out of sight behind before they could have traveled a hundred yards.

"Have you seen Chicago?" the pilot asked, "It's still a going concern. New York had to give up and be abandoned. Too many of the skyscrapers were weakened by the big waves coming in off the Atlantic. But Chicago's been building waterproof walls against its big buildings as fast as the water rose."

"Is it much out of the way?" Neal asked.

"Not much."

Below, the black landscape changed. Miles of forestland slipped past. Here and there, becoming rapidly more common, were geometric diagrams spread out—the farmlands of Canada.

And then, suddenly, there was nothing but the lead gray of water underneath—Lake Superior. Only now it was no longer a lake, but the northernmost reaches of the Mississippi Sea. For an instant there was a brief view of house roofs sticking above the surface, and the twin spires of a church.

"That was the old shoreline," the pilot said.

Neal watched the water. From twelve thousand feet it looked like sheet steel. It was hard for him to imagine that three years ago this would have been the farmlands of Michigan or northern Wisconsin, and even a year ago there were still large sections of dry land.

"There's Milwaukee," the pilot said, nodding toward it.

Neal looked. A few buildings rose from the water, with white breakers washing against them. He studied it until it was far behind, then turned to look ahead, and there were the familiar outlines of Chicago.

"Up until six months ago they could still use the elevated tracks," the pilot explained. "The depth of the water now is forty-seven feet."

He had dipped down and was making a circle around downtown Chicago. Neal could see hundreds of small boats with V-shaped wakes behind them.

"Looks like the motorboat has replaced the automobile," Neal grunted. "But what do they want to hang on for? Chicago can't be of any use any more without its railroads."

"Well," the pilot said. "They have about two million people here yet, and they're trying to become self-sufficient. They have three atom power plants. Half of what used to be offices is now converted to hydroponic gardens." He shook his head sadly. "But if the water comes up much more they'll have to flood the bottom levels or the pressure will push in the walls. They've had to flood a couple of buildings already."

He straightened out toward the southwest and went into a slow climb. Shortly Chicago was left behind. A few minutes later a landmass could be seen far away to the left.

"The Ozarks," the pilot said, "Tough down there. People wouldn't stay away. Flu epidemic now." He was silent for a while. The Ozark Islands moved around to the east. "Look down there," the pilot said.

Neal looked down where he pointed. Two stern paddle ships were there, pointed west.

"They're loaded with people going that way," the pilot said. "They'll take them to the Rockies. On the trip back they'll bring cattle to be butchered."

Abruptly there were clouds underneath. An hour later the plane dipped into them for a precarious landing on a rain drenched airstrip.

A JEEP with a flexible coupling towed the plane to a hangar. The huge hangar doors were sliding shut against the wind driven rain as the pilot slid back the cowling so Neal could stand up and stretch.

In a far corner past a partly dismantled passenger liner sporadic blue flashes from behind a partition told of a welder at work, and added an eerie touch to the scene of quiet industry.

Three men in the uniforms of majors were approaching. There were welcoming smiles on their lean faces. Neal watched them, sensing a difference in atmosphere. This was Army. This was Air Force. It was divorced from human misery and rivers of human ants. It was an island of something he hadn't seen or felt during the year and a half he had been in the north.

Eighteen months fell away. Neal stepped out of the cockpit onto the wing and dropped lightly to the smooth concrete floor, a smile of pleasure lighting his features. He came smartly to attention and saluted. Then the three men were introducing themselves. Majors Mark Andrews, Steve Davis, and Milt Altman.

They were moving toward the side of the vast cavern of industry while somehow they were getting out of him the details of his trip and a rough sketch of conditions *up north.*

"We have a way to go yet, Neal," Major Steve Davis was saying.

"But Chicago..." Major Milt Altman murmured.

And then they were closely jammed in a covered jeep on a concrete highway where huge raindrops bounced against the pavement in the light of the headlights, and a huge truck passed them going the other way, with its retinue of impatient sedans strung out behind.

Hills and wide curves, and a brief dip into a two block long street with a neon lit supermarket and a brief glimpse into bright windows with almost alive ladies in trim housedresses under a large *Grayson* sign.

"The death toll's been terrific," Major Mark Andrews said with impersonal sadness, his face lit up briefly by the *Phillips 66* sign of a busy service station, "Considerably over a million in the Mississippi Valley. China and India are the worst hit of all though. An estimated five hundred million dead from floods and the oceans going inland alone."

Red blinkers ahead in the rain. Slowing down to a crawl, they passed a wrecker pulling a sedan out of the ditch. Then they weaved around a number of slower moving cars while climbing a steep switchback. Moments later they braked abruptly to almost a complete stop. This was followed by a slow lurch over a ditch. They caught a brief glimpse of a shack and a soldier in raincoat with a rifle. For the next few minutes there was continued lurching, occasional skidding, and always the pounding of the rain on the roof.

And then, abruptly, like something in a dream, a flash of lightning driving its jagged course down from above to terminate at the peak of a trim pointed shape rearing from the unseen vagueness of the ground, up and up, until Neal's mind reeled in unbelief.

He took a deep breath and said, "Gawd, that's beautiful!"

"Like it?" Major Steve Davis murmured smugly. "You've had your first glimpse of your ship."

"*My* ship?" Neal echoed, incredulously.

And then the jeep had skidded to a stop just under a roof. Mark Andrews had opened the door and was holding it open for the others. Beyond him was a large window. Inside were tables with men and women in uniform, eating. Faintly the sound of music drifted out to blend in with the noise of pelting rain.

"A cup of hot coffee ought to feel good to you after your long trip," said Major Milt Altman.

## CHAPTER NINE

"COME IN!" Neal shut off the water and went to the door of the bathroom, draping a towel around his middle. "Oh, good morning, Major Andrews. I'll be with you in a minute. I'm about to take my second tub bath in a year and a half. Up north there's nothing but showers."

He ducked back into the bathroom. Mark Andrews came in leisurely and leaned against the washbasin.

"I guess all this is quite a treat to you, Neal," he said. "Any contact with the enemy up there? But of course! I'd forgotten how you came to be here. You're credited with shooting down one of them…and in one of those unwieldy jetcoptors, too!

Quite a remarkable feat. Speed it up a bit. General Walters is expecting you at nine, and you'll want some breakfast first."

"He can wait," Neal said, grinning from his small sea of suds confined in gleaming white porcelain contours.

"That's treason," Mark murmured, lighting a cigarette, "By the way, I hope your reflexes are still with you? You're going to need them before long."

"I suppose they are," Neal said, "Personally I can't tell. I don't feel any faster than I ever did."

"You wouldn't," Mark said. "We'll soon find out. First on the agenda this morning is raising you to the rank of Major—which is the equivalent of yardbird in O.X."

"O.X.?" Neal asked.

"Operation Extraterrestrial," Mark said.

Neal paused the barest fraction of a second, then went on lathering his shoulders.

"Light me a cigarette, will you Major?" he said.

"THESE WILL be the pictures we took, Major Loomis," General Walters said. "Our Underground Intelligence in Siberia got word out that the attempt was to be made. We readied Palomar, and were quite fortunate."

The lights went out and the screen lit up. Neal watched in fascination. There was a ship. It jumped around as though whoever held the camera was swaying unsteadily.

"Air currents," the General commented. "The moon was low on the horizon. Evidently the Russians tried to time the landing so that we couldn't observe it. If so, they neglected to take into account the fact that refraction of the atmosphere enables us to see the moon for quite some time after it has set mathematically."

The ship was pointed into the screen at a sharp angle. Soon it began to swing about until it was broadsides. At the same time the edge of the moon appeared in the picture, blinding white, then adjusting to lesser light and more detail.

The ship continued to swing about while it fell rapidly

toward the moon. Abruptly a stream of fire shot out from its stern.

"Deceleration," Major Steve Davis commented. "Watch. You're going to have two days of tough drill on this. You can get the idea firsthand from the picture:"

Neal watched, trying to imagine himself inside such a ship, dropping down toward the moon or any other body. It was beyond imagining. Rapidly, too rapidly it seemed, the cigar shaped ship rode down on its tail of fire.

"Very delicate instruments are in operation now," General Walters said in a low voice. "The slightest deviation from the downward direction sets up a tangential velocity that must be annihilated before the ship reaches the ground—or it will land with a sideways velocity and topple over, as you will see shortly."

"Those feather touch adjustments are handled by automatic devices," Mark Andrews said. "But even they aren't perfect. Human reflexes and eyesight are faster—in your case."

Neal didn't answer. He was watching the ship on the screen as it dropped closer and closer to the now distinguishable lunar surface. There was a full minute of perfectly clear picture during which the ship could be seen undistorted, even to the hammer and sickle emblem on its glistening side.

There was a final moment during which the fires of its rocket tail were thrown back from the surface to seemingly engulf it. These ceased. The ship emerged to view, toppling over with unbelievable slowness, while the dwindling gases flowed outward along the lunar surface in wavelets until they dissipated into invisibility.

"You understand, of course, Major Loomis," General Walters said as the lights were turned on, "that this is the country's most guarded secret."

"You can imagine the effect on the morale of the people," Milt Altman said, "if they find out that Russia has already reached the moon."

"Were there men on that ship?" Neal asked.

"Yes," General Walters said, "We won't take time to show you the whole collection of films. You have too much to do during the next three days before—" He stopped, biting his lip. "Major Andrews will take charge of you for the next hour," he added. "His job is to teach your body its proper reflexes under laboratory conditions closely approaching those you will encounter on the ship. That's all here in the projection room." His tone forbade further questioning.

NEAL FELT the muscles of his face sagging downward. He tried to lift his arm as the light on the instrument panel in front of him flashed red. His arm came up slowly—too slowly.

"Get your elbow against the back of your seat," the voice of Mark Andrews came through a small square grill on the panel. "That way you aren't fighting the drag against your whole arm." Neal obeyed and found it much better. "Now let's try it over."

The red light blinked out. Neal dropped his arm and rested. The red light blinked on again. This time he was able to reach up and press the button that shut it off.

"Good work," Mark said. "That topped the best mark set so far. We'll try it again, then have some variations and see how you'll do..."

ANALYZE specific sensations," Steve Davis said. "For example, I can physically tell the force of three gravities, or 'gees' as we call them, by a sensation from my left earlobe. At three and a half, one of my teeth aches a little. Just sit and watch the dial and connect your sensations to the acceleration. By the day after tomorrow you will have to be able to tell to within a tenth of a g-force what your acceleration is—or we don't dare entrust the ship to you. We know what it takes to handle it, and you've got to have it *before* you lift her off the ground."

"I'm a little tired," Neal said. "Let's take a breather."

"Uh uh," Steve said. "You're going to be more tired than that all the time upstairs. Get used to it. It's part of your training…"

"LIE DOWN here. Quickly!"

The doctor pressed the stethoscope against Neal's chest. He listened for a moment, finally nodding his head and taking the stethoscope away.

"Good," he said. "Unbelievably good. Now the fatigue test and we're through for the day."

Neal rested his hand, palm upward, in the clamp. One finger fitted through a wire hoop. The doctor fastened the cover down.

"Start!" he said.

Neal lifted his one free finger against the resistance of a spring and let it drop. Raised it and let it drop…

"THIS IS the schematic diagram of the ship," Milt Altman said, "You don't get much from it except the general arrangement of things. There are four main parts to notice right now. The rocket, as you can see, is something really out of this world. I don't think the Russians have it in theirs. It's atomic. We wanted a neutron beam but had to be content with protons. The beam is really about eight percent deuterons. The fuel is forty-percent pure plutonium in the form of number twelve-gauge wire. It's fed through the barium oxide reflector block which is really a long solid rod two feet thick, encased in a laminated steel tube, and screw-fed along the tube as it's eaten away by the bombardment of exploding atoms against it.

"And here's the gyro setup at the center of gravity…"

"CONGRATULATIONS, Major Loomis," General Walters said, "The reports of your progress are everything we had hoped for. Ah, we're having a little party for you after dinner. Your orderly will make sure you are dressed properly."

"I wish you hadn't, sir," Neal said, "I'm exhausted."

"Nonsense! By the time you've showered and eaten and put on full dress uniform you'll feel differently. Major Andrews will call for you at eight-thirty."

"Yes, sir," Neal said. He saluted, turned smartly, and went to the door.

"Don't feel so good?" Mark Andrews said sympathetically, "It's nerves, believe me *I* know." He went over to a blonde wood, cabinet and opened it, revealing an array of glasses, bottles, and the door of a very small refrigerator. He looked slyly up at Neal and smiled at the expression of surprise he saw there. "Didn't know you had a liquor cabinet in your quarters, did you, Loomis? As a matter of fact it isn't standard equipment, but we wanted you to have everything. We're pinning a lot of hope on you."

IT WAS a large hall, fully fifty feet across either way. Folding chairs were stacked up in six-foot high tiers along two walls. On the far side, on a raised platform, was an orchestra. Neal's eyebrows shot up as he recognized Joel Cartier, the most famous of bandleaders, wielding the baton.

"They flew him all the way from Appomattox for tonight's party," Mark said at Neal's shoulder.

General Walters was coming toward him, a broad smile wrinkling his features into a mask of aged joviality.

"Was I right?" he asked. "You look great. I can't understand why you weren't made a major long ago. You look the part."

"Thank you, sir," Neal said. "I think you were right. I'm sure I won't regret a last—ah—fling."

"Fling?" General Walters threw back his silver gray head and laughed. "Yes," he said, sobering suddenly. "Tonight is yours. Do what you wish. Tomorrow you go into training seriously. Two days of that, and then—the cold gray dawn."

Neal looked at Mark, who lifted his eyebrows meaningfully. The General had had a little too much to drink.

"Well," General Walters said, coming out of the reverie he had momentarily fallen into, "have a good time. I must hurry back to my niece."

"Yes, Uncle?"

The three men turned. Neal caught his breath.

"Aren't you going to introduce me, Uncle Fred?" the girl asked, looking into Neal's eyes.

"Why—why—of course. Naturally, my dear child. Major Loomis—my niece, Dorothy Walters."

"How do you do?" she said, but the words were obviously just for her uncle's benefit. She continued to look into Neal's eyes. And somehow Major Mark Andrews and General Walters had faded away, and the band was playing…

"You dance very nicely, Major," Dorothy said.

"It must be you, Dorothy," Neal said. "I haven't danced for —" He stopped as the wail of air raid sirens rose above the sound of the orchestra. "Which way is the bomb shelter?"

"Oh, we pay no attention to raids except to make sure of blackout precautions," Dorothy said. "Our fighter protection here is quite perfect—and if it isn't, we'll never know it. They've been trying to get O.X. since the very beginning."

Neal glanced nervously at the ceiling.

"Should we get a drink, Neal?" Dorothy suggested…

"UNCLE SAYS we can't take a jeep," Dorothy said as she slipped onto the vacant stool beside Neal. "The all clear hasn't sounded. They still have an atom bomber trying to get through to here with literally thousands of fighter support planes escorting it. This is the biggest air offensive they've thrown out in two weeks. Your glass is empty, Neal. Another?"

"No," Neal said. "I want to talk to you. Where can we go?"

"We could go to my apartment," Dorothy said gravely, "but we couldn't get past the desk. Uncle said this morning—or was it yesterday morning? Well, anyway, he said that they'd installed a liquor cabinet in your apartment. But why can't we talk right here? Nobody'll listen anyway. They're all having too much fun by themselves."

"What's wrong with my apartment?" Neal asked, "But I guess you're right. Bartender…" He set his glass on the bar…

"It would serve Uncle right," Dorothy said.

Neal looked at her, puzzled, "What would?" he asked vaguely.

"If I went with you to your apartment," Dorothy said, "In fact, I've a good notion to. We could have just sat in the jeep without going anywhere..."

"Let's go," Neal said. "Though I don't think you're going to like what we're going to talk about."

He stood up. Dorothy linked her arm in his.

"Let's go," she whispered excitingly...

"I GUESS we could have talked back there," Neal said, fumbling inside the door for the light switch.

"This'll be much better," Dorothy said. "Here, let me find it," She reached past him and found the switch.

"Gawd..." Neal muttered when they were inside, "I must have had an unbelievable amount to drink," He rubbed his eyes with his fingers, then took them away and looked at Dorothy who stood a scant foot away looking up at him, smiling.

"Dorothy," he said, "What I wanted to say was—I'm married. I don't know where my wife is—or even if she's alive. Haven't known for almost a year."

"Is that all?" Dorothy said softly.

"All?" Neal echoed, "Isn't that enough? I'm married. But damn it—" He stopped, lifting his hand to his eyes again.

"But—you want *me?*" Dorothy asked.

"I—I don't know," Neal groaned. "When I first saw you tonight something happened. Maybe it's just that in three days I'm going up in that spaceship. Maybe that's all it is."

"Suppose you weren't married?" Dorothy asked, placing her hands on his shoulders.

"If I weren't married maybe it'd be different," Neal groaned. "I with I could see Annette before I go up."

He brushed Dorothy's hands away and turned, stumbling over to the davenport and slumping down, burying his face in his hands.

"Neal," Dorothy said, "Neal! Listen to me. You aren't married." She walked over to him and shook him, "Neal! Do you hear me? You aren't married!"

"Huh?" he said suddenly, the meaning of her words sinking in. "What do you mean?"

She spoke rapidly. "They wanted to surprise you. They wanted to have Annette here with you these last three days before you go up. They turned the entire Intelligence Service into the job of locating her. They found her. She's dead. She died on Ozark Island almost a year ago in an air raid."

"I don't believe it," Neal said dully, lowering his hands and looking up at her.

"It's true, Neal," Dorothy said. "They didn't dare tell you. They thought—" She stopped, a horrified light coming into her eyes. "Oh gawd!" she moaned, "What have I done?"

"Get out," Neal said.

"I have feelings for you, Neal," Dorothy said, her features cramping.

"Get out."

He watched her as she turned slowly and went to the door. She looked back at him appealingly. His expression didn't change. She opened the door and went out. It closed slowly behind her.

He looked at the closed door for several minutes. His features slowly lost their expression of grief, smoothing out. Finally he got to his feet and went to the bathroom and turned the water into the tub.

Then he looked at his reflection in the mirror…and smiled.

"Stone sober…" he said to his reflection softly, mockingly.

## CHAPTER TEN

"SHUT UP, Gabby," George Lord said tiredly.

"I wish you'd stop calling me that," Harry Drake said in an injured tone. "I don't talk any more than anybody else—or if I do it's because I think of more to say."

"I never knew anybody that could think of less to say and take longer to say it," George said. "Pass me the salt—and don't start telling me all you know about salt."

"Reach for it," Harry said. He turned his attention to Einar. "What do you think, Einar? Were those human bones your shovel uncovered yesterday? They looked it to me."

"I don't think so," Einar said evasively. "In the first place they're too heavy."

"Petrified," Harry said. "I've seen petrified ivory in a museum. Handled it. It's the same exactly. And if they've lasted a million years under the ice they'd have to be petrified."

"Okay," Einar said, "but they could be the bones of a bear. We didn't find a skull. Anyway, it doesn't make any difference."

"The heck it doesn't," Harry said. "If it was human it bears out what I was saying on the way up here—that the human race lived up here once before the ice age. That means there'll be another ice age, and everybody had better come north now."

"Let's go, Einar," George said, lifting himself up and stepping over the bench into the aisle between the long tables. He gave Einar a sharp look.

"Sure," Einar said, gulping the last of his black coffee and rising.

"Just a minute and I'll go too," Harry said. He started in on the last of his fried eggs and potatoes, saw that George and Einar weren't waiting for him, and abandoned his breakfast to scurry after them.

"He'll get a knife in his ribs some night," George growled. Then, hastily to Einar, "Things are happening pretty soon now. I've got to talk to you—today."

"If it was human bones it'll be a nice thing for you, Einar," Harry said as he caught up with them, "Maybe they'll let you off with your minimum sentence in spite of your socking that guard. They should."

"Gaaa..." George gasped in frustration. He glared at Harry and stalked away.

"It's coming pretty quick now," Einar said to Harry out of

the corner of his mouth.

"What's come over him?" Harry said, staring after George, then quietly without moving his lips, "What do you want me to do?"

"Look, Harry, he just gets tired of you talking so much," Einar said. "As a matter of fact…I can tell you that I get a little tired of it myself." Then, out of the corner of his mouth as Harry looked at him reproachfully he whispered, "just stay out of the way until noon so I can get the dope on what's going on."

Harry nodded almost imperceptibly, then in a loud voice said, "Well, if that's the way you feel…" He turned around and scurried back toward his place at the table, "Hey! Somebody swiped the rest of my breakfast…"

Einar hurried out after George.

"How the hell did you get rid of Harry?" George asked in amazement.

"I told him I was getting a little tired of him myself," Einar said, a trace of a grin on his face. "It hurt his feelings."

"Oh, that's a shame," George said sarcastically. He lowered his voice. "We're all set for the day after tomorrow."

"How do you know?" Einar asked quickly. "I mean that's awfully soon isn't it? Why didn't they set things far enough ahead so we're absolutely sure that we're all synchronized to act at the same time. This whole thing would fall apart if we gained control here but all the other labor camps were a day behind us."

"The warden's radio operator is one of us," George said, "That was the hardest job of all, getting our men in as radio operators at all the camps. He got the code yesterday and passed it to the specific guards that are in it with us."

"That makes me feel better," Einar said quickly. "That's one thing I was worried about. I was afraid if something leaked out, the radio op would be able to call for the army."

"Not a chance," George said, "Not only that, but he's got a small explosive planted in one of the power tubes. If the radio's turned on and operated by anyone that doesn't know how to keep it from blowing up—poof! No radio."

"Then everything's set," Einar said, "Day after tomorrow morning eight of us leave the breakfast table early and instead of going straight out to the jeeps we turn and run to the arsenal. It'll be open. We'll have a couple of minutes to get guns. Then I fire a shot in the air. That's the signal for the riot back in the mess hall."

"That's enough," George said. "We both know how it goes from there. One of our guards shoots the warden. The other will go from the arsenal as soon as we show up. He'll see that the guards in the block are delayed until we can all get armed and herd the other prisoners out into the yard. Pass the word along today and tomorrow."

EINAR brought the giant shovel over the waiting truck and released the trip that sent its load dropping, expertly placed. He swung the shovel around and brought up another scoop. His eyes searched the crumbling embankment for signs of anything solid too long and narrow to be stone. There was nothing but the black, clay-like mud, heavy and totally devoid of vegetable matter except for the microscopic flecks of carbon that might have been coal at one time before it was picked up and ground to an almost atomic dust by the grinding pressure of ice.

He brought the shovel to a stop and dumped the second load, filling the truck. As he swung the shovel away he looked idly at the number on the truck. Twenty-three...Harry Drake's.

The truck started up, went a few feet and stopped. It started up again after a moment, went another few feet, then stopped again.

Its door opened and Harry dropped to the ground. The prison guard came running up. Einar saw Harry point toward the motor hood and shrug.

Another truck stopped in place for loading. Einar started to load it while keeping an eye ion Harry and the guard. The guard talked to Harry a moment, then climbed into the truck. After a moment he got out and went over to the driver of the other truck that was being loaded and spoke to him.

Harry wandered over and hopped aboard the shovel.

"Engine trouble?" Einar said, smiling.

"Yeah," Harry said. "Gawd…I thought I'd never get that wire twisted in two. It'll take the mechanic a few minutes to find the break, but not long. Better not waste time."

"This little uprising has been very well planned. It's as we've suspected all along, but it's happening sooner than we anticipated. Everything starts the day after tomorrow right after breakfast," Einar said. "The scale of this is huge. It involves all the labor camps. But we've got something we didn't expect. The radio operator is in on it."

"The radio operator?" Harry said, suddenly very serious. "How are we going warn our people? There wouldn't be any way to get this to GHQ. Are you sure about this? I mean the radio operators in every camp are screened pretty closely."

"George said every radio man in the labor camp setup is in on it—the organizers of this little revolt made it one of their prime objectives."

"We don't know for sure who to trust then," Harry said, "Even the warden himself may be in on it."

"There are orders to shoot the warden," Einar said grimly. We can't let that happen. We've been tracking this sabotage effort too long to have it blow up in our faces now."

"Then I'll have to try to get through to him," Harry said. "I can demand my rights and insist on seeing him. It might work."

"Let me try it," Einar suggested. "After I socked that guard I was interviewed by the warden so he could hear my version of the incident."

"No," Harry said. "Your job is to play along with them until it's over. Those are our orders. I'll get to the warden and convince him. Then we'll take over the radio, contact GHQ, and let them know how this uprising is supposed to unfold."

Einar shook his head, "The radio has a hidden explosive in it," he said, "Only the operator knows how to operate it without detonating it. You'll have to get away in some kind of a vehicle

—a truck maybe—and find a way to contact GHQ outside the camp. If you can get through to the warden he should be able to help you."

"Leave it to me," Harry said. A slight smile came to his face. "If George only knew that we're agents for the U.S. government. I'll bet he'd—" He began talking in a louder voice as the guard returned. "They'll find more bones around here. My guess is that this hill's an old prehistoric cemetery and there's lots of bones."

EINAR SAT down, looked across the table at George, then gazed questioningly at the empty place where Harry usually sat. When he looked up again George was grinning wolfishly.

"Pass the salt, Einar," he said. Then George glanced sidewise at the empty chair. "You know...I'm an impatient man...sometimes."

Einar picked up the saltshaker and held it out. George's hand was sure and steady as he wrapped his fingers around it. Einar looked up into his eyes and a chill shot through him as he realized what the man was trying to convey to him.

George had killed Harry.

Had it been because he knew who Harry really was? Einar studied him through half-closed eyes. A suspicion that had lain dormant at the back of his mind emerged. There had always been a certain *something* about George that was out of place. It came to him now what it was. A well concealed arrogance.

George Lord was a Russian spy.

The thought crystallized in Einar's mind, and a thousand little traits rose from memory to make it a certainty. Einar now knew that the entire nerve virus "attack" had indeed been Russian. It had served as a ploy to incite rebellion in the labor camps—but to what further purpose?

That was neither here nor there for the moment, though. What mattered was that Harry was to have warned the warden, and Harry was dead.

"Knife?" Einar asked, holding out his hand.

"Huh?" George said, startled. He did a double take. Picking up his knife and handing it across the table to Einar he said, "Yes."

Einar forced himself to eat and be casual while his mind searched frantically for some answer. GHQ had suspected something was amiss in the labor camps. They had allowed Einar to follow his own plans for rooting out any anti-government plot. He had staged the fight and been arrested so that no one could possibly suspect him of being a secret operative. Harry had been assigned to accompany him to Camp Fifty when it was certain there was something definite in the works.

Now everything was falling into place like the parts of a jigsaw puzzle. George Lord was the key man, the Soviet spy in charge. It was now apparent that he had come to this advance labor camp so that it could serve as his base of operations after the planned revolt succeeded, while the revolutionaries were still battling the small land army farmed out up here to help the refugees get settled.

The uprising could very well succeed if GHQ didn't know when the blow was about to fall. There could also be thousands of Russian jet fighters and troop transports ready for a backup thrust after the uprising—anything was possible.

Einar forced the last bite of fried egg down and stood up. George stood up too. They met at the end of the table and walked casually toward the exit.

"I'd have done it tomorrow anyway," George muttered, "But I decided not to wait. I'll be too busy tomorrow to worry about that."

Einar shrugged. "It's fine by me," he said out of the corner of his mouth. "But it could ruin things if they put us all in our cells while they investigate the murder."

"They won't," George said, "They want the mud bricks too much."

He was right. Einar knew that. They had to have them. They were sentencing anyone able to work for the mildest of offenses so that they could garner enough workers to turn out the millions of blocks it would take to convert this vast wasteland into the beginnings of a livable country. It avoided the technicalities of setting up a vast civilian army of workers, and what was more important, it took a crippling load off the already bankrupt government treasury. It also kept the vast population moving to the north from building up a false wealth in worthless dollar savings.

"Everybody knows?" George said.

"I passed it to the truck drivers as they got their loads yesterday," Einar said.

"Good," George said.

He grinned knowingly at Einar and moved off, hands in pockets, whistling an off-key melody.

EINAR GLANCED at the jeep speeding across the ground toward him. A guard was in it—one of the two who were in on the revolt plot. His attention was forced back to the delicate task of dropping the shovel just right to scoop into the embankment and bring up a full load. When he had swung the loaded shovel around to the waiting truck he took another quick glance. The jeep had stopped. The guard was coming toward him.

He tripped the release that dropped the two yards of mud neatly into the truck.

"Hey! Einar!" the guard shouted above the noise of the motor. "You're wanted at the warden's office!"

Einar felt a surge of new hope. This would be a chance to let the warden know what was going to happen. But immediately his heart dropped. Why would the warden be sending for him? There was but one reason, Harry's body had been found. They were bringing him in to question him, or were they going to charge him with the murder? That would be a touch typical of George Lord. More than once Einar had felt that George knew he was a GHQ operative, and that that was the source of the amusement that lay deep in his eyes when he looked at him.

"Right," he answered.

He swung his shovel around and brought it to rest ready for the next scoop and shut off the motor. The palms of his hands were moist.

He jumped down out of the cab and got into the jeep beside the guard.

"What's it about?" he asked carelessly, "Harry's murder?"

"I don't know," the guard said, starting the jeep with a violent lurch. "Damn this clutch—it sticks. All I know is they handed me orders to bring you to the administration office. Whatever it is you don't have to worry. Even if they locked you up for murder they wouldn't shoot you today—and tomorrow you'd be out again after it's over. So don't worry."

"Yeah, guess you're right," Einar said, slumping down.

The guard stopped the jeep at the administration building.

"I'll go in with you," he said. "That way I can maybe find out—in case you don't get to come out again."

Einar glanced around curiously as they entered the building. They were in a reception room. The floor was of asphalt tile, a bright mottled yellow. Two men in the garb of prisoners were at work at the two desks in the room.

"Sit down and wait, Mr. Tharnsen," one of them said, looking up. He turned his eyes to the guard. "That will be all, Mr. Overman."

The guard hesitated, looked at Einar in indecision, then turned and left. The trusty was dialing on the phone. As the door closed behind the guard the trusty said, "Right through that door, Mr. Tharnsen."

Einar went to the door and opened it. He saw the warden sitting behind his desk and a soldier—a tall, lanky officer. Both men were smiling broadly at him. Then a familiar voice reached his ears.

"Einar!"

He turned in the direction of the voice. Familiar features, the large braid of straw colored hair curved into a nest.

"Hilda!" he said, a mixture of gladness and alarm in his voice.

His wife was reaching toward him with her arms, wanting to rush to him, afraid to display affection in public. He knew what went on inside her.

"You're free, Einar," she was saying. "Mr. Swank here helped me get you free. We have a special pardon from the President of the United States himself."

She was standing there, so erect, so proud, so happy. A pain shot through Einar's heart.

For an instant he felt regret that he had ever been born. This was a moment when decisions had to be made and acted upon. He didn't feel capable of making them. Should he warn the warden now? Hilda was no actress. They wouldn't get away alive. Should he say nothing and let them take him away, and after they were safely away start things moving?

"You're free to leave at once," the warden said. He was smiling—and Einar couldn't condemn him to his death in the revolt tomorrow.

"Okay," Einar said, suddenly making up his mind. "But—could I leave a note for one of my friends?"

"Of course, Einar," the warden said, "I'll see that it's delivered to him," He opened a drawer and took out paper and pencil and held them out.

Einar smiled at his wife. While they watched him he sat down and hastily wrote out the details of the plan for revolt, giving names. He folded the paper and wrote on the outside, *For you, warden.*

Standing up, he handed the folded note to the warden. The warden took it and glanced at the supposed name on the outside in idle curiosity. He frowned suddenly and looked sharply at Einar.

Einar shook his head imperceptibly, holding his breath, hoping the warden was shrewd enough not to do the wrong thing.

The warden looked a bit confused. Then his face cleared. He smiled. "I'll see that *he* reads it, Einar," he said. "However

—" He looked at him quizzically. "I didn't know you considered him a friend of yours."

"Let's go," Marvin Swank said.

Einar nodded and put his arm around Hilda and started toward the door. His palms were moist again. So much depending on so little. Perhaps the entire outcome of World War III concentrated on what happened in the next ten minutes. The warden would have to fight for his life, rallying the loyal guards and keeping possession of the arsenal. But that was a side issue.

But—perhaps—the fate of the civilized world depended on whether he, Einar, could reach the gates of the labor camp without being shot…

## CHAPTER ELEVEN

"MORNING, Mark," Major Steve Davis said. "Sit down and join us."

Major Mark Andrews smiled at him and Major Milt Altman and sat down. "Just coffee, please," he said to the waitress.

Milt Altman lifted his arm and frowned at his wristwatch. "Just fifty-seven minutes more," he said. "Major Loomis will be boarding his ship in another twelve minutes."

"I wish I'd had what it takes," Mark said regretfully.

"Don't we all," Steve murmured. "By the way, what's come over Major Loomis? All day yesterday he had the strangest expression on his face."

"I noticed it too," Mark said.

"So did I," Milt said. "It reminded me of the smile on a nut I saw in Los Angeles once. A guy who claimed he was God. Major Loomis had that same look—a sort of quiet smile and—"

"It wasn't quite like that," Mark interrupted. "I saw a man who looked exactly like Neal did all day yesterday. It was when I was in Africa with the Europe atom bomb detail. He was a fighter pilot and he'd had a dream that it was his day to get it. If he'd told anyone he'd have been sent back home, but he just wrote a note that was found later in his effects."

"I think you're both wrong," Steve said. "Neal knows his stuff. He's the first American to leave Earth. It's a job any one of us would give his eyeteeth for. If I had made the grade and it was the day before I was to go up I think I'd have the same smile—"

"It wouldn't be the same," Mark said. He glanced nervously at his watch. "Forty-five minutes. He's riding the elevator up right now and getting into the ship. Gawd, I'm nervous! If something goes wrong and he crashes..."

Five sharp piercing shrieks sounded in rapid succession. There was a pause, then they were repeated.

"That's clear-the-field," Mark said unnecessarily. "No turning back now. He's in there. Alone, in..." He looked at his watch. "...thirty-eight minutes."

"Hey," Milt said softly, "Look who just wandered in... Dorothy." He waved his hand at her and motioned for her to come over and join them. In an undertone he said, "I saw her and Neal leave the party together. Wonder if they have a crush on each other."

"Lucky dog," Mark mumbled, "He'll have all the breaks from now on. What's eating Dorothy? She looks like—" She was too close for him to finish his remark.

"Good morning, Dorothy," Milt said, getting up and pulling back the fourth chair for her. "You're looking pretty upset. We're all nervous, but he'll come back."

"Good morning," Dorothy said. She sat down and placed her elbows on the table, twisting a small lace handkerchief in a distracted way.

"Some coffee?" Milt suggested.

"What?" She looked up at him as though she had forgotten he was there, "No...no thanks."

She bit her lip and looked out the window at the incredibly tall, incredibly graceful projectile a mile away pointing upward at the sky as though anxious already to be free of its Earth bonds.

"Twenty-four minutes," Mark announced—and suddenly

they all realized they had been staring at the spaceship.

"Oh, dear lord," Dorothy exploded suddenly. "They can't let him go up. They can't. They've got to stop him." Her lip trembled. She sucked it between her teeth, then brought the twisted remains of the kerchief to her eyes.

"Here, now," Milt soothed. "It isn't that bad. The Ruskies have reached the moon. The ship is as perfect as man can make it."

"Oh, I know…I know," Dorothy said, "But he shouldn't go up. He's in no shape for it. He might do something."

"You're just imagining things," Milt said.

"What do you mean?" Mark asked, looking at her sharply.

"Why—why nothing!" Dorothy said.

"Yes, you do," Mark said, gripping her wrist. "Come on! Out with it!"

"You're hurting me," Dorothy said, trying desperately to smile. Mark stared into her eyes and slowly relaxed his grip.

"One minute!" Steve said tensely.

They turned to the window, everything else forgotten, their eyes on the ship, waiting for the first blast of flame…

"HOW DO you feel, Neal?" It was General Walters' voice corning from the gray grill of the radio.

"All right, sir," Neal said calmly.

He was sitting in a chair with a form fitting back of sponge rubber that cradled him against the terrific acceleration that would grip him shortly. In front of him within easy reach were all the controls. Above them was a concave dome that seemed to be transparent, bringing a clear view of the rocket field and the buildings a mile away.

He reached out and pushed in the second of four push buttons in a small rectangle of the control panel. Instantly the view of the field and the buildings was replaced by one of drifting clouds and a star studded sky. He knew what he was seeing was exactly what he would have seen if the Screen were actually a transparent dome. But it was in reality a video screen connected with electronic camera eyes fixed into the outer shell of the ship.

"I have a last minute surprise for you, Neal," the General's voice sounded. "Special line to Appomattox. The President wants to wish you luck personally."

"Put him on," Neal said. The second hand passed the bottom, moving toward the beginning of its last round.

"Good morning, Major Loomis," the President's voice erupted from the speaker.

"Good morning, sir," Neal said.

"I want to wish you God speed, Neal," the President said, his voice suddenly personal in tone. "When you get back, the highest honors this Government can give will be yours..."

His voice was drowned out by the wail of the air raid siren. At first Neal thought it must have originated at the Capitol at Appomattox. Then he realized General Walters' mike must still be on.

The sky as seen in the video dome was suddenly alive with fighter planes—Soviet jets. Target-seeking rockets sliced upwards, leaving trails of still fiery gas.

Neal glanced at the instrument panel clock. Four seconds to zero. His eyes went back to the screen and he was shocked by what he saw.

A new type of ship shot into view, coming in from high in the atmosphere. It was a giant thing that looked like a spaceship and it was less than three thousand feet distant. Neal could only imagine that it contained Soviet troops and equipment, perhaps some new Soviet secret weapon. He was terrified at the sight of it. But suddenly from the side a streak of flame shot toward the ship, at its head a flash of pointed silver.

It was a guided missile.

It drove straight into the heart of the new Russian ship. In the next instant its side opened up, seeming to melt and evaporate, rather than explode. Men and machines were pouring from the wound. The atomic fire trail of the missile seemed like some lethal ray, rather than matter, and it extended through the mortally wounded ship, up into the sky above.

Then the scene of destruction was brushed aside by an unseen hand, and incredible weight was suddenly pressing Neal back. His eyes jerked to the clock. Zero hour had passed. The ship was lifting…

There was a curtain of intense black hanging deep within the concave video dome of the compartment—a very old and somewhat dusty curtain with countless holes through which light seeped. It was the universe.

Neal kept his eyes on it as he reached for the controls. The stick was exactly the same as the ones in the planes he had used.

He pushed forward against it, feeling it resist. In his mind's eye he could visualize the gear motors slowly whirring in the gyro compartment, the long ship slowly changing direction, while the tail of atomic fire continued to shoot straight back without abatement.

Something rose into view—or was it the black curtain being lifted? It was the Earth, the curved horizon.

Neal leaned forward to look down. He had seen this before in pictures taken from experimental rockets. But it hadn't been quite the same. Those pictures had shown a recognizable North America. It was the North American continent below, but no longer recognizable. It looked more like a huge, discolored pulled tooth with two roots extending down from a corroded and blackened shell, one blunt, the other long and jagged.

The Pacific stretched out ahead like the greasy surface of a steel ball. To the north the pulled tooth was joined insecurely to another mass of black—Siberia.

There were little flecks of bright silver down there. They seemed stationary, but they were above the scattered clouds. Planes. While he watched, their illusion of motionlessness vanished. His mind made the adjustment to distance and size. There were thousands of them.

"General Walters!" he called out. "There's a mass raid starting from Alaska. Thousands of planes," He waited a moment. There was no answer, "General Walters!" he called out again.

Frantically he twisted the dial of the receiver. Suddenly a station came in loud and clear.

"Your li'l ol' disc jockey, Tubby O'Hara, broadcasting from KQTZ, the Kaintucky station that moved to the hills of Tennessee when the li'l ol' Gulf of Mexico welcomed the aintire Southland to its bosom. We'll have the news in a few minutes now, but I think we have time for a tune first—"

Angrily Neal twisted the dial off station. He looked down at the flecks of silver. They were piling up along a line in the Yukon. Here and there they were changing from silver to lengthening trails of dark etched into the white background of clouds.

In his mind Neal was translating the flecks of silver into planes and battle formations and movements. There were also troop transports—too many to count. Some of them had broken beyond the line of Western defense in the north with their fighters fluttering around them. More were coming from Siberia.

This was an all-out offensive. The thing the airforce had fondly hoped was no longer possible.

Neal searched the ground to the south. There were flecks of silver there, too—all moving northward. They were U.S. jets, hurrying to intercept the Russians. He translated their speeds and calculated that they would get there in time to stop at least some of the Soviet air fleet. But the outcome looked uncertain, perhaps even grim—

"The last hope for us," he groaned.

He twisted to watch the drama of death and lost hope as the turning globe drew it over the brink of the eastern horizon.

THREE HUNDRED miles below, the looming rim of what the hungry Pacific had left of China crept over the horizon, moving toward Neal and taking form. A shoreline and sloping hills.

Neal watched it pass below with the ponderous dignity of

vast things moving slowly. Then, abruptly, he turned away from it.

He pulled back on the stick. The earth dropped in the video dome as the gyros shifted the nose of the ship upward.

The dusty black shroud of outer space with its scattered scintillating jewels was an abyss into which he was plunging.

He touched the plutonium feed controls and smiled his satisfaction as he felt added acceleration press against him.

After a while he pressed each of the four pushbuttons that selected the direction of view in the video dome and saw in turn the sun with its flaming corona, the earth which was now a colossal globe with alien geography, and the moon, travelling in its unchangeable path to the point of rendezvous, and once again the black canopy of diamond dust whose pattern was his signpost in space.

And finally the time came to touch the gyro stick once more. There was no slightest change in the force of acceleration flowing through him, yet the universe passed across the video dome in swift departure until the earth, a globe twice the size of the moon as seen in earth's skies, hung suspended in the screen, stationary.

But to Neal it was no longer the world he had left, nor quite yet the globe it would soon be. It was an abstract direction of reference in the guidance of the ship.

Now he touched the number-four pushbutton. The earth was replaced by a faint ball of fire, which was the residue of the rocket tail not eliminated from the video composite, and by the now familiar section of space toward which he was headed. And, to one side, the moon, now an unreal and magnified globe, seemingly unmoving, yet moving as fast as he was toward the meeting place in space.

There was no room in thought for any other thing. Ptolemaeus, a crater ninety miles across, was to be his destination. It was clearly visible. Already in Neal's eyes it had become the landing field, while the spaceship had essentially become a jetcopter that must be dropped on a stationary dime with a feather touch.

Time stood still while all else moved. Gyro motors in high gear for instant response. Plutonium feed dual controls, one normal and one micro. Video eyes alternating magnification for constant checking. Neal's ship was descending onto the moon.

And then—it was done. There was the jarring thud, and for a moment Neal held his breath while the destiny of mankind hung in the balance. Atomic fire rebounded from the moon's surface to blot out all things, then wash away as he cut the plutonium feed.

The ship remained upright—he had landed safely.

He jabbed at the number two video button. Instantly the earth appeared. It was stationary in the screen, revolving with almost imperceptible slowness. It would remain there in that same spot until Neal took off again for home.

Now he reached into the right hand section of the control panel and pressed a button. A moment later a green dot of light appeared inside it—the signal that the pointed nose of the ship had retracted, to be replaced by the launching tube for the atomic missiles that filled the vast hold of the ship, tier on tier.

Neal looked up into the screen at the globe suspended there, and at the discolored tooth with two roots that was North America.

A quiet smile rested on his lips as he turned on the radio.

"Major Loomis reporting," he said quietly. "Objective reached and I am centered on target."

Five seconds passed…then, "Thank God, Neal!"

It was General Walters.

"And none too soon. We're almost lost. Russia threw an all-out at us. An old side kick of yours, Marvin Swank, and a GHQ agent, Einar Tharnsen, gave us warning in time to blunt the thrust, but—fire, Neal. Fire at will until they give up!"

The quiet smile, holding within it the culmination of the hope of all freedom-loving peoples, remained on Neal's lips as he made adjustments.

In his mind's eye was the memory of the rocket in number

one place for launching. And in his thoughts as he jabbed the firing pin a voice whispered, "it's about time!"

And in neat white letters on the side of the silver shape that darted Earthward from the nose of the ship was one word.

*Moscow.*

THE END

# *ENIGMA OF AN UNEXPLORED WORLD*

*Roy Auckland had been asked to join the expedition now on the remote planet Carolus. Despite the fact that he was a communications expert, not an explorer, he was excited about the opportunity to visit an unknown world. But he wondered why he had been requested personally by the head of the expedition.*

*Once on Carolus, Roy met the weird creatures called the Vaec and was immediately intrigued by their mirth-loving nature and their patient devotion to practical jokes.*

*But was it one of their practical jokes that almost exploded alongside Dr. James' skull? Or was it a made-on-Earth murder gimmick? Suddenly, Auckland realized that behind their "native simplicity" the Vaec were dangerously and subtly deceptive. And he also realized that somehow he had to break through their mask to understand them or Dr. James would be only the first of the Earthmen to die.*

# FOREWORD

*Back in the early 40's, I remember a bull-session that some of us had with John W. Campbell, where he stated definitively that there could never be any such thing as a science-fiction detective story in the traditional "murder mystery" sense. His reason for this proclamation was that since almost anything can happen in a science-fiction story—the villain can pull any sort of dingus or super-phenomenon out of his hat—the reader would never have a fair chance to solve the mystery.*

*I didn't quite believe it, yet I couldn't think of any counter-argument to throw at John at the time. But, as Holmes would have said, it was all so absurdly simple! Of course there can be science-fiction murder mysteries, offering the reader as good a chance to solve the crime as he has in any ordinary murder-mystery where the author is playing fair. And you can have science fiction wonders and dinguses and super-scientific phenomenon, too: you just make it clear that nothing essential to the solution of the crime is wrapped up in super-science, or intricate phenomenon and extrapolation that only a scientific wizard could be expected to unravel. The motives, methods, and clues must all lie within the range of what is clearly presented to the reader. I hope Puzzle Planet will convince you that the murder mystery does have a place in science fiction.*

**Robert A. W. Lowndes**

# THE PUZZLE PLANET

By
ROBERT A. W. LOWNDES

ARMCHAIR FICTION & MUSIC
PO Box 4369, Medford, Oregon 97504

*The original text of this novel was first published by Ace Books*



*For more information about Armchair Books and products, visit our website at…*

**www.armchairfiction.com**

*Or email us at…*

**armchairfiction@yahoo.com**

# CHAPTER ONE

IT COULD almost be an unfamiliar part of Earth, Dr. Roy Auckland was thinking as he looked out of the picture window on the right wall of the prefab headquarters unit. In fact, many parts of Earth presented far more alien and other-worldly appearance than what first met the eye here on Carolus. A blue sky with white clouds—but not quite the blue of Earth; green ground-covering that could pass for close-mown grass until you saw that this was more of a hairy type of moss; flowers that suggested terrestrial flowers, but weren't quite right—were those pansies or violets? No, not quite either; and they had center dots suggestive of black-eyed Susans. Then Ekem-ve came into view, with another native Carolinian, and Auckland stopped thinking of the resemblances of this Earth-type planet to his own world.

"Mister Five-by-Five," he murmured.

"Won't do, Roy," said Shirley Mason without interrupting the rhythm of her typing. "You're describing a fat Earthman, and no Earthman ever lived who was as agile and quick on his feet as any of the Vaec. Sometimes I think their bones must be made of rubber."

"Of course," he agreed. "And some men have large eyes, but certainly no man's pupils expand and contract as much, in response to feelings as well as light. No human beings have eight fingers; and while some of us may look cherubic, all these Carolinians look that way."

He marveled at the way she could carry on a conversation without either faltering at the keyboard or turning out less than flawless copy. "And no Earthman, however bald, sports a single hair in the exact center of his skull."

"Don't know whether you'd really call it a hair, Shirl. It's more like a tentacle—sometimes it looks short and thick sometimes long and thin, sometimes curled, sometimes straight, sometimes wriggling around their heads."

"It shows how they feel even more than their eyes," she said.

"And the final touch," he added, "is that you can tell males from females on Earth, especially when the custom is to wear no clothes above the waist. I wonder how they can tell themselves, when two strangers meet."

"Scent. They all smell just sort of pleasant to us, but there's aromatic differences between the sexes, and any Vaec can tell within smelling distance."

Auckland sighed and wondered again why Dr. Howard James had asked him to join this expedition some months after work had started here on Carolus. If a communications expert had been needed enough for James to come back to Earth (with the supply ship that covered both the expedition and the colony on Laud—the only other habitable planet in this system) there were other men better qualified. Roy Auckland could see that without self-deprecation; he was good, but not the very best in the field.

"You can handle relations with the Vaec, get to know them better than we can," James had said. "And you solved the Sparks case. I need a man who is also something of a detective." He wouldn't explain why and only talked about the report he was making. And in the few days he had been here, Auckland had discovered undercurrents in the relations of expedition members, which might or might not be too disturbing—but he couldn't yet see where they were leading.

"Is the Ambassador around?" Shirley asked as she took a sheet out of the typewriter and arose to walk over to the filing cabinet. Auckland turned to look at her and his blood pressure arose at the expanse of tanned skin visible.

"Ekem-ve's outside, talking to a colleague." He smiled. "Are you going Vaec, Shirl?"

She smiled and glanced down at the short slit skirt she was wearing; except for girth, a good replica of the costume all the Carolinians sported. "Not quite." She grinned and added, "I know you'd like me to discard the halter, but have you thought of the effect on the Vaec?

"I'm sure they're already curious about the function of these bumps up front, but they might find them unaesthetic," she added. "They consider the differences between Earthly males and females strange enough, as it is, since they're egg-layers."

Auckland chuckled. "Bumps, is it? Understatement of the decade. But you know, I think the Vaec are far more curious about the contrast between tanned and untanned epidermis. I've seen Ekem-ve look curiously at Dr. Glamis when we're inside, no doubt wondering why he's so pale while the rest of us are the color of walnuts—particularly when he saw how quickly I tanned out in this sun. More ultraviolet must get through this atmosphere."

She nodded. "Ken would be a bright red in no time at all, if he went out without protective clothing, except at night. Used to sunburn terribly on Earth, he told me, and was allergic to all the lotions."

Auckland's eyes focused and ran over the black lines with orange shadings in spots that covered Shirley's skirt. "Did Ekem-ve help yon with the designs?"

She opened a file and brushed back blonde hair from her face. "No, I just tried to reproduce some of the effects I've seen on Vaec clothes. Ekem-ve brought me some dye, but I must have muffed the process somehow. Or perhaps it's only good on Vaec fabrics. There's a riddle for you to solve, Roy. We've never seen any trace of industry on their part, yet they have fine cloth, their own dyes, and a very good variety of colored inks which don't run."

"They also have artifacts, but no sign of anyone making them, I'm told. About all anyone sees them do is fish, play Earth-type games which they adapt to suit their pleasure, play practical jokes on each other, and gather food… What color are you using?"

"The light blue…But they can work, Roy. I've seen them out at the diggings; they're as industrious and efficient as beavers."

Auckland smiled faintly. Just simple observation could give you the reputation of being a detective at times. "Haven't you noticed, Shirl? The blue tints wash out under fluorescent light. Which reminds me, we don't need them on now. I've been up since dawn." He reached over to the wall and switched the lights off. "There. Now you can see your pale blue background. Goes very nicely with your eyes."

She didn't answer and he sensed that she was both pleased and disturbed at flattery. "What's going on outside?" she asked, looking through the window. "Are Ekem-ve and Hcent playing jokes on each other?"

Auckland swung his chair around sidewise to check. The Vaec could be distinguished from each other easily, if you took the trouble to look. Hcent's face was narrower than Ekem-ve's, and though a roly-poly when seen alone, she was slimmer than the Vaec's liaison agent to the Earthmen.

Hcent was handing Ekem-ve one of the small, decorated boxes that Auckland had seen another Carolinian carrying a day or so before. Hcent's hair was short and thick now, while Ekem-ve's was long, thin, and looping and unlooping slowly. Now Hcent's hair followed suit.

"No. If Ekem-ve were about to play a joke, he wouldn't give himself away like that. Hcent must have told him a pun, or something else funny. What's the *ve* stand for, Shirl?" I should have found this out days ago, he thought.

"Sort of title," she said. "It approximates our idea of *ambassador* and *chief* at the same time. He's as close to a status of authority in the clans as they ever get."

Hcent had turned and was about to stroll away. Now Ekem-ve dipped a hand into the pouch that all Vaec wore at their belts, just before he gave Hcent the traditional slap of farewell. When his hand left the other Vaec's shoulder, there was a sticker attached to Hcent.

"What does it say—*Kick me?*"

Auckland shrugged and thought of the stickers that had been attached to him when he was a boy. It was somewhat hard to realize that practical jokes were a way of life among the Vaec and that Hcent would feel no resentment on discovering what had been done—although Hcent would try and score with Ekem-ve, if this jest left him behind. No, left *her* behind. Hcent was female. "More likely something insulting," he said. "The Vaec don't seem to go for directly violent horseplay. They prefer more subtle jokes."

Shirley frowned, and he realized that she had been looking more sober than usual this morning. "They're like children," she said slowly. "Only they aren't. I can't make them out, Roy. Their sense of humor seems to be at a moronic level; practical jokes and puns. They 'assist' us in return for toys and games. Even Ekem-ve, who seems to have a lot of natural dignity, was immediately fascinated when he saw a pad of gummed labels. For mirth, as he calls it."

"They love poker," Auckland agreed, "and especially all the variations with wild cards and such. They like games with boards and equipment and complicated methods of scoring, although one of their favorites is a childish variation of whist called 'Red Mustache,' in which everything is twisted around. You have to lose to win, and you have to knock on the table before you make any kind of play at all. Most of the game consists of the players yelling 'Red Mustache' when they call penalties on someone who has forgotten to knock—real bedlam."

"Yet," he went on, "they're highly intelligent. Really on a par with us, I'd say."

"Long-lived, too," she agreed. "Ekem-ve and a couple of others we see around submitted to the language-transfer apparatus when Leitfred first discovered Carolus, and that was over thirty years ago. But now all the Vaec know our language, even if their manner of expression sounds like a cross between broken English and the pseudo-Confucian manner you found in the old fiction that Leitfred was so fond of. I wonder just how much more they picked up from the transfer apparatus than the language itself."

"Perhaps it was just a joke," she murmured as she replaced a folder in the files. "Perhaps someone didn't realize…"

"Didn't realize what, Shirl?"

She turned around and faced him. "I shouldn't tell you, Roy, but really I think you ought to know. Phrecle just brought back Doc James' thermos container with a note. Doc thinks that someone is trying to poison him. Phrecle smelled *dodlig* right through the container and told Doc that the soup would made him sick."

"Sick! Just one drop of *dodlig* juice to a gallon would kill any man." Auckland bit his lip. "And you think one of the Vaec did it for a joke, Shirl?" He shook his head. "No, that's out of character. They don't go in for that sort of humor. If someone put *dodlig* in the soup, that person wasn't joking!"

## CHAPTER TWO

SHIRLEY MASON said, "But that's just it, Roy. Phrecle knows that *dodlig* isn't good for us, but maybe he didn't know it was fatal. Perhaps some of the other Vaec don't even know that it will hurt us all—just thinks it tastes funny, perhaps."

Roy Auckland's eyes narrowed, and he wondered if Dr.

Howard James had been thinking of murder when he made his invitation. No, it didn't seem likely that James would have been reticent about such a matter.

"If I know the doc," he said, "he won't buy an explanation like that. Not without positive proof; in this instance, some Vaec admitting that he put the *dodlig* into the thermos. Where would the opportunity come in?"

"That's it, Roy. Doc's note asked me to run a test on the soup and keep it quiet, said it might be just a joke, that maybe Phrecle was making it all up. But Phrecle was right; there was *dodlig* in it." She blinked. "Only no one could have put it in there between the time I filled the thermos and the time Phrecle took it out of the crawler. Besides, you just can't conceal that odor."

"Is the skipper around?"

"Captain Edholm's out at the diggings. So it looks like there's no one here but us. No one's been here since they left except Ekem-ve, and he hasn't come in yet. I didn't leave the kitchen between the time I fixed breakfast and made up the soup for lunch—you're galley slave next week, by the way—and no one could have done it while I was there."

"Anybody come into the kitchen?"

"Everybody was in at one time or another. But you know you can smell *dodlig* a quarter of a mile away when it's cut or bruised."

"I know..." he mused, thinking of Glamis coming in a couple of days ago after scraping against *dodlig* and nearly collapsing when he took off his suit. It had taken hours to get rid of it.

"It isn't the odor," Shirley explained. "It's the irritating action on the nasal membranes. Glamis might have smelled it through his mask and thought nothing of it. But when you get a full whiff, it's like ammonia, only much worse."

Auckland ran his fingers through his black hair. From what he knew of Dr. Howard James, the man would probably say nothing to the others, but try to lay some sort of subtle trap. "How was it discovered?" he asked.

"Well, Phrecle says that Doc sent him to the tent for something, and he smelled *dodlig* as he passed the lunch basket. He went back to James, took him aside, and said something like—" she closed her eyes in thought "—'deplorable taste when joke render subject too sick to laugh.' Doc told him to take the thermos back here and get a replacement before lunch. I ran the test, scribbled a note to Doc, and gave Phrecle a fresh thermos a little while ago."

Auckland could visualize it. James would probably call everyone together at lunchtime and go into the usual talk about his theories, watching to see the expressions on their faces as he ate his soup and failed to drop dead. "You tested it, Shirl. But why didn't I get a whiff? I was here, and you know how that stuff penetrates."

"Phrecle noticed, and I quote, '*Dodlig* mortified by mixture with excellent Howard's soup and withdraw pleasing aroma. Just barely do this unobservant one ascertain fragrance when pick up thermos.' " She shuddered. "Apparently they like the odor—which isn't so bad, I suppose, if it doesn't react on the nasal passages—but they don't eat the plant."

"If you couldn't smell it, how did you find it?"

"Leitfred's chemists worked out a formula for spotting *dodlig* no matter how it might be disguised, because the pollen sometimes gets on otherwise edible plants and makes them deadly, too, though they don't pick up the odor."

"Just as deadly?"

"Well, no one has tried, but you'd probably have to eat more of them to get the effect."

Auckland took a cigarette from the container on the desk and tossed another to the girl. By the time he put it to his lips, the chemicals in the tip had reacted to start it glowing. "Did you check to see if *dodlig* loses its 'pleasing aroma' when mixed with the soup at any temperature, or whether it has to be boiled?"

"No. I didn't experiment with *dodlig*. I just identified its presence in the soup. Want me to try that?"

Auckland grinned wryly. "Just a thought, and not a very good one. I thought that since you boil Carolinian plants and then add powdered concentrates to it—but that's no good. Even if the *dodlig* were tossed in here—and I can think of a way it could be done without making a stink…"

"How? Don't tell me that you've figured out a way to do it?"

"Elementary. We all take gelatin capsules. One of those could have been opened, emptied out, and *dodlig* substituted. It would melt in no time when put in boiling soup. Those capsules melt fast in almost any liquid. But that isn't how it was done."

"It isn't? How can you be sure?"

"You just told me yourself why it couldn't have been that way." He grinned at her, then went on. "You said that Phrecle ascertain fragrance when he picked up the thermos bottle, which meant that he smelled *dodlig* in it from a good distance, before he picked up the bottle. Phrecle helped load the crawler this morning—I saw him—so he couldn't have missed that 'fragrance' had it been there then."

Shirley Mason stubbed out her cigarette. "I wish I could think it was just a joke, a mistake, but…"

"But you don't think it could have been. Nor do I."

"But suppose some Vaec didn't realize that the odor would be undetectable to us under the circumstances?" she protested. "Someone who thought we'd find out in time."

Auckland shook his head. "No good. I've been studying the Vaec and their humor since I arrived. This just isn't right for them. First of all, they restrain their pranks with us. Secondly, there's nothing malicious about their horseplay among themselves. They wouldn't see anything funny in spoiling food."

"But why…?"

There was a bit of a bewildered look in Shirley's eyes, but Auckland reminded himself that she might be acting. He gripped her shoulder gently. "Don't be naive. Now that it's happened, I can think of possibilities, and so can you."

"For murder? Yes…I suppose so. But not with Doc as the victim. I could see him braining Glamis some time when Ken is riding him about his theories. I could see Burleigh taking vengeance when Glamis starts spouting what Calvin calls needless blasphemy. And I could see someone poisoning Amelia James. But Dr. James as the victim? No."

"You don't think Amelia might like to be a widow?"

Shirley snorted. "What for? The only tie that binds those two is financial, and even that is as loose a binding as you can get without its falling off by itself. She has more money than he has, and she thought that coming to an alien planet—not too alien so as to be uncomfortable—would he romantic."

"She doesn't strike me as being disillusioned on that score," Roy said thoughtfully. "Amelia seems to like it here."

"Of course, with four virile and not too repulsive men around, in addition to her husband. Howard isn't really senile, despite the difference in their ages." Shirley took another cigarette. "She hasn't neglected you, either, when it comes to picking nightflowers." She shook his hand off her shoulder and went back to her typewriter.

She sounded jealous, he thought, except that there didn't seem to be any reason. He'd seen her wandering off with Kenneth Glamis, too. He looked out the window. "Hello," he said, "here comes the crawler with Burleigh driving it."

The blonde went to the window and looked out at the all-purpose vehicle approaching with its treads retracted. Before she could comment, Ekem-ve entered, carrying the box they had seen earlier.

Auckland gave the traditional greeting: "May your heart be mirthful."

"May laughter lighten your life," replied the Carolinian. He looked at Shirley Mason, and the single hair atop his skull made rippling motions. "The Earth female makes our affections sing when she follows the dress of the Vaec."

Shirley smiled. "How are the designs, Ekem-ve? I tried to make just straight lines and angles, and little shaded patches the way you do. I hope I haven't come up with anything inartistic by your standards."

Ekem-ve's hair looped and unlooped lazily. "Most pleasing to a Vaec would be such symbols. I would dance indeed to see them on the dress of a female whom I found desirable in my eyes."

She watched the single hair's motion for a moment, then studied the native's face. "What—what do they mean, Ekem-ve?"

The Carolinian's hair was looping more rapidly now, as he pointed. "This symbol says that you have laid three double-yoked eggs this season. That one says that your last few lovers were superbly amusing, and that the lover you now seek must even so be a mighty man of mirth." He paused and his hair made a side-to-side.

"About this one I am far from certain, even as our own females delight in ambiguity. It seems to my inept comprehension that you do declare that your family has proclaimed your aroma more pungent than *dodlig*, even though you are unable to lie in mud more than six hours, as our females do to improve their skins. On the other hand, it might…"

Shirley was no longer listening; she had left the room. Auckland laughed heartily. "Is that true, Ekem-ve, or are you joking?" The Vaec never lied, he knew, but what was spoken in jest among them was not considered amenable to standards of truth. However, custom required that a Vaec reply truthfully if asked directly whether he was joking.

"The female is a female still with you and me, excellent Roy, no matter however differently we were created. Seeking in wisdom to avoid souring mirth, I did not translate completely." Auckland remembered another thing about the Vaec. It was not considered a lie to withhold part of the truth; and even when asked directly, no more facts need be given than were specifically requested. Only the motion of his hair indicated that Ekem-ve was still chuckling, as it were.

"But the designs you interpreted did mean what you said they meant?" he asked.

"They did indeed, excellent Roy. I have brought with me the box that excellent Howard requested for study. May I take it to his room, or some other place, at your judicious suggestion?"

"I would not impose upon you by asking you to take it to the laboratory, Ekem-ve. If you would leave it here, it is better that I demean myself." After such a reply, the Vaec would insist upon running the errand.

"May your heart be mirthful, Ekem-ve," came Burleigh's voice as the lean, spade-bearded man entered. He waited for the response, then said to Auckland, "The skipper wants the three of you to come out to the diggings, and bring the spare Rouse cameras. Would you please excuse us, Ekem-ve, while I deliver a personal message?"

The Carolinian blinked the Vaec equivalent of nodding or shaking one's head. "This unworthy one will take box to lab and await excellent Earth people in crawler." He wiggled a finger in the parting gesture the Vaec used when leaving Earthmen. Auckland wondered what situations among the Vaec dictated the slap of farewell and the finger wiggling. He'd seen both used in what appeared to be similar occasions.

Burleigh waited until the Carolinian had gone out the other door, heading for the lab. "The situation is far from mirthful. Howard thinks that someone is trying to kill him, and things are pretty sticky—particularly Glamis. There's a fit subject for a violent end if I ever saw one, Lord forgive my spite."

"Shirley's changing costume, I think. I'll round her up." He was frowning as he started toward the door to her room, which adjoined the office. Had James revealed his suspicions so soon?

Burleigh had seated himself and taken up a cigarette. "It is all nonsense if you ask me. But you know how Doc is when he gets an idea. Came up out of the cellar where he was studying murals like something out of Dante's Hell, ordering everyone outside on the double. When he had us rounded up—except for the natives—he started talking about hearing something ticking. Says he noticed that one of the blocks in the wall was pushed out slightly. Has it all figured out that someone rigged up a homemade bomb and concealed it there, set to go off while he was working in the room."

"Did you hear anything yourself?"

"He wouldn't let any of us go down there with him in the first place, so no one knows if he saw or heard anything. The skipper takes it seriously, so we're all waiting around for an explosion!"

## CHAPTER THREE

IT WAS when you stepped outside the cluster of prefab units that made up headquarters, Roy Auckland thought, that you really knew you were on an alien world. He didn't feel much lighter, but there was a springy feeling underfoot, and it seemed as if the mossy ground-covering was propelling him into the air. His blood tingled.

And the air—not much different from Earth chemically, they said, but he smelled something that reminded him of apple-blossoms. And when the light breeze blew, he got a will of something that reminded him of the months he'd spent in the tropics as a student. The planet Carolus was almost vertical on its axis, which meant that seasonal variations would be small.

He followed Burleigh to the crawler and stood beside it, looking back at the severely functional headquarters unit, laid out like a letter "I." Calvin Burleigh took out his pipe and followed Auckland's gaze.

"Not exactly artistic," he said, "but not too bad. The dull, gray finish stands out amidst all the greenery without looking like too much of an intruder, though I haven't seen that shade of gray anywhere else here."

"Plenty of greenery," Auckland agreed. "And I suppose somewhere on this planet there's grass or trees or shrubbery the shade of green that looks right to an Earthman. All I can see is a bit too yellow, too white, or too blue to be my idea of vegetation—where it isn't some tone of red instead." His eyes narrowed as he fixed the layout of the building in his mind. "You know, whoever designed this was a genius at avoiding convenient arrangements."

Burleigh smiled faintly as he lit his pipe. "Tired of having to take a walk to the shower room? At least we all have our own sanitary equipment." He held the match in his hand, as if uncertain whether it would set fire to the moss, then let it drop. "Well, I'm more fortunate. At least I don't have to step outside to get to the kitchen, rec-room, or office."

Auckland nodded. "You and Edholm at the upper end, and Ken and Shirley at the lower end have doors connecting with the three rooms in the shaft. The lab's like the shower rooms, inaccessible to any others. Doc James and I have no connections with any other rooms at all."

"And everyone has to hike to the storage sheds… Well, the weather here's pretty good, although there are sand storms out in the desert where we're heading. Up here, though, we just get ordinary rains and moderate winds. It won't be much different in winter; hardly noticeable, I'd say."

"We all have ample windows with shutters, and none of them look on to each other. I suppose that's something to be grateful for."

"Except for the lab. Anyone in the lab can look into James' quarters, if he hasn't closed his shutters. And each room has its own individual power unit for light and heat, so it's almost impossible for the entire building to be blacked out by any accident."

Shirley emerged from her room wearing shorts, and Ekem-ve followed. Auckland sat beside her, in back, trying to fix the various inter-room connections in his mind. Each room was accessible to any of the others via the intercoms, but the important thing was that someone watching the single door to the James' quarters could tell if anyone tried to slip in there. Which might be an important point if things were shaping up as Dr. Howard James suspected.

Something like a bumblebee buzzed by the crawler. Auckland ducked instinctively, and Burleigh chuckled. "Don't worry to much about them. A couple of us got mild bee-stings—they're not really bees, of course, but fairly close to them, and they act a lot like Earth-type bees—but they weren't much worse than mosquito bites. The insects haven't bothered us at all since the first week or so, and Glamis never had to worry about them at all, since he wears that suit every time he goes outside in daylight.

"Now there's something for you to look into. I know you're no entomologist, but we suspect that the Vaec control them in some way."

He took a cigarette from his case and passed it around.

"Carolus is going to be a fascinating field for ecologists, by the way. We've seen only two kinds of insects: the 'bees' and a kind of praying mantis thing that keeps them down. Nothing of what you'd call pestiferous insects at all, very few birds or animals—the last two keep away from our vicinity."

"Plant life is abundant—" he indicated the outcroppings of flowers, shrubs, and various trees that resembled weeping willows in bloom—"and seems to have been arrayed in a sort of order. You don't find fruit or nut trees in amongst the willows, and that goes for the flowers, too. Whatever sort you want to find, you've got to look for a group. Oh, they're not bunched together—what I mean is, you'll never find just one willow, say, in an area that has other kinds of trees."

Auckland nodded as they started out and noticed that the indentations made by the crawler were soon lost. It was as if the—grass-moss?—pulled itself in just before being crushed than gradually rose again. Which meant that it was almost hopeless to look for footprints if the occasion ever arose; he'd seen very few bits of bare ground with its faintly violet soil.

"I boned up on Carolus before I came," he said, "but there doesn't seem to be much information on the planet."

"There isn't," said Shirley. "After all we're only the third group of visiting humans. Leitfred discovered two planets in this system which would be suitable for occupation, and named them after early Anglican martyrs: Carolus, who was a king, I think, and Laud—wasn't he a cardinal?"

"Archbishop," corrected Burleigh. "This was back in the days when the church was all split up into sects and the various rites weren't in communion with each other. Virtual warfare between them at times."

The terrain was reasonably smooth, though far from flat, and seemed to have a general incline. Despite the lack of bumps, crawler-riding was hardly comfortable, Auckland thought. Well, at least the top was down.

"Well," Shirley went on, "Leitfred established relations with the Vaec and his report made Planet Control decide that there would be no colonization until we learned more about them. Leitfred considered them primitives, but others didn't agree."

"Ah, yes," broke in Auckland, then stopped himself and looked embarrassedly at Ekem-ve. "This isn't very polite, I'm afraid,

The Carolinian's hair waved slightly. "No need for apology, excellent Roy. Humble native have no pride of culture. We were in fact greatly pleased that excellent Jonas —" Auckland blinked then realized that he was talking about Leitfred "—taught us fascinating language of Earth people. Far more interesting than Vaec tongue, so with humble joy we adopt same for ourselves by generous permission of excellent visitors."

"That was when Dr. James came back with Leitfred's second expedition," Burleigh said. "He persuaded Leitfred to stop here for a little while—Leitfred was en route to another system—to test his theory that the Vaec weren't really natives of Carolus, but were descendants of a race that had established a colony here in the very distant past. The Old Martian records mention a star-empire which they discovered when they went traveling in space, and James thinks that the Vaec are remnants of it."

"Excellent Howard inquire of us maybe about old time Vaec history, but we unable to tell much." Auckland frowned, wondering why Ekem-ve lapsed into this sort of diction every now and then, when he could speak as good English (allowing for differences in thought-patterns) as any of them. "Long time, Vaec find history poverty-stricken in mirth. We show excellent Howard some furniture from old time dwellings."

"James tried to find traces of an earlier civilization here," Burleigh continued. "But he couldn't find any in the time he had. Took him nearly ten years after returning to Earth to convince Planet Control that something might be found, due to Vaec references to what might be considered a buried city in the desert."

"Great was our distress," said Ekem-ve, "that we could not assist excellent Howard at that time, for we could see that much mirth would attend his finding of same. While we wait for excellent Earth people to honor us with further visit, we look around planet ourselves. What joy that we are able to help excellent Howard now."

The crawler was passing a stream that made a wide pool at this point. A lone Carolinian was sitting on a rock, fishing, with some sort of container beside him. Ekem-ve said, "May we not pause, excellent Calvin, and observe Syeltan in his unawareness?" The Vaec's hair was now waving a little more vigorously.

"Afraid not, Ekem-ve. There may be mirth to spare out at the diggings. We have to get there before we miss it." He explained the hidden bomb, avoiding any hint of intent to harm the victim. "What sort of joke is being played on Syeltan?"

"Every day, Syeltan fish in pool for time-space of three baits. He uses *vlagin* nut for bait, that the fish may have a fair chance for happy feed and escape. It occurred to this dull person that the pop-ball resembles *vlagin* nut if little operation be made. So this one performs operation and secretes pop-ball among bait. When Syeltan intrudes hook into disguised pop-ball…" He broke off, and his hair looped wildly.

"What happens then?" asked Auckland.

"Ball makes loud pop and perhaps startles Syeltan into pool. Juice from pop-ball splatters allover Syeltan, covering him with red splotches. Juice very tenacious, does not like to leave what it touches. Syeltan wear juice for long time. Will know when he pops ball, but extra mirth if can see him do it."

"Oh, you put the pop-ball in his bait last night?" asked Auckland.

"No I didn't. Secrete pop-ball when Syeltan fill container four months ago, as excellent Earth people say. Bait last for exactly fifteen more days, as even this short-thinking person realize that number of bait must remain the same. Maybe today, maybe tomorrow. Every day, this one comes to watch."

"Heavens," said Shirley. "To wait nearly five months to see if a practical joke comes off! But Ekem-ve, suppose he drops the pop-ball into the water accidentally, or recognizes it despite your skill?"

"Long joke make for most exquisite mirth, excellent Shirley. If ball is lost, then this person must try again. If discovered, then this person is caught on own vine."

"They lay sticky traps for each other," Burleigh explained.

"When one of them discovers a trap—custom decrees that it be identifiable as the work of a particular person—he moves it to another spot where the one who made the trap may step into it. Next to being the perpetrator of a joke, the Vaec consider it most mirthful to be caught in one's own trap. These vines aren't harmful, but they're hard to get off once they stick to you. And there doesn't ever seem to be hard feelings when a joke comes off, either on the victim or rebounding on the perpetrator."

"Of course no hard feelings. Mirth too precious to be spoiled by overestimation of self."

And if a Vaec didn't realize that the *dodlig* would lose most of its odor when mixed with James' soup, thought Auckland, he'd think it a first-class joke. He remembered how he had walked into a sticky trap himself, the first day he was out alone. He'd managed to remove all traces of it before he returned to camp, and none of the Carolinians had referred to it since.

Yes, might not some native have reasoned that James would open the thermos and—*phew!* No danger of him eating it, and they all knew it would take only a little while to replace the lunch.

Burleigh's comment answered the question he was about to ask. "They've pulled things on all of us, too, but they seem to realize that we don't find some of the more undignified jokes they play on each other as funny. I must say that they haven't overstepped the bounds."

Before he could pursue the thought any farther, Shirley broke in. "We're coming to the rise now, Roy. You'll see the desert from the top of it."

They were out of sight of the pool now, where Syeltan still sat fishing. Their last glimpse of him caught him in the act of pulling his empty hook out of the water and putting his hand into the bait-container. Auckland felt a twinge of sympathy for Ekem-ve, along with admiration for his patience and stoicism. The Vaec didn't seem put out at all by such disappointments.

Now the crawler was at the top of a plateau. They turned and headed for an edge where the slope was fairly gentle. As they passed the rim, Auckland gasped at the sight of what looked like an expanse of pure gold, in mounds and hills and flat stretches much like the Sahara.

"Put on your desert glasses," said Shirley as she donned hers. "Five minutes or less looking at that without filters and you'll find that snow-blindness is mild by comparison."

He obeyed sheepishly, as they'd told him about this before.

The beauty of the scene remained even when the glare had diminished. "I wonder how Leitfred could have missed this, or failed to have mentioned it," he said.

"Didn't land in this part of the planet," Burleigh explained.

"Talks with the natives seemed to indicate that there was a desert where the original settlements had been. But that was during the second trip. Ekem-ve assured James that the Vaec would be very, very happy to help if we wanted to send out an expedition." He mused for a moment as the crawler started down the incline. "Ekem-ve and his clan migrated thousands of miles and resettled, in order to be here when we came back."

"They must have very long lives," said Auckland. "Ekem-ve and the others were here when Leitfred first landed, and the Vaec don't seem to show signs of aging."

"There're the diggings, Roy," said Shirley.

Auckland could see tents, machinery, and a large group of people standing or sitting around the excavation.

"Archaeology is slow work," sighed Burleigh. "Even with modem excavators which make for fewer aching backs and risk of damage to buried objects."

"How many Vaec assistants do you have?"

"About twenty are all we need at a time. They take shifts, each putting in three days at a stretch. We've been here about four months now, and we're ahead of Doc's timetable. But now…"

A dull, booming sound came to them.

Burleigh turned to Auckland, his face suddenly pale.

"Lord, Doc was right. It sounds as if someone did plant an explosive in that room."

## CHAPTER FOUR

THE FAMOUS deserts of Earth held rich deposits of history, Roy Auckland was thinking as the crawler, now on treads, its wheels retracted, headed for the scene of operations. Voices cried out in Earth's deserts, exhorting men to turn their thoughts to eternal matters; trumpets blared and men clashed and slew each other for temporary and elusive advantages, often not their own. And the desert grew slowly, eating up once-beautiful cities and gardens. Did these golden sands of Carolus conceal the remains of similar events, and long-forgotten glory, as Dr. Howard James believed?

A strange question, he thought, remembering the events of his first day with the expedition, which he had spent examining the records, while the others went out to the diggings. Just before they left, Dr. Glamis came back into the office and said, "There's some cans of film we've taken here in the closet. Doc didn't want to tell you until they were edited, but you might learn more if you see them as they stand. Don't let on that I told you."

Auckland lost no time in looking the film up, and running it off.

The three-dimensional effect was as good as he had ever remembered seeing, and the battery of speakers around him brought every sound from its proper direction, and incorrect tonal proportion. After a moment or two, Roy Auckland wasn't sitting in a darkened room watching a screen; he was out in the Carolinian desert.

Calvin Burleigh climbed up into the small Bronstien

Omnicraft, waved to Dr. James, Kenneth Glamis, and Shirley Mason standing nearby, and closed the hatch. All wore sun helmets and tinted glasses, except for Glamis; his entire protective suit was tinted, and the top of his helmet was white.

An instant later, the Omnicraft rose in a straight vertical line, until it was some fifty feet above the golden sands, which were nearly level at this spot, but took on ripples and hills farther out. The Omnicraft shot off to the west in the cloudless blue of the sky, then began to make a circle, drifting along.

"More pictures?" asked Shirley. "I thought this area had been mapped."

Howard James unrolled the blown-up print he carried. "Those were just preliminary photos yesterday, taken from half a mile up." He indicated dark areas in the glittering sands. "See these spots? The Rouse wave catches anything below the surface, but at that distance it's more like an old time dentist X-raying teeth. At fifty feet, we'll get definite outlines. Saves time to do it this way, because we can see now just what areas are worth more careful examination."

"We can't tell what's there, Shirl," said Glamis. "It's most likely rocks, or even beds of minerals. What we're looking for is some outline that might not be a natural formation by its shape. Buried cities, you know." He sniffed.

"And why not?" James said stiffly. "The Vaec admit being here for many centuries. Ekem-ve said that the desert has expanded since his people first came to Carolus, and that some of them may have lived in this area when it was still fertile. There are many parts of Earth, now desert, which were once fertile land; certainly no reason why it couldn't have happened here."

"The fact that it could have happened is no proof that it did."

James turned away abruptly, and Glamis grinned after him. "The brow is the brow of Shakespeare, but everything else is ham. He's got it all figured out; and if we do find anything, he'll fit it into his neatly-preconceived pattern."

"Why do you hate him so?" Shirley asked.

Glamis shrugged, "I don't really hate him; I just find him irritatingly ridiculous. He's no charlatan, but he's too eager to make a solid reputation, so he'll believe what he wants to believe and manipulate the evidence to fit. He wanted me to come along as a balance-wheel, he said. Which shows he has some idea of his weakness, I suppose."

"The loyal opposition is supposed to be loyal," she murmured. "You're just opposing."

"I'm trying to keep him sane. He got a rough deal back in the days of the Marlene scandal. Howard was Jules Marlene's assistant, and while he wasn't prosecuted, there's still a feeling of guilt in him. Maybe they think he did help Marlene pull a *piltdown*, or that he should have known what was up. He's lived just to make some unimpeachable discovery of his own, but his obsession is driving him to ludicrous tricks."

"Then why aren't you helping him?"

"How can I? He says he wants me to keep him in check but what he really wants is to know as many objections to his theories as possible in advance, so he can work his way around them. Very scientific."

Glamis was looking up at the Omnicraft, and did not see the expression on Shirley Mason's face.

The six of them—Howard James, Amelia, Glamis, Shirley, Burleigh, and Edholm—were standing around a table in the big tent, looking at the photographs that littered it.

"Now here's the pictures of the nearest Vaec village," Dr. James began.

"If you can call it a village," Glamis put in. "The Vaec

don't build their dwelling places close enough together so that the term 'village' would apply."

"Oh, stop it, Kenneth!" Amelia James said wearily. "If it helps to think of all their homes in this locale as a village, then let's call it a village."

Glamis bowed slightly. "As Madame desires."

James cleared his throat. "Now look at this picture. You can see that the darkened areas beneath the sand are in the shape of a large diamond, with a smaller square next to it. Then another diamond, another square, and a final diamond. They're all connected into one unit, and just for convenience, until we can think of something more apt, we'll call it a villa. Okay, Ken?"

Glamis shrugged. "So long as no one gets the idea that calling it a villa makes it a villa."

"Are you likely to get that idea, Dr. Glamis?" Captain Edholm asked sharply.

"No."

"Then kindly allow us similar intelligence until and unless you have evidence to the contrary, sir." Edholm looked again at the pictures. "I have noticed that the Vaec dwellings are all perfect squares."

Calvin Burleigh pointed to another photograph. "And you can see that in some places, this pattern of diamond, square, diamond, square, diamond does pop up. The natives tend to create in terms of Euclidean geometry. Consider the decorations on their clothing. You see this sort of pattern there, too.

"Considering the number of dwellings in this area, it would be more unusual if some such pattern couldn't be found somewhere," Glamis observed. He glanced at Amelia, and added, "But that doesn't take anything away from the shape of this area below the sand. It does suggest artifice."

James smiled. "Thank you, Ken. I know you do not think

highly of my hypothesis that the Vaec we see here are descendants of a stellar colony. Of course, we cannot call this a theory as yet. But let's keep the possibility in mind."

"Not much danger of our forgetting it, Howard," Burleigh put in, and James smiled as chuckles broke out.

"Well, it's agreed that this is the place we start work?" Everyone nodded, and James started out of the tent.

Glamis caught Amelia's arm and said softly, "You don't have to take it personally."

She didn't answer; she looked at him and her lips parted slightly. Then the half-sensuous expression left her face, and she shook herself free from his grasp and walked away. Shirley followed her, looking as if she considered the two of them beneath contempt.

Shirley Mason painted in the letter *n* in the legend. It was a red JAMES EXPEDITION on a white banner, containing a blue Earth. She wiped the red paint off the brush. Three similar banners were stretched out on the table in the tent.

Burleigh and Glamis strode along the golden sands, Burleigh carrying a long, thin metal shaft with one of the banners at its top, and Glamis holding a small instrument with two light-buttons. A faint buzzing sound came from it; the sound stopped abruptly, and Glamis said, "You've deviated Cal. Step to the right a bit."

Burleigh obeyed, and the buzzing started again. A short time later, the left-hand light flashed on. Glamis stopped "Here. Come left a little more." He waited until the right hand light also glowed. "Exact spot."

Burleigh pushed the pole down into the sand, and Glamis assisted, after putting the finder into his pocket. They looked around the expanse of desert at the other three poles that were the comers of a rectangle marking the boundaries of the diggings.

Glamis looked up at the banner. "Shirl could have put in a cross behind the Earth," he said.

Calvin Burleigh's eyes narrowed. "That was supposed to be a humorous quip, I presume. From someone else, it would have been amusing, but not from a person who find everything about religious faith amusing."

"Think I'll be struck down some day in the midst of blasphemy, Cal?"

"If you're looking for a lightning bolt aimed specifically at you, no. But the mocker usually finds himself mocked one way or another. How old are you, Glamis?"

"Sixty-eight or thereabouts."

Burleigh nodded. "You started rejuvenation treatment in your thirties, then. Well, I'm ninety-six. Took the treatments first when I was forty, so I'm almost forty-six physically if you hold to the rule of aging one year in ten after treatment. Doc James is one hundred and twenty, which would make him relatively forty-eight or maybe fifty. Perhaps if you live to his age, you'll begin to grow up."

He walked away, his pointed beard out-thrust, looking as if he should be wearing a burnoose and riding a white horse or camel, leading desert tribes into holy war.

Under the direction of Dr. James, the Vaec set up the excavators. The bodies of the machines looked like huge sausages from a distance; sausages with blisters at top center, and air holes punctured along the sides.

Burleigh was saying to Amelia, "They're really nothing but glorified vacuum cleaners. Each one has its own power plant, works on the Bending converter principle."

"I'm not a scientist, Calvin. You might as well say it in Old Martian."

"Oh, you've heard of hydrogen fusion, haven't you?"

She nodded. "I've studied history. But isn't that dangerous? I thought it was always accompanied by tremendous radiation."

"Bending found a way to get around that difficulty. His converter did the job without emitting any radiation at all—well, no more than is normally present in sunlight—and it draws the hydrogen from the air. Doesn't need too much. Even the moisture-content of desert air like this will suffice."

The Vaec were bringing long, flexible tubes—light, for all of their eight-inch diameter—over to the orifices in the excavator and fitting them in.

"Looks like a many-tentacled monster now, doesn't it," said Burleigh. "Who's going to run them?"

"Howard demonstrated them to Ekem-ve yesterday," she said. "I mean, he just showed him a model and took him into the control turret, and Ekem-ve got the idea at once. He said that any of his people could handle them after a single bit of instruction."

Calvin Burleigh frowned. "I don't like it."

"Why not?"

"There's no doubt about the natives' intelligence. Reminds me of that old jingle, 'The people are bright, and very polite.' Applied to the Japanese at one time, I believe, when the western powers discovered how quickly they learned methods centuries in advance of their own culture, once shown.

"However, whenever we've brought advanced technology to so-called primitive or backward peoples on Earth we've destroyed their own ways of living in the process. We've killed the virtues they had and replaced them with our own highly advanced vices. And sometimes they've improved upon our vices and surpassed us in all kinds of evil."

"You think we should avoid the Vaec?"

"I think we should use such decency as we have, and not

foist our values upon them. And technology is part of our values and our corruption accompanies it."

He gazed in the direction of Howard James, and Burleigh's entire aspect seemed to exude anger.

"You'd like to see this expedition stopped, wouldn't you?" said Amelia. He didn't answer her.

Now Ekem-ve and Phrecle walked up to the excavator, and Phrecle climbed up the notches in the body that led to the control turret. A moment later he was inside and seated at the board.

Burleigh said, with ungrudging admiration, "You'd think that eight fingers would be in the way. Actually, the natives can spread their hands far wider than any of us, and they can handle all the important buttons simultaneously. Their coordination is superb. What pianists they would make!"

Amelia gasped as the four tubes lifted simultaneously, like snakes, and moved closer to Burleigh. The excavator moved on its treads over to the boundary pole, then stopped. The foot-wide mouths of the tubes came down to the sand, which seemed to be sucked up, carried through the body of the machine, then expelled in a high golden stream.

"It's hard to remember, when you see that, that a vacuum has no sucking or lifting power," Burleigh said.

"That's one thing I do remember from science," Amelia replied. "Atmospheric pressure, or artificially produced air-pressure, makes the effect. It's like water rushing through a hole in a dam, carrying everything along with it."

"But it still *looks* as if those snakes are sucking up the sand," said Burleigh, smiling.

"Couldn't larger tubes be used?"

"Of course. At least four times as large, but that would be too dangerous. As it is, don't let yourself get caught within several yards of those openings when the power is on. You could lose an arm or leg or head before you knew what had happened."

Ekem-ve had come up to them as Burleigh was speaking.

"Excellent Calvin speaks wisdom," he said. "Must keep respectful distance from excellent tube which cannot tell Vaec or excellent Earth person from sand."

The reel of film came to an end; Auckland could see that considerable editing would be necessary before it was shown to the general public. The second reel was a more expert job of film making, he soon found; the work of days compressed into minutes.

Four sizeable pits filled the screen, the excavators at their bottom, the tubes slithering like serpents eating up the golden sand, and the ejection spray higher and farther-carrying. The Vaec were shoring up the sides.

Ekem-ve, his single hair straight as a ramrod, came up to Dr. Howard James. "Erring Vaec misinform excellent Earth people. Storm season over, but latecomer approach." He pointed.

Over toward the east, a black dot had appeared against the blue of the sky, and it grew larger as they watched. James looked startled. "How long before it reaches us?"

"Late-coming storm hurry to make up lost time. Must leave desert right away."

James spoke into his wrist-communicator. "Phrecle, Hcent, Syeltan, drive the excavators out of the pits and head for the bluff." He pressed a button. "Attention, everyone. Pick up as much equipment as you can carry easily, and get to the crawlers. Close the tents, but be sure the finder is set. The pegs are long and deep enough so the tents won't blow away, but we may have to excavate it." He sighed. "Well, at least the shoring should hold; we'll just have to dig around it."

The black dot had now spread until it nearly filled the sky, and a gale was rising. No one was running now; all were walking, leaning against the wind, and the sand was swirling around them. There was still some light as they reached the crawlers. Ekem-ve said, "Do not worry about Vaec, excellent Howard. Vaec not get lost in storm. Pleasant to ride in excellent vehicles but not necessary. Nsenol take pictures as long as possible. Can excellent Earthmen find way?"

James nodded. "We tune our finders to headquarters, and they will show us the way." The Vaec wiggled his fingers and helped Amelia climb in, then turned away.

The excavators were a bit ahead as the crawlers, completely covered now, started out; then all were but dim shapes vaguely seen in the swirling sands.

The excavators were uncovering the tents, which proved to be intact. Now they were on the floor of still larger pits than those made before the storm. The black edges of a triangular shape were emerging from the golden sands.

The villa stood out, sharp and clear, as if it had been carved and painted a glossy black; the sands around it were level with its base. They were standing before a large triangle outlined in red.

"Whatever it's made of," Edholm said, "will certainly have to be determined by spectroanalysis. You've found that it's harder than diamond, about a quarter of an inch thick, and resistant to every sort of heat we've applied. And you can't scratch it or dent it."

"Those triangles appear to be doorways of some sort," said Burleigh. "There's one on each of these buildings—no windows." He shrugged. "And no indication of how they open."

"Open sesame," Glamis called out. "You know, it might be amenable to some sort of thought control. Suppose we all just concentrate on wishing it would open."

"Nothing to lose," said Burleigh. The group fell silent. A spot appeared in the eight-foot triangle. It widened rapidly until they could see that the material was sliding into frames.

"Since I'm wearing a protective suit, I'll go in first," said Glamis. He stepped into the opening, and a moment later, the place was filled with light.

Now all were inside the room, which was illuminated by a soft glow, revealing light-toned walls that seemed to change subtly in value as the camera moved about. It was a triangle-shaped room, empty except for objects that could be chair frames.

"Well, we've found out a bit," James said. "The lights go on when anyone comes in; so long as anyone is in, they stay on unless we 'think' them off. As soon as the last person goes out, they go off by themselves. The air in here is perfectly good. What's the measurements of the room, Cal?"

"Fifteen feet to a side, and the partition over there is made of something that looks like children's building blocks. They seem to be a sort of brick."

"And those chair frames," James went on, "are very similar to the ones the Vaec use, though the material is different. These are metal, while the Vaec use a sort of cane and matting material."

"I wonder if they're solid enough to sit in," Amelia said. "My feet hurt."

"You might draw a cultural diffusionist conclusion from those chair frames," said Burleigh. "Since the natives have artifacts similar to these, the natives must have gotten the designs from whatever civilization created this villa. Still, there's no reason for not assuming that the natives arrived at their designs independently."

"There is even less reason," said Glamis, "to postulate that the Vaec are degenerate descendants of the same—"

A cry from Amelia interrupted him. They turned to see

her sitting in one of the frames. But the frame was shifting, its contours sliding to conform to her shape. And from the frames, a thin material was issuing, something that resembled web-work.

She struggled out of it; and as soon as she was free, the chair began to revert to its former shape as the webbing retreated back into the frame. Glamis laughed. “Now that is what I call service.” He sat down on the frame, and the process repeated itself. “The last word in comfort,” he said.

They stood outside the second building in the villa, the square attached to the far diamond, and watched the doorway open. “Obviously,” Burleigh said, “there's machinery around here somewhere and it's still working after how many Carolinian centuries? It operates the doors and lights to thought-control, and keeps the air pure and the temperature comfortable.”

Dr. James was writing in his notebook. He closed it, looked at his stylus, and said, “Let's see if any object passing that doorway will put the lights on. It might not be thought control for them, after all.” He tossed the stylus through the dark opening.

Nothing happened. “There's your answer,” said Glamis.

He stepped through the doorway. Then they heard him exclaim. The lights came on as they followed him, to see blocks scattered over the floor. “Someone didn't straighten up,” he said.

Over in a comer, was a partly dismantled wall that had cut it off when it was complete. Burleigh went over to it, and pushed against one of the remaining blocks. It moved back easily. He pulled on the block next to it, and it came out just as easily. “Quite light,” he said. “Though only about half the length of the one I pushed.”

“About six by four inches, wouldn't you say?” asked

James, making the entry in his notebook.

"Look at this," called Amelia. She had started to pick up the blocks on the floor, and was piling them up. It was a perfectly straight pile. She put another block on the top, a little less than true, and it seemed to slide into place by itself. They watched until she had a single column as high as she could make it. She stood back and looked at it a moment, then pushed against it. Nothing happened.

The others tried, with similar results; that single column wouldn't topple. Glamis pushed a block partway down and it gave easily, but he couldn't push it entirely free. Burleigh went around to the other side, grasped the recalcitrant block, and pulled. It came out in his hand, and the blocks above it tumbled obligingly.

"Here's something," called out James, and they saw that he had climbed over the remnants of the wall of blocks. He held what looked like a good-size box in his hands. It was covered with intricate geometrical designs, all straight lines. "Do these designs look familiar?"

"They look like the designs on the natives' clothing," said Burleigh. "See if you can think that carton open."

"Looks like it's fairly heavy," said James, leaning over the wall and depositing the box on the floor. "Oops, I think I've got it—heard a sort of click."

The top of the box opened. "I'd say it was some sort of books," he announced happily.

They were in a room whose walls were completely covered with murals, designs, and sections devoted to groups of dots and lines, with occasional diagonals. The murals looked like abstract paintings in every possible color and tone.

"Poetry, perhaps," said Glamis, indicating the groups. "It's the same characters that are in the books."

"And also more of these walls of blocks, complete or

incomplete," mused James. "More boxes of books in these cellar rooms. I think these murals may tell us something, in relation to the books, perhaps, if we study them. I'm going to spend some time in this cellar. I have a feeling..."

Roy Auckland shook his head, and brought himself back to the present. Those unedited films had given him important background details on the expedition and its members. But now the crawler had reached the edge of the diggings and was going down the ramp that had been constructed for it. He could see Howard James, Amelia, Glamis, and Edholm standing near one of the triangular doorways, and it looked as if they were arguing.

But Auckland had no eyes for them at the moment. Even though he had seen the villa in the films, there was something about it that literally took his breath away. For size, it couldn't compare with the temple of Karnak, just the first of many remains he had seen on Earth. For durability, it seemed less wonderful than the Roman viaducts still in operation—had it been France or Spain where he'd seen them? For a feeling of alienness, it couldn't compare with Aku-Aku. What was it then?

It was the aura of newness about the villa, he decided. It had the appearance of having been built tomorrow, then time-transplanted back into yesterday. It looked like a demonstration building—the very latest in architecture—never occupied, perhaps never intended for occupation. Auckland looked around at the golden sands, brighter still against the gleaming black walls of the villa. He found himself thinking of a sand pile dumped in a backyard at night to surprise a child when he awoke in the morning; sand which covered a toy the child had left outside.

Captain Walter Edholm was talking as Auckland neared the group. The spaceman stood there, half an inch shorter than Kenneth Glamis, a shade slenderer than Dr. James, and apparently between their ages. He didn't bark out commands, but there was authority in his manner.

"It's moot whether these attempts were inept," Auckland heard him saying. "Until I am satisfied that there are no more booby traps in the villa, excavation and exploration is suspended. I am responsible for the safety of you all."

He turned to greet the approaching quartet. "Miss Mason, I want you to take Rouse wave photographs of every building in the villa, and of every object which has been removed from it."

"More objects?" asked Auckland.

"Just boxes and chair frames and blocks," said Tames, seemingly unperturbed. "I hadn't opened some of the boxes."

"Precisely," said Edholm. "Someone else may have done so." He turned to give Ekem-ve the traditional greeting, with a slight grimace. "I think you can see that this is no joke."

The Vaec's hair was perfectly still now, belying the benevolent look on his face. "Mirth departs when harmful desire enters, excellent Walter. Yet sometimes young Vaec unaware of harm—perhaps Earthman unaware?"

The question could not be evaded, for that would leave a worse impression than the truth, Auckland thought. Edholm nodded. "Sometimes Earthmen cause harm to each other and themselves in search of mirth."

Just what did the Vaec include in that word? More than laughter; that was certain. Not folly; the adult Carolinians showed no signs of it, however foolish some of their jests might appear to Earthmen. "Forgive our foolish ways," Auckland thought.

Edholm continued, "Someone has gone too far in mirthful plans, Ekem-ve, and we must look for dangerous sticky traps. Will you and your people help Dr. Auckland look for traps, and anything else he needs assistance in doing?"

"Vaec happy to help excellent Roy," Ekem-ve replied.

"The point J was trying to make—before you arrived, Roy—was that things aren't as they seem, and shouldn't be taken at face value," Glamis put in. "I say this applies to both alleged attempts at murder. They really shouldn't be taken too seriously."

Edholm looked at him sternly. "On the contrary, Dr. Glamis, they cannot be taken too seriously. Dr. Auckland is in charge of the investigation and is to report solely to me. I expect every one of you to cooperate." He glanced around at each of them. "Except one, of course, and no doubt that person will put up a good show of cooperation."

Here it is, Roy Auckland thought. It's my baby now!

## CHAPTER FIVE

EDHOLM CONTINUED: "You will all return to headquarters. I shall remain here to examine the bomb fragments."

Roy Auckland cleared his throat, "On the contrary, Captain, since I am in charge of the investigation I'm going to have to veto one thing you've said and amend another. There will be a full report only when I am satisfied that the case is solved, and then everyone will hear it. Until then, I shall tell any of you as much as suits my purposes. And until then, everyone is under suspicion, including the captain."

He lifted a hand as Edholm bristled. "When I say everyone is under suspicion, I do not mean that I consider the guilt of everyone equally probable but rather that I am not starting out with the assumption that anyone is to be considered above suspicion. That is the amendment. From time to time, you will all be asked to assist.

"Right now I would like Doctor James to take charge

while Captain Edholm and I examine the room in question. That is the veto. Please get ready to return to headquarters, but no one will leave until we return."

He followed Edholm inside the doorway and felt the strangeness of the room, which was as he had seen it in the pictures. There was one difference, however; over near the wall that faced the adjoining unit, a section of the floor had slid back, revealing a flight of steps leading down.

"You can't wish the lights out so long as this is open," said Edholm. "There's one flight leading down, and another leading up to the next building. This is the only way to get from one of these units to another without going outside."

At the end of the steps was an entrance like the entrance outside. They passed through and Edholm turned and faced it. "Watch," he said. He lowered his head as if he was in deep concentration, and the opening closed. "I have shut the door and turned off the lights in the upstairs room."

Now he saw the walls around him, filled with designs in color, and groups of dots and bars and lines. It was certainly like nothing he had ever seen before except perhaps a collection of abstractionist paintings, and he had to force himself not to stare at them and try to trace the shapes and make them fall into some sort of pattern. The alienness of it was both pleasing and disturbing. Auckland shook his head and forced himself to ignore the murals. Edholm, he saw, paid no attention to them at all.

The peculiar blocks were scattered about the floor, one of them resting by the far wall. The wall of blocks, he saw, had not been entirely knocked down.

Edholm pointed to the single block. "That one was propelled with a lot of force, though it didn't dent the wall or even damage the surface," he said. "Just how badly it would have hurt anyone it hit is hard to tell. If it had only made some sort of mark, we'd have something to go on."

"We have quite a bit to go on," replied Auckland, picking the block up, astonished at its lightness. He took a stylus Out of his pocket and tapped it. "Doesn't sound hollow, though."

It took a while to gather the fragments of the improvised bomb. "Any ideas about these?" he asked the captain.

Edholm nodded. "Yes. I can tell you that it was rigged from various toys and gadgets we brought with us for the Vaec. Extremely simple. An explosive pellet was put in a mousetrap, and the trap was attached to a little wind-up timer of some sort. When the timer went off, it released the trap and exploded the pellet. Want to take the remains back to headquarters?"

Auckland shook his head. "No. It's simple enough for anyone, including me, to have rigged. These little timers all make a ticking sound, don't they."

"Yes. Well, no, we did have a few silent ones, but the Vaec didn't care for them so much."

"Very interesting. And everyone, of course, has access to the storerooms. I take it the Vaec find mousetraps amusing, too." Edholm nodded. "Tell me, if a pellet were exploded out in the middle of the room, do you think the concussion would be fatal to us?"

Edholm mused for a few moments. "It would shatter our ear drums, that's certain. Whether one of them would kill us, I'm not sure. Wouldn't want to take a chance on it. Of course, there may have been more than one pellet attached to the trap."

"We heard it go off from a considerable distance. I take it that Doc left all the doors open when he came out of the cellar."

"They make a lot of noise. The Vaec had used them for fireworks—Leitfred gave them some on his second trip here. But they seem to have lost interest in them. I suppose it's because these things are a bit too dangerous for practical jokes. Anything else you want to look at here?"

"No, so we may as well head back." It was clear that the improvised bomb might have been dangerous had James been in the room, but the question of how dangerous remained open. That would require tests, and he made a note to have Ekem-ve take care of it.

In his quarters, Roy Auckland spoke into the microphone of his recorder as he rimed through the personal dossiers of the expedition members.

"Question one," he said. "Why is Shirley Mason with this expedition? Why did she resign from the space service to join it, when she had a far more promising career ahead of her, since she received the citation for bravery beyond the call of duty, trying to rescue a sick passenger in the wreck of the spaceship *Scriabin?*

"Question number two: What is Calvin Burleigh's present connection with the Fowler Committee on Alien Contacts? When he was committee chairman, the line was that Earthmen should run away fast the moment they saw aliens not clearly their equal, lest fallen and wicked human beings corrupt simple and pure natives. He is the only one here who refers to the Vaec as natives and acts as if he would like to put an end to the expedition.

"Question three: Would Edholm also like to stop the work? He testified before the Fowler Committee and tried to get this planet declared off-limits for Earthmen. But he does not regard the Vaec as primitives. He seems to distrust them, for all his politeness toward them.

"Question number four: What is Amelia James' real attitude towards her husband? She met him at Sanderson's Rest in Alaska shortly after the Marlene affair, and they have been married over thirty years. He does not seem to take her infidelities seriously, but relations between him and Glamis and Burleigh show signs of strain. Is he jealous? Would Amelia like to be free of—"

The intercom started buzzing, and Auckland switched off the microphone and turned the room speaker on. Dr. Howard James' voice came through, excitedly.

"Will everyone please come to the recreation room? I have something to show all of you."

Everyone else was there, except James, when Auckland arrived in the rec-room. Dr. James entered a moment later, bouncing in with the air of one who has found the Lost Chord. Auckland felt an irresistible urge to needle him at the earliest possible opportunity. Could this, and this alone, be the meaning of Glamis' behavior toward the chief?

It was certainly possible, but Glamis wasn't wearing his usual sardonic smile as Howard James held up an object they all recognized as one of the books found in the villa. James placed it on the table silently, and they all gathered around him.

Gazing at the object gave Auckland that feeling of looking at tomorrow again. There was a simplicity and beauty and implication of durability in the covering material that made all Earthmade books, even the finest, seem shabby and impertinent by comparison. As if the books of Earth were a mockery and negation of the very idea of bookmaking. There was the breath of eternity in this object and Auckland thought, *Heaven and Earth shall pass away, but my words will never pass away.*

James opened the book, and the substance on which the contents were impressed augmented the impression of the outside. He did not have to touch the pages; he had handled these volumes and knew that the pages were light, flexible, and impervious to normal applications of heat or moisture. The spark from a cigarette could fall upon them; water, acids, alkalines, grease could be spilled on them and wiped away, leaving no trace. They were almost white, taking on a slight tone which varied with the light falling upon them.

He looked at the matter on the pages, and it was like a glimpse of yesterday—yesterday's yesterday.

He thought of illuminated manuscripts, because he knew without any further evidence that these pages had not been "printed" or otherwise reproduced by mass mechanical means. This was handmade.

James turned a page and it lay there flat. The books could be opened and left thus at any page. There was no tendency in the book to close itself, yet no matter how hard one pressed upon open pages at any point, the binding remained unharmed. He looked at the dots and lines and bars, some in different colors, that made up the left column, then gasped at what he saw in the right column. It was…

"Looks familiar," came Glamis' voice, breaking into his thoughts.

James nodded appreciatively. "I was hoping you would say that, Ken. Go on don't let me suggest what it looks like."

"Reminds me of Old Martian."

"My thought, too," said Burleigh in an awed voice. Auckland looked at Shirley and then at Amelia. Both of them ignored the book on the table. Both of them were watching Kenneth Glamis. Shirley's face was calm but it made him think of a mask. Amelia's ripe lips were parted slightly and she was having more trouble in suppressing emotion.

Edholm said dryly, "Gentlemen, it is Old Martian." He nodded at James stiffly, reluctant approval in his voice. "You have found a Rosetta stone, sir."

Auckland felt himself breathing a bit more quickly, as the feeling came to him that he was present at a moment of history. When men first explored Mars, they found traces of a long-vanished civilization and a few decipherable inscriptions that were close enough to Sanskrit to translate more or less intelligibly. The indication was clear that either the Martians had once been on earth, or that Earthmen had set up a civilization on Mars. A civilization, not just a colony. Colonies do not develop the type of art forms that were found on Mars until they have passed the stage of dependence and are no longer colonies. There were factions among Earth's archaeologists as to which was the case; at the moment, the party which believed the Old Martians to have migrated from Earth was in ascendancy.

Later explorations uncovered fragments of records, partial translations suggesting that the Old Martians—to distinguish them from the simple, insectoid creatures now dwelling on the fourth planet—had had something like a stellar empire. The records referred to contact and friendly relations with another (humanoid?) culture, which also covered many worlds.

You had to put a question mark after "humanoid," because there was no description of either the other beings or the Old Martians themselves. The phrases describing these other beings broke down to "much like ourselves in form," which meant that these others were humanoid if the Old Martians themselves were human or humanoid.

Where the Old Martians had gone, or why, was still a riddle. There was a fragment of what was believed to be a poem, of which one line read something like "when we bid farewell to this system." Context suggested that "this system" was our own solar system, and opinion was that the Old Martians had migrated en masse to the planets of another sun or suns.

"The evidence," James was saying in a satisfied tone of voice, "is entirely circumstantial. However, circumstantial evidence can sometimes be very convincing. I refer you to the classic example of the trout in the milk, which is still used in elementary law. Now you must admit that the circumstances indicate a connection between the Vaec and the villa. We have seen the numerous similarities.

"And I further suggest the similarity of pointlessness. The Vaec do innumerable things which seem pointless or childish to us, and the wall of blocks we found seem to be the same sort of pointlessness."

"Meaning, really, that we just do not see the point," said Edholm. "I think there is a lot before our eyes that we are just not seeing."

"Of course," James agreed. "We haven't the proper perspective. A trout in the milk is convincing evidence that water was added to the milk. But it does not positively state why, nor again, how much. To torture the analogy, in some milieus the trout may have added because people like the flavor trout gives to the milk. In others, the trout may be accidental, but the addition of water is considered desirable. In the frame where such things happened in our own history alone, was it proof of adulteration with intent to deceive?"

"And what do you think this volume may indicate, in addition to being a Rosetta stone, Doctor?" asked Auckland.

James smiled. "I expect to find some indication that the Vaec here are remnants of that other culture referred to in the Old Martian fragments. Oh, by the way, did Ekem-ve bring the box I asked for?"

"It's in the lab," said Shirley.

"Very good. I was going to study it tonight, compare the designs with the designs in the photos I've taken of those murals in the villa. I think we may find some definite connection between the Vaec and the builders of the villa."

"My guess is that you will find a very close resemblance," said Glamis. His voice wasn't mocking, but he was secretly amused about something, Auckland thought.

"Well, that can wait," James said. "I'm going to take this

book to look over later tonight. Want to see if there is any noticeable similarity at any point in the characters of the two scripts." He picked up the book and started out.

Glamis looked after him and said lightly, "For a man who's apparently escaped two assassination attempts in one day—"

"The assassin overlooked one essential," broke in Burleigh. "If he had left that book lying on the floor, he could have put his bomb in the middle of the room, and James would have never heard it."

Amelia James, who had started toward the door, paused and threw a withering glance at the two men. Then her eyes met Auckland's and her lips parted. She didn't speak but her eyes said, "Please come with me."

## CHAPTER SIX

THERE WAS no moon in the sky, but the stars were thicker than you would ever see them on Earth, and the patterns were mostly unfamiliar. The amount of dust in the air wouldn't be the same as in Earth's atmosphere, but there was enough to produce rain very much like rain on Earth; and stars twinkled. The light was stronger than starlight on any moonless night on Earth, but never as bright as even gibbous moonlight.

They walked over the spongy ground-covering to a grove of willow-like trees, beneath the shade of which nightflowers grew, opening slowly as soon as light began to fade. The leaves were outlined with phosphorescence and the long-stemmed flowers had raised their heads fully by now and most were completely open. They, too, glowed in the night and swayed gently with or without a breeze. Around them droned insects that, to Auckland's perpetual surprise, did not alight upon Earthmen. He looked at the nightflower whose wide-open calico was speckled with moving dots. As he watched it began to close; one or two of the insects darted away before the trap was shut, but most of them remained.

Unlike the flytraps and carnivorous plants of Earth, the scent of the nightflower was fragrant.

Amelia sank down upon a patch of moss-grass and Roy Auckland joined her. "Thanks for coming," she said. "I have to talk to someone and I can't talk to them any more… They hate him. They all hate him."

"You think everyone here hates your husband?"

She smiled faintly as she took the cigarette he offered her.

"You don't. You don't particularly like him, Roy, but you have nothing against him."

"Hate is a negative thing expressed in a positive way," he said. "There are all kinds of degrees. Some hate kills, some wants to preserve its object and will never kill, some is too afraid to strike, some doesn't consider its object worth the involvement which murder requires." He thought a moment, then added, "And there are those who will kill without hatred."

She shook her head. "Never that. It may not be personal, but hate is there just the same. That's Calvin. He would kill any of us for principle and pray for our souls a moment later. He thinks we're all evil and the only reason he's here is to try to ward off the corruption we're bringing to his precious aliens. Oh, he doesn't love the Vaec, you can be sure of that. He loves to fight evil and he's always looking for it."

"But then why would he try to kill Howard?" Auckland persisted.

"To put an end to the expedition. He tried to stop all contact with Carolus, you know. He couldn't fight that any more, so he joined us. But if anything happened to Howard, the expedition would be over."

"It would be over if Burleigh killed Glamis," Auckland

said, "and Ken is the much better choice. By Burleigh's standards of evil, Glamis is probably the better victim. He's the one who mocks religion and amuses himself with theology. And he's the one who would corrupt the Vaec, to use the expression, just out of curiosity." He looked at her. "Or is there another reason why he might want to dispose of Howard?"

"Me? You think Calvin would imperil his soul by making love to me, another man's wife?"

"Missionaries aren't always totally sex-proof."

She shook her head. "He's no Reverend Davidson out of 'Rain.' To Calvin, sex is a means, not an end. It's a way to get a woman, to convert her through love. Oh, he'd seduce me in a moment to serve his ends and justify himself on the grounds that pleasure wasn't his object."

"While Glamis has no such ulterior motive. Why would he want to kill Howard?"

She was silent for a moment. "Don Juan was simple and single minded. He wanted very little from women, really, and they didn't realize how little he wanted. But some men want to make their women into replicas of themselves before they go on to the next campaign. Kenneth can't endure to have any reminder of failure around him."

"He wanted you to look at Howard the way he does—as a buffoon, as a target for his wit? He wanted to destroy your husband in your eyes as a human being?"

"He wants me to divorce Howard."

"And marry him?"

"Of course not," she said. "You don't think I'd believe any such proposal how often he made it? Edholm, now, he doesn't like it here. He doesn't trust the Vaec."

"Thinks they'll suddenly turn on us?"

"I don't know what he thinks, but he wants to leave this planet and see to it that no one comes back here. He thinks they're dangerous but he won't say how or why."

"Hardly sufficient motive for murder, though."

"He's like Burleigh—nothing personal, you understand. But…no. No I can't see him killing anyone without legal justification. But it wasn't necessary to stop the work, you know. Captain Edholm seized the opportunity, and if he has his way he won't let it resume."

Auckland sighed. "Well, that leaves only Shirley. Why do you think she hates Howard?"

Amelia's mouth writhed into an expression of distaste.

"Shirley, in case you haven't noticed it, is Dr. Glamis' own puppet."

There was certainly no love pretended between the two women, he thought. If it hadn't been for what he had noticed this afternoon… Still, Amelia could be right in that Shirley Mason was an unwilling ally of Glamis. He couldn't accept anyone's judgment as final, but that was something to look into. Whatever the tie between Mason and Glamis, he was sure it wasn't love.

"Didn't those two attempts on your husband's life strike you as somewhat inept?" he asked. "Both of them were caught with the greatest of ease."

She was closer to him now as she said, "There's such a thing as two for the price of one. Why couldn't I have been an ordinary, plain woman, Roy. I wish I had been. I wish…"

Looking at her upturned face in the starlight, Roy Auckland didn't wish anything of the kind.

Roy Auckland swallowed an anti-fatigue pill as he studied his notes, sprawled out on his bunk, and tried to coordinate what Amelia had told him with what he'd learned from the others and from his own observation. She'd started to say something about Glamis working on something he found very amusing. She knew what it was, but he couldn't get any more out of her, except that she did not find Glamis' private project amusing at all. What else was there? It had something to do with the Vaec, for earlier she'd said something about his wearing a smug look after an all-night fishing trip with Ekem-ve.

It didn't seem to make sense that someone could be trying to murder Dr. Howard James so inefficiently. What was the purpose in even pretending that Dr. James' life was being threatened? "Two for the price of one," Amelia had said. That would fit in well enough if the object were to make it appear that someone was trying to kill James—if this were a frame-up. But that didn't account for the childish naivete of the attempts; someone trying to frame another would have rigged up something that looked much more real.

How had the *dodlig* been put into the soup? What else about Carolus was relevant? There was something nagging at him that he couldn't put his finger on. He'd studied the general report on Carolus—the Leitfred report—before he came. Was there something in it? He went in to the office and took the folder containing it out of the files.

Not more than half an hour later he discovered that two sheets had been removed from the loose-leaf folder. Interesting, he thought. Particularly since he remembered a good deal of what had been on those missing pages. Yes… *dodlig* could have been extracted from some other plant on which its pollen had rested. It would take a bit of lab work but the resultant poison would not have had the overpowering odor associated with *dodlig* itself.

The only trouble was why should the two pages containing this information have been excerpted? He pictured the two sheets, recalling that the specific paragraph relating this was broken at the bottom and continued on to the top of the second missing page. But everyone here was aware of this; everyone *would* think of it had it been brought to their attention.

As it had. Was that the reason for the pilfering of these pages?

The explanation of mysteries was usually simple when you got the right angle, but this was too simple. Auckland turned off thc light and closed his eyes feeling that he was being misdirected for a purpose. He wished now that he had waited to see who would draw his attention to the missing papers.

How imbecilic can I get, he asked himself. I can still find that out. He got out of bed and tucked the folder under his arm.

In the morning, Auckland's four watchers reported.

Ekem-ve, Hcent, Phrecle, and Syeltan (the last-named hadn't yet been caught by Ekem-ve's pop-ball trick, Roy saw) trooped into his quarters, their single hairs lying flat on their skulls. That, and the slight expansion and contraction of their pupils, indicated interest and fascination; although at any moment, something might cross over the thin line that separated mirth from not-mirth in their eyes.

"Ineffective watchers offer different report, excellent Roy," began Ekem-ve. "Hcent watches north, Phrecle watches east, Syeltan watches south, and this unobservant one watches west. We come together when day begins and arrange list of happenings from ace to king."

"Oh, chronological order," said Auckland. "Very good.

That can make a lot of difference. My ears wave happily." He hoped that was the idiom he meant, and followed Ekem-ve's glance to Phrecle, whose single hair quivered a bit then lay flat again. It could be appreciation of his exactness or the equivalent of a snicker at his malapropism.

"After meeting in recreation room," Phrecle began, "excellent Kenneth comes out of excellent Howard and

Amelia's room walking with steadiness to own room."

Not hurriedly or lazily, Auckland translated.

"Excellent Howard and Amelia have windows shuttered, thus depriving watcher of wisdom," Phrecle added.

"Excellent Kenneth does not keep windows shuttered," said Syeltan, "and is struck by haste after entering room. Seeks object which conceals itself from him. Darkness opens like nightflower and excellent Kenneth shutters window, then turns on light."

"Excellent Kenneth and excellent Shirley come out of office and go west like brook," said Ekem-ve. "Excellent Shirley not filled with mirth but play follow-leader with excellent Kenneth."

They didn't walk in a direct line, and took their time, thought Auckland.

"Excellent Howard comes out of excellent Calvin's rooms when lights go on in room," said Phrecle. "Excellent Howard walks with steadiness to own room."

So Dr. James had some sort of conference with Burleigh, then retired to his quarters.

"Excellent Howard carries object with care," Phrecle continued. "Object has appearance of book found in villa." Phrecle paused for a moment, then continued: "Excellent Roy and excellent Amelia come out of recreation room and, go east like brook. Excellent Roy not filled with mirth, but play follow-leader with excellent Amelia." Auckland gulped.

"Now unworthy assistants remember excellent Earthman's watches as darkness has opened and dials glow like nightflower," said Ekem-ve, "This negligent one looks at dial when excellent Kenneth and excellent Shirley return walking with steadiness and dial shows 11:00. They go into excellent Shirley's room."

"Excellent Kenneth comes out of his own room at 11:13 and walks with steadiness into lab," Phrecle said. "Does not shutter window. Admires object under microscope and writes letter to self. Excellent Roy and excellent Amelia return walking with steadiness at 11:32. Stop for two breaths to look at excellent Kenneth, then excellent Roy parts from excellent Amelia at door to room and walks with steadiness to recreation room.

"Excellent Kenneth looks up from the microscope and delivers instruction to self. Then puts microscope away and takes out camera. Puts box on table and starts to take pictures of box. Excellent Howard unshutters window and excellent Amelia walks like river to window.

"They look at excellent Kenneth. Excellent Kenneth sees them and makes gentle breeze with hand. They make gentle breeze with hand but excellent Amelia not very mirthful. Excellent Howard shutters windows and excellent Kenneth shutters window, thus depriving watcher of wisdom."

So Dr. Glamis was doing microscope work, muttering to himself now and then taking notes. James called Amelia to the window. She came quickly, and Glamis waved—to Amelia, no doubt—and they both waved back, but Amelia wasn't pleased about it. But why should James call Amelia to the window to look at Glamis?

"Was Dr. James wearing his glasses when he came to the window?" he asked.

"No, excellent Roy. Excellent Howard wore two eyes only."

That could account for it, then. James wanted to be sure just what it was Glamis was taking photographs of. Wanted to know if it was the Vaec box or some other, probably (the Vaec boxes being four-inch cubes, approximately, and James was a bit near-sighted).

Ekem-ve took up the report. "Excellent Roy comes out of recreation room at 12:00, carrying object, walking with steadiness to own room. At 12:33, lights go off in excellent

Roy's room. At 12:37, lights go on again, then excellent Roy comes out of room walking like river taking object to office. At 12:38, comes out of office walking with steadiness, and returns to own room."

"Shuttered windows in rooms of excellent Earth people deprive watchers of wisdom, except for that already told," said Syeltan, and Auckland realized that the Vaec considered this a peculiar practice.

"No wisdom offered to this lowly one," said Hcent. "At no time do excellent Calvin, excellent Walter, or excellent Howard and Amelia unshutter windows at north."

"I take it, then," said Auckland, "that Captain Edholm and Dr. Burleigh did not step outside the building at any time after the meeting in the recreation room last night."

"That is the way it grew, excellent Roy," said Ekem-ve.

"And excellent Shirley did not unshutter windows at any time, nor did you."

Auckland glanced at his notes. "You have helped a great deal, all of you," he said. "We suspect that an unwise sticky trap is about to be prepared by someone, and that is why I need to know where everyone is at night. If indeed the trap has been made, what you have told me may help to uncover this unwise person."

He swallowed. "But it would help me more if you take note of the time even in daylight. For example, Mrs. James and I actually started out before it was very dark. Dr. Glamis was in the recreation room when we left, and your timetable would seem to indicate that he and Miss Mason went out a little before we did.

"But that cannot be the case. Dr. Glamis was talking with Dr. James in his quarters at that time. Phrecle saw Dr. Glamis come out of Dr. James' room and walk to his own room, where he was looking for something—and it was getting dark enough to turn on the lights. About how long would you say he was looking before he turned the lights on?"

"Only very short time after he enter room," said Phrecle. "And it was dark enough so that the watches would glow well around 8:30—after Dr. James left Dr. Burleigh's quarters and returned to his own. When did the light go off in Dr. Glamis' room?"

"Excellent Kenneth discover object soon after lights are turned on," Syeltan said. "Then turn off lights."

"But he did not go outside right away. He must have gone to the office and met Miss Mason there, or walked with her to the office. But, you see, we cannot be sure that Dr. Glamis actually found what he was looking for, because no one saw whether he was carrying anything when he came out of his room. He might have just given up the search."

"We hear wise words, excellent Roy," said Ekem-ve.

"So it is important to report only what you actually saw and not make inferences as if they were something you had seen. Of course," he added hastily, "inferences can be helpful , So long as we know that they are not something you really saw. But what the evidence really implies is only that Dr. Glamis and Miss Mason went out later than Mrs. James and I."

Auckland scratched his head. "And that—somehow—does not seem right. Are you sure, Phrecle, that it was Dr. Glamis who came out of Dr. James' quarters, went into his own room, and started looking for something?"

"He was wearing the special suit, excellent Roy."

Auckland grinned wryly. "But he wasn't wearing it later when he went out with Miss Mason, was he?"

"No, excellent Roy," said Ekem-ve. "Excellent Kenneth heard to say at one time that protective suit protect from mirth, as well as sorrow of sun burn."

Auckland arose and put his notebook away. "You have

done very well and I am grateful. Can you continue the watch and keep track of all movements with the time they took place?"

The four Vaec indicated their fascinated assent.

There was no answer to Auckland's knock, but the door to Kenneth Glamis' room swung open. Nothing unusual about that, he thought; the single men's doors were rarely locked here. He stepped inside, just to be sure that Glamis wasn't still asleep.

The room was unoccupied, and the condition of the bed indicated that Glamis had not slept here. That was one thing about Ken: he insisted on a neatly-made bunk, although he never got to making it up before noon, if he was around headquarters, or after returning from the field. Otherwise, Glamis was not very tidy, and last night's search hadn't helped any.

The desk was usually a litter of papers and knick-knacks.

Glamis was continually bringing back stones and bits of wood from the surrounding territory. Now the desk was a spread of confusion. There were the usual empty and partially filled containers of coffee standing around, being used for ashtrays, as Glamis preferred to use the latter for wastebaskets. One container had been overturned, and cigarette butts scattered. Another had coffee remains, and had splashed some papers with sketches and doodles on them. Photographs, usually piled under an ashtray, were scattered.

A small stack of paper had been knocked off the typewriter stand. The tape-maker was underneath it. Auckland sighed. If someone other than Glamis had been searching the room, you couldn't tell the difference, he thought. Glamis himself had done the same thing in the past, looking for something which he had left somewhere else.

The only thing definitely implied by the condition of the room was that a small object had been the object of the search—one which might have been lying under papers, or mixed in with a pile of photographs. It might have been in the file box, which was likely to contain everything except papers. Auckland still wondered if Glamis had been deliberately overdoing it the last time he'd talked with the man in his room. That pulling a sandwich out of the file under U for unfinished business sounded like a gag, yet it was in character.

There was little point in trying to decide whether anything that he had seen before was missing, because, with Glamis, hardly anything important was likely to be where you would normally expect it to be—except for a few hours after he'd straightened everything out.

"Auckland!" came a voice, and he looked up, to realize that it had come through the intercom. "Dr. Auckland!" It was James' voice; nothing had happened to him during the night, as Roy was sure nothing would. "Please come to the lab. There has been an accident to Dr. Glamis. Please come to the lab right away. Dr. Glamis is dead!"

## CHAPTER SEVEN

THEY WERE all in the lab when Auckland arrived: Amelia, Shirley, Burleigh, James, Edholm, and Ekem-ve. The latter stood apart gravely, while the rest were gathered around the body that was sprawled on the floor by the table. Glamis was dressed as Auckland had last seen him in the recreation room the night before, although stains indicated that he had been outside in various postures of ease. Edholm was down on one knee, examining the deceased.

He looked up as Auckland joined the group. "Hello, Roy," he said. "Things seem to have taken a different turn than we expected. It's ironic that for all his care in wearing a protective suit outside, Ken still had to be stung by an insect and that finished him."

"Are you sure about that?" Auckland asked, looking down at the body.

Edholm stooped and, lifting Glamis' right hand, rolled his short sleeves back. "Puncture in index finger," he said. "Black indicating poison. Entire hand and arm swollen. Very much like a snake bite, you see. Ekem-ve tells me that little animals stung by the wild bees look a lot like this when you find them afterward. There's a dead bee on the table," he nodded to his left, "and it's pretty clear that it stung Ken, and Ken swatted it before he succumbed. It hit him fast; he didn't have time to call for help or get to an antidote himself, if that would have done any good."

"But—but how did the bee get in here?" Amelia asked. She was shaken by the event, but there was no sign of grief about her. He glanced at Shirley, whose face was white—no sorrow there, either. James had an abstract, somewhat puzzled air about him, as if he was not quite sure whether he was dreaming this or not. Only Burleigh seemed to be affected with anything like regret.

"A native box was brought in here and it is on the table now." He pointed to the open artifact. "Ken was photographing it, as you see from the pictures there, and he must have opened it. And the natives make pets of the bees and often carry them around with them." He turned to Ekem-ve and said softly, "Why was a bee left in this box, Ekem-ve? And I thought you said they wouldn't sting us."

"Wild bees told not to sting excellent Earthmen," Ekem-ve replied. "No Vaec tell wild bee to sting for mirth. Bad joke not mirthful. Pet bees not able to sting. May examine remains of unfortunate insect, excellent Calvin?"

Edholm and Burleigh nodded, and the Carolinian carne

forward and picked up the dead insect gently. He held the small body in his fingers and pressed the abdomen.

"This is pet bee," he said. "Unfortunate insect cannot sting because Vaec give pets a most gentle operation for own protection. When wild bee sting, stinger remain in wound of victim and insect soon die from loss of stinger. Is stinger in wound, excellent Walter?"

Edholm took a magnifying glass from the drawer and bent over Glamis' body again. The breath whistled through his teeth as he said, "No. I should have noticed that before. There's no stinger."

"If you will please observe stinger of unfortunate insect under magnifying glass, while this one press abdomen."

Edholm held the glass on the dead bee as Ekem-ve repeated the operation. Auckland peered over the captain's shoulder and it was evident enough. The stinger was ridiculously short and blunted. It could not have penetrated Glamis' skin.

"Then," began Amelia, her eyes becoming wide, "it wasn't an accident."

"Very unlikely." There was a pencil-light on the table Auckland picked it up and played it around the inside of the Vaec box. "Dr. Glamis pricked his finger on something sharp, something pointed, something coated with an alkaloid poison, very possibly. He was examining a box which ordinarily you would have been examining. It's empty now. You two saw him working on it?"

"Yes," said James. "I opened the shutters to see if he was in the lab. I was going over to ask him something—really can't recall what it was now. He was photographing an object on the table, and I couldn't be sure what it was since I didn't have my glasses on. I asked Amelia to look."

"What did you see?" Auckland asked.

"This box," she answered.

"I mean, what did it look like from your window?"

"Oh." Amelia blinked and thought a moment. "The light was clear and I could see a cubical object with designs in black around the outside on a rather pale blue background. The designs looked like the designs I'm looking at right now, although I could not see them all as clearly."

"And Dr. Glamis waved to you, and you waved back?"

"Yes," said James. "I was a little miffed, I'll admit, as I wanted to examine the box, then I realized I was being silly. There was no reason why he should not take photographs of it. He'd finished one roll—just torn off the last one—and was about to put another roll of film into the camera when he looked up and saw me. He waved, and I waved back just to show there were no hard feelings. Then I closed the shutters and went to bed."

Auckland picked up the camera and examined it. "There's a fresh roll in here," he said. "So we know it happened before he could take any more photos. Was the box closed when you saw it?"

Amelia nodded.

"There are a lot of questions, then. I take it the box was open when you found him?"

"Yes, it was open," James said. "I came in here and saw the box open, the first thing. Thought that he'd gone to bed —he didn't always put things in order, you know." Auckland nodded. "Then I saw him lying on the floor and I called everyone."

"Did you see the bee then?"

"No," James replied. "I didn't see it at all until Edholm examined the body. He called our attention to it. It was on the floor just a little under the table. He picked it up and put it where you saw it when you came in."

Auckland's head nodded. "You can see this much clearly someone did not know about the Vaec pet bees—the only person I can now be sure did not know is Roy Auckland—and this party thought that if Ken were found thus, we would assume that he had been stung. We all knew that he was very allergic to insect stings. The indications were all there."

He turned to Burleigh. "I remember you said something about being stung by the wild ones and it not being very serious."

Calvin Burleigh shook his head. "Not the large bees. No one here has been stung by them."

"Then that kills one theory," said Auckland. "I was about to say this indicated that Glamis was not an accidental victim of murder aimed at someone else. If it hasn't been established whether the bee stings might be fatal to anyone

"A couple of Leitfred's men were stung by bees," said Edholm. "One died. The other didn't."

A stricken look crossed Burleigh's face. "I didn't know that," he said to Auckland. "And I misinformed you, quite unintentionally, when I told you that a couple of us had been stung, but that it wasn't at all bad. It wasn't the bees like this one," he nodded toward the table, "but the smaller type, and we'd bothered them. I assumed that this kind wouldn't be much worse, except to Ken of course."

"What about this, Ekem-ve?" asked Auckland. "Why I should any bee sting one of us unless we were trying to harm it? I thought you had control over them."

The Carolinian blinked rapidly, the Vaec manner of shaking one's head or nodding. One had to guess which, in each instance. "Unfortunate insects not large in intelligence, excellent Roy. Cannot be told not to sting, can only be told to keep away from excellent Earthmen. Very easily frightened. If wild bee put in box then released with suddenness to see stranger bending over, unfortunate insect follow instinct; perhaps flyaway, perhaps sting."

"That makes a difference," said Shirley. "Why, I might

have tried to capture or pick up one of the bees, particularly one that came out of a box and I thought was tame."

Ekem-ve's single hair straightened, then drooped slightly.

"This thoughtless person overcome by remorse at stupidity. Did not think of such contingency."

Amelia asked in a low voice, "Are you going to leave him there?"

"He was the doctor," said Auckland. "More irony. Ken is the only one who could have established the approximate time of death, which may be important, or performed an autopsy." He looked at Edholm. "Space officers have to have some medical training. Can you give us any idea how long he was dead when you examined him?"

Edholm shook his head. "We really don't have that much training, Roy. The body was cold, and rigor mortis had pretty well set in. Obviously, he'd been dead for some time when Doc found him."

"Just a few more questions, then we'll lay him out. What is the rule, by the way? Can he be buried here, or must the body be returned to Earth?"

"The men who died out on the first expedition were brought back home," Edholm said, "but such matters lie in my discretion. Has anyone any idea of what his preference might be in this matter?"

"I think he would prefer to stay here," Shirley said. "And I think he would appreciate a funeral service."

"That is always done unless the deceased expressly abjures it," Edholm said. "Can you finish the questioning now, Auckland?"

Auckland picked up the pile of photographs on the table and glanced through them. "Anyone examine these?"

Apparently no one had, outside of Burleigh's cursory glance. He nodded and put them in his pocket. "I'm holding them for the time being. What was the time when you saw him working here last night?"

"About midnight, wouldn't you say, Amelia?"

The woman nodded. "It was before midnight, but not very much before."

"And no one else came into the lab, or saw him, from midnight until Dr. James found him this morning?"

The question was rhetorical, Auckland knew. No one would admit either seeing Glamis or entering the lab between midnight and the time he was found. He said to Edholm, "I'll be back in a few moments," and nodded to Ekem-ve.

The box rested on the table in the recreation room, and the others sat around in various postures and attitudes of unease. None of them had liked Kenneth Glamis, and all but one feared unjust accusation, however they assured themselves that their innocence left them nothing to fear.

"There have been times," Howard James said, "when I could have killed him with the greatest of pleasure." He did not look at Amelia, who was chain-smoking.

"I think," said Edholm, "that the first question we have to resolve is whether Dr. Glamis was really the victim intended. I admit, sir," he nodded at Auckland, "that I was dubious about the previous alleged attempts on Dr. James' life, but now it seems to me that they might make more sense. I think they were deliberately botched, so as to give the impression of ineptness. I think that a competent person was posing as incompetent because that person had tipped his hand earlier, or thought he had, and wanted to misdirect his victim."

Howard James frowned. "You mean that if it had not been for the *dodlig* in the soup or the bomb in the cellar, I might have been careless about opening a Vaec box?"

"Regardless of whether Glamis was the intended victim, we are still faced with a murder to solve," Auckland broke in. He switched on the lights. "I would like you two to look at this box again and tell me which side was facing you when you saw it in the lab last night." He got up and started to turn the box slowly. He hadn't gotten far before a scream came from Amelia.

"She's fainted!" snapped Edholm, but James was already by his wife's side. "What's the meaning of this, Auckland?"

"Something very simple," said Auckland. "So simple that no one noticed it, even if anyone did examine the photographs on the table." He took the color pictures out of his pocket and spread them out. "You will observe that the pictures show a box with black designs and orange shadings, on a pale blue background; and Amelia said she saw a box with black designs and orange shadings on a pale blue background."

"But it *is* a blue—" began Burleigh then stopped and stared. "Good heavens, it isn't. It's white…but I could have sworn."

Auckland glanced at Shirley who was visibly pale now.

"You were right, Cal. The box actually is pale blue. But as Shirley and I discovered yesterday, the Vaec blue tends to wash out under fluorescent lights."

A slight moan came from Amelia, then she sat up again. "I'm all right," she said faintly. "It was just the shock of realizing…

"Yes, you see there are two possible explanations," said Auckland One is that you actually saw Glamis working there by daylight, without lights on—which would make the time you saw him this morning, rather than last night—or that the box you saw him working on was not the box before us now."

"But why should we lie to you, Roy?" asked James.

"Fortunately, we don't have to bother about that, Doc. Ekem-ve, did Hcent find what she was looking for?"

"Yes, excellent Roy," replied the Carolinian. "Is it your

wish that she bring it in now?"

Auckland nodded, and Ekem-ve wiggled his finger in the parting gesture as he left the room. "As soon as I heard Amelia describe a pale blue box, I thought of a substitution, so I asked Ekem-ve to see if he or one of the others could find something that looked like a Vaec box anywhere around."

Ekem-ve entered carrying a box the same size and shape as the one on the table. At a gesture from Auckland, he put it beside the white one.

"I'll be damned," said Edholm. The box Ekem-ve had just brought in had black designs with orange shadings, not unlike the other, but its background was clearly a pale blue. Auckland switched off the lights, and both boxes showed a pale blue background. Set side by side, the difference in tone was just barely noticeable.

"So you see," Auckland said, "the second explanation of the discrepancy is the simpler one. Where did Hcent find this box, Ekem-ve?"

"She says box concealed in shrubbery outside shower rooms."

Auckland glanced around. "So now we begin to see the mechanism of murder. Dr. James asked for a Vaec box to examine—" he switched on the fluorescents again "—and Ekem-ve brought this box which now appears white into the lab. Presumably, no one here had examined these boxes closely before, but this presumption must be discarded.

"Dr. James intended to examine the box last night, but the unexpected discovery of the book made him put it off. Dr. Glamis went to the lab, as he very often did, and after puttering around with whatever he went there to do, decided to examine the box himself. But someone had substituted what you can see is a very clever imitation."

"But, I don't understand," James interrupted. "What was

the danger in the imitation?"

"Glamis pricked his finger on something sharp. Do you know how to open the Vaec boxes, Doctor?"

"Of course." James arose and went to the table, and picked up the box with the blue background.

"Not that one," said Auckland.

"Oh, Heavens, it is easy to forget the difference, isn't it."

He put the imitation down and said, "You'll see that there are large solid black squares on opposite sides. You just press them." He squeezed and the lid Hew open.

"Exactly," agreed Auckland. He opened a drawer and took out a small cutting tool with a cord, which he plugged into a socket on the desk. "I'm sorry to damage a work of art, but this is necessary."

A moment later he had the top off the imitation. "Now, if you will all look inside." They gathered around the little box, and gazed in fascination at the slender object projecting from one of the sides.

"This needle," Auckland said, "was set so that the person pressing the solid black squares to open the box would prick his finger."

Shirley Mason was gripping the edge of the table, her knuckles white. "But I didn't…I didn't…" she whispered.

"When did you make the imitation, Shirl?" Auckland asked.

"I…it was a month or so ago. Then I put it away. I haven't seen it for a couple of weeks. I didn't think about it. You've got to believe me, Roy. I didn't make it for a death trap."

# CHAPTER EIGHT

EVERYTHING was so damn convenient, Roy Auckland thought: the poisoned soup which was sure to have been discovered because Phrecle always brought the thermos' to the party when they knocked off for lunch; the obvious bomb, placed *after* suspicion had been aroused by the first attempt. Careful questioning had revealed that anyone might have put it there during the lunchtime siesta when no one was paying much attention to where anyone else went.

Dr. James had said he hadn't considered the possibility of another attempt so soon, and that he had been trying to give the appearance of normality. Yes, it was in character.

But others might have tried to open the fatal box, which must have been substituted for the original before supper. Burleigh and Edholm had not gone out; either might have gone to the lab, seen the box there, and started to fool around with it. If your fingers happened to cover both solid black squares simultaneously, and you squeezed, the top flew open. It wasn't likely to happen by accident, but it could happen.

The obvious conclusion was that three persons knew how to open the boxes: Shirley, who had made an imitation; Dr. James, the intended victim; and Glamis, the actual one. Shirley or James could have told Glamis how it was done.

And there was one more possibility: the person who had rigged the needle, if that person were neither James nor Shirley. But he had to consider the possibility that Howard James had planned the murder of Kenneth Glamis from the start, that the preliminary matter was stage-dressing.

But even if so, it was such bad stage-dressing. He had interrupted Edholm, who was getting too close to stating something that Auckland didn't want to come out into the open as yet.

Either way, one thing seemed clear: one murder, while an end in itself, had been planned as the means to another end. Someone was being framed, and cards were being forced upon Auckland. He had the feeling of having been meant to find everything he had discovered so far.

Was there anything that might not be knowledge common to several people here?

Glamis had known about Shirley's imitation of a Vaec box; he had taken photographs of an original, while visiting Ekem-ve at the Carolinian's dwelling, for her to use as a model. She had destroyed the photographs after finishing. The basic patterns on the box that Ekem-ve had brought were the same as on Shirley's copy, but there were small variations. Auckland took the photos out of his pocket and compared them to the genuine box. At a quick glance, they seemed to be the same, but close inspection showed minute differences in shading and line.

But why didn't Glamis recognize the imitation when he saw it? And who else not only knew about Shirley's project, but remembered it? Edholm claimed he didn't know about it in the first place. Burleigh and James both acknowledged that they had seen it or heard about it in the early stages, but had forgotten. Amelia apparently neither knew nor cared.

Coincidence: Shirley Mason had a wooden box the general size, shape and weight of a Vaec box. It took a little ingenuity to engineer it so that the top would fly open when the sides were pressed. Ken had done that part of it, Shirley said. The painting was her contribution.

Then why, why hadn't Glamis recognized the box?

It would have been simple enough had Glamis prepared the death trap for James; then his apparent non-recognition would make some sort of sense. He could claim that it was just a joke and that he knew nothing about the poisoned needle. But he wouldn't have committed suicide in order to prove his innocence.

Or could it be that it a childish joke, and that he didn't suspect the needle of being anything but a sterile, harmless needle which would prick someone's finger, but nothing more? In that case, he surely wouldn't have opened it to photograph the inside, stinger and all.

Obviously, the plan was to substitute the Vaec box with his deadly imitation, then re-substitute the original early in the morning. Someone had gone to the lab and made the change. Had that person been surprised to find the body of Kenneth Glamis, rather than Howard James, on the floor?

"Does this thoughtless one disturb flow of thoughts, excellent Roy?"

Auckland looked up to see Ekem-ve and Hcent, their single hairs standing stiff at the bottom, but drooping and not moving at the top. This, then, must be how the Vaec displayed regret.

"The thoughts flow, but the stream is muddy, Ekem-ve. Disturbing them couldn't make things any worse than they are."

Hcent said, "Muddy stream may become clear if watcher wait for a time."

"Very true," Auckland agreed. "And that, I'm afraid, is what I shall have to do, as if I were playing a long joke."

"Excellent Kenneth was man of fine mirth. Vaec look for him with sorrow."

Somehow, Auckland was glad to hear that Glamis had not passed entirely unmourned.

"Most doubtful mirth to put poisoned needle in box, where victim will prick fingers," said Ekem-ve.

It was quite clear that the Vaec disapproved of Earthmen harming each other, yet what sort of jokes did they consider fine mirth, but not harmful? Where did they draw the line?

"What is fine mirth, Ekem-ve? Most of us consider

murder doubtful, to say the least. It isn't funny in the first place, and it is doubtful whether the person who perpetrates it will really achieve the advantages or happiness he thinks he will obtain from it. But what was there about Dr. Glamis that made him a man of fine mirth?"

The Carolinian's pupils expanded and contracted for a moment. "Good joke always beneficial to victim, excellent Roy. Show victim something that is good to see, perhaps that not see otherwise. Sometime perhaps force victim to revise opinion of self."

"But what if the victim doesn't get the point? What if the victim merely becomes angry over the joke?"

"Then joke unwise, excellent Roy."

Auckland nodded. "And that is often the case with us, Ekem-ve. We don't always get the point, nor does the person who plays the joke always have the best interest of his victim at heart." He frowned in thought a moment.

"I do not know if Dr. Glamis had the right idea of what humor was for. In the light of what you said, in fact, I doubt it. And more than that, I doubt that his victims were always able to benefit by his mirth, even if it was well-intended. Earthmen are more likely to be harmed than helped by jokes —and sometimes we want to harm each other. Sometimes we think it is very funny."

"Excellent Kenneth prepare long joke much needed by victim," said Hcent.

Auckland nodded. "But you see, Hcent, the victim may not realize the need, even when it is shown to him. I wish this were not so. I wish we could be more like you." He shrugged. "But wishes do not change the facts."

Ekem-ve blinked. "You speak wisdom, excellent Roy. Are Earthmen who cannot see point of joke many?"

"Far, far too many," Auckland sighed. "I, myself, might become angry at some well-meant jokes, although I would not if I knew in advance that no harm was meant, or, more particularly, if I was sure that good was meant, and that the person who played the joke really knew what was good for me." He smiled. "I would not be angry at the Vaec because I trust them. I cannot say the same for all Earthmen I know.

"I came here, you see, to try to prevent harmful and unwise mirth, and I have failed. Now all I can do is to try and see that folly is not rewarded by success."

"We know," said Ekem-ve. "We have seen. We are filled with much sorrow that Vaec could not help excellent Earthmen. We see that Vaec is foolish, too, and must now leave Earthmen to unravel own nets."

"You're going back to the village?"

"Yes. Unwise to stand in path of Earthmen. Not help mirth, perhaps do harm."

"Can you tell me what Dr. Glamis' long joke was?"

"Wait until muddy thought becomes clear, excellent Roy, then ask clear question."

The reactions of the others to the departure of the Vaec from the Earthmen's vicinity was roughly what Auckland had expected. Edholm was considerably relieved, and made no bones about it. Burleigh, too, thought it was a good thing, and heartily approved the Vaec's intelligence in withdrawing themselves outside the range of human contamination. Shirley was regretful—she'd grown fond of Ekem-ve and Hcent—and Amelia thought they could have waited long enough to help with the burial.

The exception was Dr. Howard James, who said nothing and appeared completely withdrawn as they gathered in the recreation room and Captain Edholm, wearing the cassock of a licensed Reader, read the first part of the funeral service out of the English-rite prayer book.

Auckland glanced intently around, trying to look behind

the expressions and demeanor of the others. Burleigh listened with bowed head, nodding every so often; Shirley looked calm and somehow relieved; Amelia dried tears, and he wondered whom they were for. James seemed to be watching and listening for something beyond the words.

Edholm closed the book and nodded. The other four picked up the prefab coffin and started toward the grave that the other two men had dug in a grove of trees resembling red maples. The texture suggested hard rubber, and the oval leaves bore white striations, but the impression of maples remained. James and Burleigh bore the coffin ahead, while Auckland and Shirley took the rear end, Amelia and the captain walking behind them.

Here was a new world, Auckland thought, and so soon contaminated by old evil. Somehow, Burleigh seemed very right in his attitude. Did Glamis' blood cry out from the soil of Carolus as surely as that of the first victim of murder when Earth was new to man? Was someone hearing a voice within him asking 'Where is thy brother?' as surely as a murderer on Earth, however he might turn his hearing from it?

They set the coffin down and listened while Edholm began, " 'Man, that is born of woman, hath but a short time to live, and is full of misery…' " Was someone wondering when and how he would come to this end, or rather confident of avoiding all unpleasant consequences and looking forward to the benefits of his action? What was the motive? What was the good that someone expected to reap?

Edholm had laid down the prayer book, and picked up a small pamphlet. "The missionary bishop of Arcturus, whose diocese we are in, has authorized this prayer for burial of the dead in worlds afar."

Auckland blinked, then he remembered that extra solar-system dioceses were laid out by arbitrary divisions of star maps, and there was no implication that Carolus was actually in or near the Arcturian system. At a nod from the officiant, he and Burleigh took shovels and filled in the grave, as Edholm read the prayer of committal. Amelia set the marker in place, and Shirley placed a simple wreath of Carolinian flowers around it.

They started back to headquarters and James caught Auckland's arm, turning aside. "Why did you let them go, Roy?" he asked, after the others had passed beyond earshot. Couldn't you have persuaded them to stay?"

"I don't know if I could have. In any event, I didn't try. I think they have done the right thing, both for them and us. This is our problem, and they can't help any at the present stage of it."

"But we need them, Roy. You need them, I need them. They're tireless watchers, and so long as someone knows that they are watching..." He paused and breathed deeply. "I don't think that it is over yet, and I don't think you do, either. There's something diabolical here, something that still has to come to its conclusion."

"You still think someone is aiming at you, Doc? Why? What's the motive?"

James shook his head. "I don't know. Can't figure it out. I thought, well, I had a strong suspicion that he was behind it all. But he wouldn't have fallen into a trap that he set for... Not that easily, But he was jealous, Roy."

"Of what?" Auckland asked brutally.

"Men have murdered over women before, when there was really no need for it. But not..." He shook his head again. "Try to get them to come back, won't you, Roy?"

"When it is time, Doc. Tell me, have you considered the possibility that Glamis might have been the intended victim from the start and that the attempts on you were a blind? What if the culprit wanted us to think that Glamis was accidentally the victim of an attempt upon you?"

"But that doesn't make sense, Roy. The poison and bomb bit were pretty crude, but I think someone was just playing with me. A bit of subtle torture before the genuine attempt was made. I'd be torn between doubt and fear, wondering on the one hand if it was just an execrable joke, or whether something was coming my way in earnest." He frowned. "And that was the way his mind worked, too."

"I'd have said Glamis was more subtle than that."

James took a cigarette from his case, brought it almost to his lips then threw it away. "I see poison everywhere," he said, "It's cowardly and foolish, but I can't help it...Yes, he was subtle in his way. But he could be crude, too."

"Of course, there is another possibility." Auckland picked up the discarded cigarette and put it to his lips.

James didn't seem to be listening; he was intently looking out towards the desert. He turned suddenly and said, "Here's a tip, Roy. I've no proof, but I have a strong conviction that Glamis was blackmailing someone."

## CHAPTER NINE

THE QUESTION was, what had the death of Kenneth Glamis accomplished, besides removing him from the scene? If blackmail had been afoot, then that was stopped. Was there anything else?

Auckland looked into the deadly box, and remembered that it had not yet been established that the needle set inside it had really been the cause of death. Shirley would have to examine it, under Edholm's supervision.

The train of thought halted abruptly and he turned around.

"Ekem-ve...?" he started to say, then stopped as he realized that the room was empty. Why had he thought a Vaec had entered?

But what else had the murder accomplished? Well, the digging had been stopped and the expedition was virtually at an end. The supply ship was due to arrive soon, and it was almost certain that Edholm would insist that they leave if the mystery hadn't been cleared up. Everyone wanted it cleared up, but someone was promoting a false solution.

Anything else? He had been planning to spend some time with the Vaec. Could that have any connection?

He snapped his fingers suddenly as Shirley came in. "I was just going to look you up," he said. "There's something you can help me with."

She nodded listlessly and followed him to Dr. Glamis' room, which he had sealed with a special lock of his own. He produced the key and ushered her inside. It was as he had left it earlier.

"I want you to look around and see if anything appears to be missing." As she hesitated, he added softly, "Don't pretend you're not familiar with this room. You have spent quite a bit of time here."

There was a pleading look in her eyes as she said tiredly, "It's not what you think, Roy."

"How do you know what I think? I didn't say you went to him willingly. He had something on you, didn't he? That's what I think."

She sat down on the bed and buried her face in her hands, and he knew she was crying soundlessly. "You don't have to tell me what it was," he said. "Although you may have to tell someone else." He sat down beside her and put his arm around her slim shoulders. She didn't flinch; her body relaxed against him. "Think now, Shirl. Could anyone else have discovered what it was?"

She raised her face, tear-stained. "Thanks, Roy. He wasn't like that; he would have demanded to know everything."

"You don't have to tell me," Auckland repeated.

"But I want to," she said. "I've been afraid too long."

"Something to do with your resignation from the space service?" he asked.

She nodded, and the story came out between bursts of tears. She hadn't tried to save the passenger in the space-wreck. She had been in the sick man's room when disaster struck, had panicked and started to run. She'd struck her head, knocked herself out. By sheer coincidence, when the others found her, it looked as if she had hurt herself in the attempt to get him to safety.

No one suspected at the time, but accepting a citation was too much. Yet, she hadn't the courage to tell the truth. She didn't think that anyone save Glamis had found it out.

"How he knew, I'll never be able to figure out," she finished. "And the worst of it was that he didn't really care. He never liked his brother, and the inheritance came at a very convenient time for Kenneth Glamis. I guess I must have given myself away when he called on me to thank me for trying to save his bother—to thank me for failing, really. I knew then I would have to do whatever he wanted me to do."

It was not an unpleasant task, comforting blonde Shirley Mason.

Eventually, they got back to the situation at hand. "He was untidy, yet he always knew where everything here was," she said. "Have you any idea of what it is you're looking for?"

Then it wasn't Glamis who had been seen leaving James' quarters, going to his own, and searching. It was merely a man wearing a protective suit, walking in Carolinian twilight. Could either of the two women have dressed in such a way as to conceal the differences in outline which the Vaec found so interesting and curious? It didn't seem likely that either

Shirley or Amelia could have passed for Glamis in the eyes of a Vaec watching, even allowing for dim light and distance.

"Was Ken playing a joke on someone, Shirl?"

She nodded, bending over the open drawers of the desk.

"He didn't tell me who or what, but I knew he was up to something."

Auckland picked up a scrap of paper covered with doodles. "Could he have been writing something?"

"He might have been," she said, then straightened up suddenly, and said, "Of course!" She went to the file and started to finger through it. "He kept a reel of tape filed under 'Projects, Miscellaneous'—which was his code for humor. It was the only file he really kept in order." An instant later, she added, "No tape."

Calvin Burleigh looked haggard, as if he had spent a sleepless night on his knees, and there was a quality of tired resignation in his voice. He closed the door of his quarters and motioned Auckland to a chair. "I suppose you think I'm secretly glad about all this," he said.

Roy relaxed in the chair, wishing that they had brought some of the seemingly magical chairs from the villa. "Are you?"

Burleigh shook his head. "There is spite in me and I disliked him very much; my first feeling was one of satisfaction, Lord help me. But I'm not really glad he's dead. I'm only relieved that we'll be leaving Carolus."

"You really think man is so evil that he must be kept away from alien beings?"

"Not evil, Roy. Just foolish and unready. I'm a scientist; I believe that the universe contains many secrets that will be unlocked to whomever asks the right questions. My life has been spent trying to learn some of the right questions to ask. But we humans are too impatient. We rush out and ask questions, the answers to which are dangerous because we've not asked the right questions about ourselves yet—as a whole.

"Like a man who discovers that it is possible for blood to be transfused from one person to another, but hasn't bothered to learn, or even thought to ask, about the possibility of antagonistic blood-types." He shrugged. "And sometimes you'll get away with it, sheerly through luck."

Auckland nodded. "I see the point. But I don't see what you and I can do about it, outside of trying to get some measure of humility ourselves and trying to influence anyone else who will listen. And always remembering that we may be awfully wrong just where we're sure we are most right."

Burleigh smiled. "I couldn't have put it better myself."

Auckland was surprised at the warmth of that smile. "But I don't think you came here for a philosophical and theological discussion, as much as I would be willing to engage. I know that I'm a suspect, so go ahead and examine me."

Auckland took out his notebook and leafed through it. "Doc James dropped in on you after we broke up last night. What did he talk about?"

"The Rosetta stone book, mostly." Burleigh closed his eyes, "I had a feeling that there was something else on his mind, something else he really wanted to talk about but just couldn't get around to."

"Amelia, perhaps?"

"Perhaps."

"You've known him longer than I have, Cal. And I gather that Amelia is something of a flirt." Burleigh said nothing, but there was the slightest suggestion of a quirk around the corner of his lips. No doubt he had noticed Auckland's own nocturnal excursions with the woman. "Was James jealous? Was he jealous of Glamis, or you?"

"He had no reason to be jealous of me!" came the answer sharply. "Unless, of course, she lied like Potiphar's wife about Joseph. But I don't think that happened," he added after a pause. "She wants men but she doesn't strike me as the kind who gets frantic if she can't have a particular man, especially if there are other acceptable ones available." The slight quirk appeared again.

"Do you think he was jealous of Glamis?"

"I don't think James is jealous that Amelia has any particular affair in itself. But there's such a thing as carrying on in a manner that's offensive in itself. I think he found Ken's manner insufferable. And I think that she did, too, after a while. It had stopped before you arrived, and for once, I don't think he was the one who broke off."

"Any idea why?"

Burleigh tapped on the desk with his finger. "Amelia James is more than you would suspect. In all other areas, she is a loyal and devoted wife. I think that is why Howard isn't jealous of her." He looked out the window. "I suppose you have your own theories about this business."

"I'd like to hear yours."

"Hmmm. Well, it seems to me, Auckland, that there's one very deceptive thing about it all. You know the old fallacy, 'After it, therefore because of it.' I think that trying to connect the alleged attempts on Doc James and the murder of Ken Glamis is a trap."

"Then what was the meaning of the *dodlig* in the soup and the bomb in the basement?"

"Practical jokes, meant to be discovered. He was capable of pretty sophomoric humor. But someone else either saw a use for them, or fitted them into plans already made."

"You think Glamis would have been murdered anyway?"

"Possibly—no, I'd say more surely than that. But someone thought they saw how it could be passed off as an accident in another attempt on Howard." He declined a cigarette. "I'm not opposed to tobacco, just don't go for it. Of course, there is the possibility that someone did want to get Howard, and that Ken did get killed by mistake. But if that's so, I still think that Ken perpetrated those two attempts out in the field, and the real killer made use of them."

Auckland's gaze rested on the desk and his eyes ran down the side to the intercom box. Suddenly he stiffened; the switch was on. Had Burleigh been talking to someone else earlier, or…?

"Have you been in all the time since we came back, Cal?"

"Yes. Why?"

He stood up and looked out the window to see Edholm coming from the storage shed. Then he wasn't the listener. "Nothing. Just a thought. I think a good part of the key lies with the Vaec, but I don't see how yet. I have an answer but it doesn't make sense, yet. I have a feeling that Ekem-ve knows. He said to ask a question when the muddy thoughts were clear; think I'll go over to the village, after a bite to eat."

There was one more thing to do before he left, Auckland thought, as he said good-bye and stepped out into the sunset. He found Edholm in the office and maneuvered him outside, telling him about the open intercom. "I told Burleigh so that whoever was listening would hear, too. Keep an eye out, will you? I have a feeling that someone will follow me later.

## CHAPTER TEN

BEYOND THE meadow which held the headquarters unit was the Carolinian equivalent of woods; a series of clusters of trees, each cluster containing only its own kind, with high bushes in between. There were patches of fungoid growths that glowed in the darkness and took shapes that would offend the eyes of the prurient.

It was stillness that made the Carolinian night so unlike that of Earth's countryside in summer. There was no chorus of insect voices, no frog singing from the marshlands to the east. He wondered again if the planet did have such life forms and if they had withdrawn when the Earthmen came. The Vaec had indicated that most of the animal and insect life had retired thus.

Except for fish, of course. Syeltan and others did some fishing in the stream.

He took out the map that Edholm had sketched for him and looked at it with his pencil-light. This was the grove of bird-trees, so called because the long thin limbs bore short-stemmed leaves that stood up and nearly looked like feathers. During the day they spread themselves fan-wise, closing up at night.

At the end of this grove, he should turn right and go straight until he reached the stream. Then a left turn, and he would follow the banks until he came to a grove of the willow-like trees shaped like a letter V, with the point at the stream itself.

Bushes now, and these, unlike the trees, were not in homogeneous clusters. Some spread along the ground, forming patterns not unlike spider webs. But most of them were as tall as a man. He stopped by one that was filled with globes about a quarter-inch in diameter. He started to pick one, curiously.

And jumped at the report as it burst in his fingers and he felt it spattering. Pop-balls! His fingers were covered with a dark substance, thin as ink and his shirt showed stains. *Damn!* he thought, and then grinned. So this was what had been planned for Syeltan. I suppose it won't wash off easily, he thought.

The stream was a little way distant, and provided the first sound he had heard outside that of his own soft footfalls and breathing. A few bushes more and he was at its bank. It stretched brightly before him and he shook his head; this didn't seem right. There was no moon to make water silvery. Then he realized that the brightness was the glowing forms of innumerable water bugs skating over its surface. The stream flowed sluggishly here, and he watched for a few more moments.

There was a slight stirring in the water and the surface broke momentarily; a patch of lightness scattered. Some fish was feeding. He watched for a while, seeing the sparkles of the bugs as they broke apart then drew together again. He wondered where they hid themselves by day.

Might as well see if I can wash this off, he thought as he knelt beside the stream and plunged his hands into the cool water. The brightness drew away in a wide circle as his hand neared the surface. He rubbed his fingers for a while then dried them on the grass-moss on which he was kneeling. No soap, both literally and figuratively.

Auckland gave a heavy sigh, rose, and continued his journey, avoiding clusters of rushes he encountered from time to time. They shot up like icicles, and from spiky-looking branches at top, pear-shaped flowers depended like Christmas tree ornaments. By daylight, they would open and spread out like tiny pancakes. *Dodlig.*

The *V* of the willow grove was in sight when a voice said, "May your heart be mirthful, excellent Roy."

He looked around to see a Carolinian standing to one side, the single hair on his skull looping. There were mottlings on the Vaec's face and mare spots in his chest. Auckland smiled. "And may laughter lighten your life, Syeltan. Muddy thoughts have settled and I would ask a question of Ekem-ve. But I would not ask you to demean yourself by being my guide."

"This careless one seeks Ekem-ve also," replied Syeltan.

"Much happiness in walking with excellent Earthman."

Ekem-ve's dwelling was a large, unadorned square, like the units in the villa, Auckland saw, and rested in a small clearing. Light spilled out of the triangular doorway, the white light he had seen in the villa. As they crossed the clearing toward it, Ekem-ve appeared in the doorway and welcomed them, his hair waving gently. Auckland thought of a dog that is not quite sure whether he is approved, but hopes that all will be well, then discarded the thought. The Vaec's eyes rested on Syeltan and his hair increased its motion. So, he's just learned that his trick worked, Roy thought.

"Excellent Roy makes heart of humble Vaec sing with visit," Ekem-ve said as he motioned them inside.

"Earthman's heart is humble with realization of ignorance," Auckland replied. "I come seeking wisdom."

The room was triangular, he saw, with a partition down the middle. Simply furnished, only chairs much like those in the villa were visible. He could find no source of the light, which was bright enough to read by, yet soft and comforting to the eyes. The walls were covered with Vaec designs and walls and floor seemed to be a single sheet of substance. It did not feel as hard as that of the villa, however, being a trifle springy underfoot, but it didn't creak.

Clearly this was not the dwelling-place of a primitive.

There was an advanced technology behind its simplicity. The chairs looked much like the magic chairs, except that the cane frames were filled in with a sort of matting. He settled into one at Ekem-ve's bidding, and Syeltan took another. It was just barely short of one of the villa chairs for comfort.

"Excellent Roy has thirst which is enemy to mirth," Ekem-ve said. "Will deign to swallow liquid of Vaec?"

As Auckland hesitated, the Carolinian added, "Excellent Earthmen accompanying excellent Jonas imbibe same after many tests and declare not harmful. But prefer own liquids."

"I shall he happy to accept," Auckland said.

Ekem-ve strode to the partition that opened from the bottom, fanwise, when he stood before it, then closed after him. The room was dark behind the opening, but Auckland assumed that the light would go on immediately—unless the Vaec could see in the dark, which he suspected.

In a moment, the door reopened, light spilling out, and Ekem-ve returned with three cubes set upon each other. He handed one to Roy, then a second to Syeltan, taking the third himself. As if reading the Earthman's thoughts, he said, "No mirth in spoiling liquid, excellent Roy."

Auckland lifted the cube to his nose and sniffed gingerly. The odor was vaguely pleasing, but he couldn't decide what it was. There was a faint suggestion of cinnamon, and a suspicion of vanilla, but not quite either. He shook the cube slightly and noted that the liquid had about the viscosity of water.

The first impression when he sipped was one of coolness, and a definite feeling like that of spring water though not as cold. There was a very slight pungence and a very slight sweetness, neither unpleasant. It seemed to have the thirst-slaking properties of water.

"Vaec liquid clasps hands with mirth, something like Earth liquid," said Ekem-ve, "but does not promote false wisdom or seek more of itself. One cube takes thirst on long journey."

Auckland felt that he wanted to drain the cube steadily, neither gulping nor sipping. He finished and set it down on the floor, as he saw Ekem-ve and Syeltan doing. He could feel mild euphoria setting in, but nothing akin to intoxication; and he knew that if the cube was refilled he would not have the slightest desire to take another swallow.

"Ekem-ve," he said, after praising the drink, "the Vaec

have been very friendly to Earthmen. We have tried hard to be friends with the Vaec. We have shown you much about ourselves, and you have seen much that we did not wish to show. Yet we have not concealed anything from that you asked us about."

"Excellent Roy speaks words of truth."

"Yet you have told us nothing about how the Vaec live, about your technology, when we asked. Why is that?"

The Carolinian's hair was motionless now. "Excellent Earthmen have custom, not answer some questions. Wise Earthmen not ask some questions. Some Earthmen shut away from answers that other Earthmen obtain when admitted to clan that knows answers."

"Yes, I think I see what you mean. Captain Edholm is not permitted to tell me some things which he could tell another captain."

"Answer excellent Roy seeks grow on similar tree. Wisdom can be gathered only by member of Vaec clan."

Roy Auckland frowned. There was something strange about this, something that did not fit. With a truly primitive culture, it would be understandable, but the Vaec were not primitive. Nor could all aspects of their technology be security matters. He looked at Syeltan and Ekem-ve, whose single hairs were now quite still, the eyes giving no signs. But he had the feeling they were expecting something of him.

"Long ago, on Earth," he said, "there were people who lived in clans, and each clan had its own ritual of acceptance. Many things were forbidden to those who were not members, but a stranger who had proved his worth could be adopted into the clan, or by passing tests could qualify himself as a special friend of the clan. Is it possible for an Earthman to be adopted into the Vaec, or qualify as a special friend of the Vaec, one who is entitled to wisdom?"

Ekem-ve looked at Syeltan, and both Carolinian hairs

stirred. "Wise question brings happy answer, excellent Roy. Earthman undergo tests, may be brother of Vaec."

"And what are the tests?"

"Same as given to young Vaec on doorway to adulthood. Test of skill, test of mind, test of understanding."

"Among these early Earth people," Auckland said, "it was often necessary to undergo periods of waiting and special preparation before the candidate would be given the tests. Are such preliminaries required with the Vaec?"

"Excellent Roy has fulfilled preliminary requirement," said Ekem-ve. "Test of skill in morning if excellent Roy would be happy to spend night with humble Vaec."

"I would indeed by happy."

Ekem-ve arose. "While we talk, friends come to visit. Will play excellent Earthman's games."

Syeltan arose and picked up his chair, carrying it outside. Auckland followed suit, and saw several Vaec approaching, two of whom he recognized as Hcent and Phrecle. Syeltan introduced him to the other two: Rycur and Nsenol. Nsenol was somewhat narrower of face and a trifle slimmer than the others, except for Hcent, and Auckland wondered if this indicated sex differentiation. Hcent was the only Vaec they knew as a female, since Ekem-ve and the others referred to Hcent as she. Not very often, though, as the Vaec used the proper name in preference to the pronoun.

Ekem-ve was coming out with the top of a table, shaped in the form of a regular heptagon. Like his dwelling and the villa, it appeared to be utterly black and in one piece; but from the way he carried it, it was very light. He carried it like a waiter carrying a tray. When he stopped and lowered it slightly, Hcent came forward and pulled seven long, thin strips from the underside and rested it on the ground. The two Vaec pressed their hands on the table and the supports sank into the grass-moss. Auckland touched it tentatively;

apparently it was set solidly enough.

He turned and started back into the dwelling to help with chairs, but Syeltan said, "Excellent Earthman guest; not work."

He watched while the rest of the chairs were being brought out and decided that there must be a lot of furniture in the farther, closed-off part of the dwelling. That seemed somewhat strange, though.

Now Ekem-ve was bringing out a globe about the size of a muskmelon. He raised it at arm's length and drew out a single strip much like the legs of the table, setting it in the grass-moss a few feet away from the table. Behind him the light in the dwelling faded and the door closed. Syeltan had brought out a pack of cards, boxes of chips, and a windup timer similar to the one which had been used in the bomb in the villa.

Auckland wondered whether they realized that he would have a difficult time reading the cards in this light, but his apprehensions vanished as the globe began to glow, casting a clear but glareless radiance over the table. Ekem-ve motioned all to he seated, and as he took his chair, Auckland noticed that seven equal piles of chips had been laid out.

"Excellent Earthman set value on chips," said Ekem-ve. "Game of skill, no possessions at stake; winner accumulate chips of all."

"The white chips equal one unit," said Auckland. "Red chips are worth five white, blue chips worth two red or ten white. I assume the game is to be poker."

"Even so, excellent Roy."

"Then I will gladly play by your rules, but need to know what they are. I assume the value of hands is standard, but you will have to tell me what kinds of poker we will play, and what are your rules for betting and dealing."

"No limit on amount wagered, excellent Roy, but player

with insufficient chips may remain in hand until showdown; if lose, is out of game. If win, restore to table shortness of bet. Dealer choose rules for hand; rules continue until future dealer declare change."

"And is there a time-limit on the game?" asked Auckland, looking at the timer.

"No, excellent Roy. Some dealer create mirth by use of timer in own deal." He passed the cards to Auckland. "Will excellent Earthman begin?"

Auckland picked up the deck and shuffled it. "First ace will deal," he said, starting to pass the cards around face up. The ace fell to Nsenol, and Auckland passed the deck to her —he found himself thinking of Nsenol as female, even though he had no proof as yet.

The first few hands were orthodox draw and stud, and Roy lost three, his own deal of seven-card stud included, the last time bowing with aces high to Rycur, who had filled an inside straight. Then the wild hands started, and the Earthman found himself a little dizzy trying to keep up with the complications. On the sixth, he took the pot, finding himself a few white chips ahead in the process. Vaec betting was uninhibited to say the least.

After another two losses—small because he dropped early, as he noted some of the others did at times—he began to get ideas. Poker was to the Vaec a game of wits, each dealer making complicated rules that favored him strongly, although the dealer did not always win, he noted.

Now it was Syeltan's deal, and the temporarily spotted Carolinian took the timer, which Auckland now saw was double-faced, and placed it where all could see. The Vaec had taken two timers apart and made one of them, with the windup mechanism on the side, rather than the back.

"Seven-card stud," Syeltan said. "Red seven wild between 12 and 15; black three wild between 15 and 30; jack triumph over king, and deuce over 7 between 30 and 45; low hand high between 45 and 60." He set the timer and started to deal, then stopped it when the last card in this round was up. Red sevens wild, Auckland thought. The timer was started again, after the betting.

Before the deal was over, his brain was reeling and he felt a little dizzy as he watched his own hand, the other hands laid out, and the ticking timer. He felt a little stupid at the time he took to make bets, but noticed that no one else was in any hurry. Yet, despite the complications of these recent hands, he managed to win two of them, and was still a little ahead. But this one took the prize.

The final wagers started and Auckland watched the still-ticking timer as the bets went around. Now the jack beat the king, and the deuce was higher than the seven. He looked at his hand and sighed, then studied his hole cards and the hands around him. He seemed to have a winning low if he could make a showdown at the right time. Then he remembered: Phrecle had instituted a rule permitting anyone to equal the bets on the table and declare final showdown once the deal was finished and a complete round of bets had been made. As dealer, Phrecle had done this himself at the end of the first round. That rule had not been rescinded, so was still in force. And Auckland would bet right after Syeltan.

He waited for Syeltan to raise, then glanced at the clock.

Two seconds more; he had it. He pushed his chips to the center of the table and said "Final showdown."

Syeltan's long fingers snaked out and stopped the timer.

Auckland looked at it, and cursed himself silently for a hasty fool. He had forgotten to ask when that final stopping would take place, and the hands rested about a half-second short of 45. The almost-perfect low he held was useless. As Phrecle, the winner, swept the chips from the center of the table and added them to his own pile, Auckland had a sinking feeling. Somehow, he felt that a great deal depended upon his making a good show in this game, and he'd just displayed himself as the crassest of bunglers.

## CHAPTER ELEVEN

LOOPING HAIRS around him indicated that his companions found the game most mirthful. Auckland struggled valiantly, but the mental pace was beginning to tell. He not only had to bear in mind what rules governed the hand he was playing now, but which rules carried over from before. And the shifting of wild cards with the timer, which was brought in every few deals, virtually had him gibbering.

Syeltan passed the cards to him and he looked at his pile of chips. If it could be called a pile, he thought. An orthodox hand was his only hope, yet he felt obliged to introduce something new.

A thought came to him and he smiled as he shuffled the cards. "There was a town on Earth, many years ago, where they played this variation with unwary persons," he said, "who thought they understood the game. Five cards were dealt, nothing was required to open, and nothing was wild. Everyone was permitted to draw five new cards if he wished.

"Then, when the sucker—a term for a naive person who, I am afraid, was regarded as one to be cheated if possible—laid down his cards—somehow he always got a very good hand in these instances—someone else declared that he had a lallapaloozer, which beat everything. I hereby introduce the lallapaloozer—the first one counts—which is what some Earthmen call 2-4-6-8-10, suits irrelevant."

A quick glance around showed that the party found this interesting, and Auckland noticed that only one of the Vaec kept a pat hand. He drew three cards himself and put the last of his chips into the pot when his turn came to bet. At the showdown, Hcent spread out a perfect 2-4-6-8-10.

Auckland laid down his own hand, a pair of sevens, a three, jack, and eight, and said, "My lallapaloozer wins, friends."

"But excellent Roy," protested Hcent, "I have 2-4-6-8-10. Is that not what you called a lallapaloozer?"

"No, Hcent. If you will remember, I said, indeed, that the lallapaloozer beats everything and that some Earthmen call 2-4-6-8-10 a lallapaloozer." He grinned. "But I didn't say that I called 2-4-6-8-10 that; this is what I call a lallapaloozer." He indicated his own hand. "You neglected to inquire, just as I forgot to ask exactly when the timer would be stopped when showdown was called on Syeltan's deal."

He looked around and saw looping hairs everywhere.

"Excellent Roy catch us all in sticky trap," said Ekem-ve. "Said clearly that naive person unwisely neglect to obtain necessary information. Lallapaloozer win as he call it."

It was a good pot, and he was well ahead now. Hcent had raised considerably on every possible occasion, and no one had dropped. He noticed that subsequent dealers neither cancelled the lallapaloozer nor changed its value. A few hands later, Phrecle and Rycur had been wiped out; but they watched with unabated fascination as the dizzy variations continued.

At the end of a most baffling one, wherein the degrees of wildness of the down cards in seven-card stud varied with the majority of suits of picture cards showing, he found that he had somehow managed to put together a royal flush. Only Syeltan fought it out with him, and then at the showdown, produced Auckland's own version of the lallapaloozer.

Auckland grinned and shook his head. "Sorry, Syeltan," he said, "but I distinctly stated that the first lallapaloozer counts. Only one is permitted a night."

The looping hairs about him looked like they were tearing

themselves out of their owners' heads as he gathered in the chips. Apparently nothing was too tricky or even childish for the Vaec. He remembered their fondness for that silly game called Red Moustache, and grinned as the deal came his way again.

He said, as he shuffled, "This is called Happy Dealer. The second rule in this hand is that you must follow the dealer exactly, or put a white chip into the pot. The third rule is that it will be played like seven card stud, eights wild up. The first rule you must deduce for yourself, but I will give you one hint: it has nothing to do with the cards you hold."

He then set up a mad system of knocking with different numbers of fingers and numbers of knocks, scratching his head, clearing his throat, bending forward to peer at cards at times, shifting his hole cards from one hand to another, and so on, which resulted in a flow of penalty chips into the pot. When showdown came, everyone was in to the hilt.

Auckland laid down his hand and said, "My friends, the pot is mine. I do not have to show my hand, as I told you that the first rule had nothing to do with the cards you held. The first rule of Happy Dealer is that the dealer wins. You should have declined to play."

As he suspected, he had not only won the game, but also made a smashing hit with his tricks. .

After the cards were put away, Ekem-ve suggested that some entertainment be provided for the guest, and he and Syeltan proceeded to put on a show of legerdemain that would make the finest terrestrial stage magician weep and tear his hair with envy. Despite his most skillful watching, through which he had managed to spot a great deal of stage magician's tricks, Auckland found himself completely baffled more often than not as to how they managed to make objects appear and disappear. And the shell game they showed him was magnificent, for the little white ball under the small raised ovals could not be compressed and slipped out from beneath a shell. Nor was there anything to make it adhere to the top of the shell when it was lifted. Nor was there a double shell. Nor could he see it being abstracted at any time.

Yet, it was never under the shell he lifted. On invitation, he tried to see if he could stump his hosts, and failed one hundred percent. Despite the fact that he was positive, at times, which shell contained the little white ball, there it was under a different shell, which a Vaec lifted after brief scrutiny. And Ekem-ve assured him, when he asked directly, that none of them could see through the shells; none of them could smell the ball or hear it rattle, and none of them used any mechanical devices in order to detect its presence.

It couldn't be mind reading, either, he thought; he'd lost track of the ball several times when he shuffled the shells. Auckland lay on the cozy mattress that Ekem-ve provided for him, and drew the light, warm blanket given him over him. The texture was something like silk and would either cling or lie softly upon him as he wished.

Auckland sighed and drifted off to sleep, wondering what the physical test would be.

In the morning, the party assembled again after a quick and simple breakfast, which Auckland found both palatable and satisfying. The Vaec food, which Ekem-ve assured him had been found harmless to Earthmen, did not have much flavor to his taste, but the texture of the little cakes and fruit that composed it was pleasant. The meal was concluded with a cube of the liquid he had tried the night before; as his head was quite clear, he decided that Vaec liquor produced no hangovers.

"Other members of clan to meet us at testing place," Ekem-ve said as they started a leisurely hike along the banks of the stream. The terrain was gradually uphill, he recalled, and the stream widened as they proceeded. He noticed different types of fungoid growth in places, and observed that everyone skirted patches of *dodlig*, the flowers now spread open flat in the sunlight. They were a light blue in color, and looked more like flat ovals covered with caterpillar fur. The wild bees swarmed around them, but paid no attention to the Vaec and their guest. He had hoped to catch a glimpse of some animal life, too, but there was none visible.

The stream became a small lake as they came to the top of a bluff, some thirty feet above the water. They stopped at a point about a hundred feet from the opposite bluff, where a large crowd of Carolinians awaited them. Ekem-ve greeted them and explained that the Earthman was about to try the test of skill. The crowd parted to let Ekem-ve and his party through, their single hairs swaying gently as if a light breeze was blowing from several directions at once.

Then Auckland saw the "poles." They crossed the chasm, about ten feet from each other, and each one was about six inches in diameter. Hcent stepped up to the farther one and waited. Auckland gulped. Was the test the old greased-pole ordeal? "Skill" was a most inadequate term for it!

"Test of skill, excellent Roy," said Ekem-ve, "is to cross finish line before Hcent." He pointed to the other side of the stream then looked down at Auckland's ripple-soled shoes. "Contestant may wear clothing to choice."

Auckland removed his shirt and trousers, which Syeltan took, and noted that the Vaec were interested in the designs on his red and black shorts. He decided to retain his shoes, which would help give him purchase, and noticed that Hcent retained hers; the buskin-like foot-covering that all Vaec wore. His watch was water and shock proof, and he decided to use the stop-watch section.

He started toward the other pole, then turned as a thought struck him. "Is it permitted to use other equipment?"

"What would you, excellent Roy?"

"A straight stick, about so long—" he spread his hands apart "—which assists in keeping balance. Of course," he added, "I would expect Hcent to have the same advantage."

"This one not desiring stick in hands," said Hcent, "but would not deny same to excellent Roy."

Ekem-ve blinked; Nsenol walked away toward a cluster of willow-like bushes, returning in a little while with a wand the exact length Auckland had indicated. He'd forgotten to mention the thickness desired, but it seemed just right. He looked at the end, neatly cut, and wondered how that had been done—he'd never seen a Vaec carrying a tool.

Auckland sighed, and stepped up to the pole. "All ready," he said. "Will there be a signal?"

"May mirth attend your starting," said Ekem-ve. "Begin."

Auckland pressed the start button on his watch, balanced the wand in his hands and stepped forward. The surface beneath his feet was hard and slippery like a polished, but not waxed, hardwood floor. He breathed a sigh of relief; it wasn't greased.

Hcent, he saw, was walking slightly bowlegged, with an air of perfect naturalness, her toes just a trifle more turned out than usual. If she had toes, that is, Auckland thought. He remembered that he had never seen a Vaec without buskins.

It was difficult going, in that he knew he must not hurry, but Auckland found that his shoes compensated for most of the slickness of the surface beneath him. The morning sun was warm on his head and torso, and he was grateful that the occasional breezes were light.

For a time, the two remained roughly parallel, but Hcent gradually began to forge ahead, without stepping up her pace. Each step must be a light fraction longer than his, he thought, so that the difference eventually showed up. He tried to increase his own stride, and only the wand in his hands kept him from disastrous loss of balance. By the time they were nearing the halfway mark, Hcent was several feet ahead of him.

No sound from behind. The Vaec watched in silence, possibly to avoid distracting their guest, he thought. He tried again to lengthen his stride and this time was successful, but it still looked as if there would be no catching up.

Suddenly, Hcent fell. He didn't see her slip, or make an effort to regain balance; she was just plunging off the pole. The shock almost made Auckland lose his balance; he stopped momentarily, watching. As she plunged downward, he saw that she was curling herself up, so that by the time she hit the water, the Vaec was practically a ball.

Moments later, her head appeared and she was swimming leisurely on her back. Auckland sighed in relief, gripped his pole and continued, cautiously. Obviously, the Vaec could not be hurt by a thirty foot fall into water, but it could be entirely a different story with him.

In a short time, he was ahead of his swimming competitor, and after a couple more narrow escapes he reached the other end of the pole and stepped off. Exactly two minutes and seven seconds. As he stood there, looking down, Hcent, who was nearly at the shore—there was a shelf about two feet wide before the walls of the bluff started—dived under the water and came up at the bank itself.

She came out, doffed her buskins—he saw that she had toes—and then began to climb the nearly sheer sides of the bluff without hesitation. Auckland watched for a moment, then decided that Hcent would have no difficulty in joining him. He wondered how the others would get across. Swim probably. Then he turned, and gasped; the entire company was there, awaiting him!

"Excellent Roy is most skillful," said Ekem-ve, his hair waving. "Few Vaec cross all the way."

"It was hard," Auckland said, "and I couldn't have made it without this wand. Even so, she'd have beaten me because I just couldn't have caught up." He smiled. "But I did win, didn't I?"

"No, excellent Roy, Hcent is winner. Hcent touch finish line. You did not."

"But, but…" he sputtered, then remembered something and closed his eyes in chagrin at his own stupidity. He had forgotten to ask a specific question. "Where is the finish line?" he asked weakly.

"Finish line is bank of stream, under water, excellent Roy."

Well, there was no use complaining. He'd had sufficient warning about this sort of thing, and had beaten them at their own game in it the evening before. "Then it wasn't necessary to walk across the poles at all?"

"No, excellent Roy. Contestant may swim all way, but often like to try skill at pole."

"Then I've lost," he said tiredly, then straightened as a thought came to him. The chairs that seemed to be too many for Ekem-ve to have in his dwelling, the legerdemain and vanishing little white ball, the wand cut without a tool, the sudden appearance of the company on the other side of the bluff—it all fell into place.

"Ekem-ve," he said, "you Vaec can all teleport, can't you? Transport yourselves and objects various distances by some sort of mental power, without touching them?"

"This is truth, excellent Roy."

Auckland's mind was now working furiously. What else had he forgotten to ask? Nothing could be too elementary, he decided. He smiled and said, "I told you that among some old-time Earthmen, an outsider must pass tests before becoming a member of a clan, or a special friend. You told me that the Vaec had three tests: the test of skill, the test of mind, and the test of understanding. But you did not say that all three tests must be passed, and you did not say that I had to beat Hcent in order to pass the test of skill."

He looked around him and saw signs of pleasure.

"Much wisdom in Earthman's deduction," said Ekem-ve.

"We return now and after refreshment candidate may ask one question about the Vaec. Answer truthful and complete."

They had given him ample time to think. Roy Auckland ate with them, drank a cube of Vaec liquid and put his thoughts in order. The test of skill was over. The test of mind—wasn't the mad poker game of the night before a test of mind? And the test of understanding . . . Understanding what?

It would seem most logical—and the Vaec were quite logical in their own way—that the "understanding" here referred to understanding the Vaec themselves. And the Vaec were difficult to understand.

Why? Because they seemed to be two incompatible things. They understood English perfectly, yet spoke in a caricature of the English like some old-time fictioneer's idea of how "ignorant" natives spoke to the superior white man. They lived simply and effortlessly, yet there was no doubt that they had a technology far in advance of Earth—a power source so simple and efficient that everything resembling machinery could be kept out of sight.

They were clearly advanced in philosophy, and had a genuine sense of humor in well-balanced personalities. They were sympathetic and friendly with the Earthmen, willing to act virtually as servants. Yet there was nothing servile about them.

Again, like the stories of old-time Earth—a combination of the happy, ignorant, childlike "natives" who loved practical jokes, and the dignified "savages" who served the "lords from beyond the seas" with genuine respect and liking but without losing their own values.

His one question, he was sure, would be crucial. And this, he felt, would be the only test that really counted.

He set the cube down beside the chair as they sat outside Ekem-ve's dwelling. The others who had been there the night before sat around quietly, and he wondered if they were the testing committee. Very likely.

"Ekem-ve, and excellent testers," he began, "I have been curious about certain matters for a long time." He told them about the peoples of Earth that they seemed superficially to resemble. "This," he said, "is how many, perhaps most, Earthman see the Vaec. But I think their vision is mistaken."

He took out a cigarette, and put it in his mouth, and puffed a few times after the tip started glowing. The hairs around him were perfectly still.

"I think," he said, "that you have been hoaxing Earthmen, that you are playing a long joke upon us, and that the villa in the desert plays some part in that joke. But my question is: Am I the first Earthman to tell you he had come to this conclusion and ask you about it?"

Now the hairs were in motion as the committee turned to Ekem-ve, and he saw various blinking.

Ekem-ve arose and held out hath hands. "Welcome to fellowship with the Vaec, Roy Auckland."

## CHAPTER TWELVE

EKEM-VE continued, as the single hairs on the others stirred in approval, "We can speak naturally when there are no other Earthmen around, Roy, but it is best that we continue to talk like 'natives' in the presence of Earthmen who assume us to be like that. To answer your question: You are the second Earthman to put it to us; and your deductions are correct so far as they go."

He felt that they expected him to come up with more, wanted him to think more deeply and see still other things that they thought should be most apparent to a man of understanding.

"Then you have actually been testing all of us, all the time," he said. "I suspect that you learned a good deal about us when Leitfred used the language helmets—unless you can read our minds and learned it before the transfer was made."

"We can read your minds when you are trying to tell us something," Syeltan said, "but that is very limited. We can read only what you want us to know. We cannot extract anything you try to conceal from us. If you concentrate on telling us something, we can pick up your thought."

"What about things which we might not want you to know, but which we cannot help thinking about? Or things which we might not be aware of ourselves consciously?"

"The desire to communicate the information has to be present," Phrecle said. "The most we would obtain from unconscious thoughts and attitudes, or thoughts you wanted to hold back, would he a sense of disturbance on your part But we could not determine what caused the disturbance or whether it had anything to do with us."

Auckland looked around him, wondering what to do with the cigarette butt. Rycur passed him a small dish. "Thanks," he said. "Then you must have gotten something special from the language transfer process."

Ekem-ve blinked. "The helmets are much more powerful than you realize, Roy. They bring up and amplify a great many things which you might not want someone to know. We thought at first that they effected mutual understanding but it was soon apparent that Leitfred had learned nothing about us from them."

"We saw his pictures of us, in terms of 'simple natives' as you put it," Hcent said. "It amused us, and we decided to conform to it just enough to satisfy those who felt we should be that way. Leitfred's attitude was picturesque, you might say, but it was soon apparent that the others were not much different. And they were all relieved that we were not too advanced, as they thought."

Auckland nodded. "Then you saw some of our bad points but some good ones, too. You saw that some of us—all of us to an extent—take ourselves too seriously. Pride. The man who has too much pride has too little humor. He can't laugh at himself, which is often essential in understanding other people. Your practical jokes on each other were clues for us to follow if we could. And we did notice that none of then were really harmful, which is not the case with practical jokes some Earthmen play on each other."

"We were not astonished, but it did make us feel sad whet we discovered this," Nsenol said.

Auckland took out another cigarette. "Bad habit," he said "but it does help to settle the mind. There is one danger here. A man who cannot laugh at himself resents being mad, the victim of a joke, however well-intended. You say one other Earthman came to you as I did. Was that Dr. Glamis?"

"Yes," said Ekem-ve. "He was a man of excellent mirth, which is the simplest way of putting what we mean into your language."

"But there is one member of the expedition," Auckland mused, "who cannot laugh at himself, who cannot bear the thought of being taken in by people he considers 'natives' and inferior. Ekem-ve, where did Hcent really find the imitation Vaec box?"

Hcent answered, and Auckland found that his suspicions had been confirmed. He talked at length about the case, and his opinions. Finally, he rose and said, "I must be getting back. I think something dangerous is about to occur already, but I've been counting on a belief that someone will try to stop me from getting back safely first."

"We will help as well as we can without unwisely interfering," Ekem-ve said. "You must not think that the Vaec are all-powerful. The Creator has given us some abilities that you do not have, but you will find that you have abilities we do not have. Even though we can read minds at times, we can be deceived." He arose and added. "Some of us will try to guard your return."

He gave Auckland the slap of farewell, and the others followed suit.

"It is best that you do not see the guards," Ekem-ve said.

"May you come to us again, perhaps under more mirthful circumstances."

He started away, thinking that he had learned nothing about the Vaec technology, but somehow that seemed to be of very secondary importance in comparison to what he had learned. Now he had to be on the watch—for the Vaec could not he expected to know all the ruses of a murderous human being—and try to think like the one he suspected was the culprit.

Putting himself in this person's place and figuring out the best moves could help to a certain extent. But you could be led into a trap of your own making. What you thought was the most logical move for another to make might not be so at all; and even if you were right, there was no guarantee that the other person would make the best move. It was better to try to think of your opponent's characteristic moves, always keeping the best possibilities in mind.

The sky had started to become overcast that afternoon, and Auckland realized that he had yet to experience rain on this planet. He'd been told that rains were quite similar to those of Earth. The light was very dim now, and the disadvantage would work both ways, so far as his hunter was concerned. If someone were hunting him. He couldn't be sure that this would be the case at all, but it was likely, and it made sense.

They had helped him make a much more accurate map of his return route, then showed him how he could follow the course off the "paths." There were no paths in the sense of beaten down trails through woods. There were clear areas, where only the grass-moss grew. It did not hold footprints, not even the marks of the heavier crawler, and this would be to mutual disadvantage. And footfalls were soundless.

The evening around him was soundless, too, except for his own breathing and the pounding of his heart, which seemed unusually loud in his ears. When he touched a bush, it sounded as if he'd made a terrific clatter, although he knew he hadn't.

He knew tht there were friendly followers around him somewhere, but that didn't decrease his apprehensions much. All the important little questions that he should have asked the Vaec, but hadn't thought of at the time, now came crowding into his mind. How well could they hear? How sharp was their sense of smell?

Well, he thought, they could smell the faintest touch of *dodlig*, undetectable to human nostrils—but, somehow, he felt that this was misleading. There was something about this he knew, really knew, without knowing; something he needed to remember and coordinate with other observation.

Did the Vaec have senses which men did not—or which, in the human being, were degenerate, vestigial, or potential and as yet undeveloped—beyond the abilities which they had acknowledged? There was telepathy and the ability to teleport, but these were both qualities which many human philosophers and some scientists believed to be in man, too. Vestigial or potential, perhaps present in that large area of the brain for which no function had as yet been assigned by specialists.

What were the qualities that Earthmen had which the Vaec realized they did not have? Was pride and the foolish desire to be God a corruption of one of these qualities?

His adrenals were reacting to danger signals, but such physical response could come just as easily from an imagined peril as a real one. He stopped by a large maple-like tree, stepped behind it and took out the map, holding the pencil-light up against it and hoping that the faint flow would not reveal his presence. Yes, he seemed to be on the right track; he must bear left from here, and his next landmark would be a roughly triangular-shaped patch of fungoid growths.

He stepped out from behind the tree, and a touch of giddiness assailed him. It was only momentary, and he must have staggered to his right a bit before it passed. He reached out to lean against the smooth trunk for support, wondering what had happened to him. His finger touched something cold and thin.

It felt like metal, a thin sliver of metal. Then he caught his breath as he realized it was metal indeed, and the thickness and length of a small needle. It had been fired from a needle-gun, which was soundless beyond a few feet and accurate for about a hundred yards. The needle would not penetrate deeply, however, beyond a third of that distance and it was not unusual for them to be poisoned.

He drew it out. There could be no certainty, without more careful examination than he was able to conduct here, but it might be useful for evidence. Then he realized that he had nothing in which to wrap it, and it wouldn't be safe to carry any other way. Auckland momentarily blasphemed the progress in fabrics that made his clothing tear-proof, so far as his own abilities were concerned. A strip from his shirt would have been quite handy.

What to do with it? It would have been better, he thought now, to have left it sticking in the tree. He settled the problem by stooping down and pushing it deep into the grass moss, then using his pencil light to ram it down into the soil. It would stay there.

When he stood up, he realized that he'd missed another bet. The sensible thing to have done was to have feigned being hit and put on a show of quick decease. Yet, as he thought more on this, starting ahead again, there were risks. He was unarmed and if the hunter were equally sensible he would not come too close without firing another needle into his victim for certainty. That's what I would do under the circumstances, if I were the hunter, Auckland thought, and grinned at the comforting realization.

The giddiness hit him again, and when his mind cleared, he realized he was well off his course. What was happening? Was the Vaec food having some effect that his hosts hadn't foreseen, due to some personal allergy? He saw clumps of unfamiliar growths and little patches of water; he'd stumbled into the marshlands, so he had to bear roughly north-north-west. He glanced at the compass dial in his watch and made the turn indicated. The way led to a good size bare patch.

He had not traveled far into it, when he realized that he was sinking. Quicksand! But if it were like quicksand known on Earth, he had a chance; he could float on the top of it as one floated in water. He tried to let himself down gently.

And found that he had lost all power of motion. He was paralyzed, and the treacherous surface beneath him slid from beneath his feet so that he sank down steadily, as if in a slow elevator. Roy Auckland closed his eyes and concentrated on one thought: "Ekem-ve! Help! Quicksand!"

They would be listening for him, of that he felt certain.

They would receive his call. But whether they would

arrive in time, whether this was the only area of quicksand in the vicinity. He thought briefly of the route he had traveled, as well as he knew it.

Auckland opened his eyes. He could not move his head but just stared straight ahead. Something was stirring beyond the patch, by a clump of tall bushes. In another moment, something came into sight. It was a figure in a protective suit. It stood there motionless and raised its arm, then lowered it. Auckland realized that the hunter had decided there was no need to waste another needle. The hunter would wait to make sure that he had gone under.

The downward motion was slow and silent. Auckland's thoughts were racing. Could he at least solve the mystery in his own mind before that mind was released to another order of existence? He thought, *"Into thy hands I commend my spirit,"* then turned his mind to clues and evidence.

Shirley Mason entered his thoughts first, partly because he knew he did not want her to be the guilty one. Yet she had a good motive for killing Glamis and she could have set the deadly needle in the box. That would mean that someone else, perhaps Glamis himself, had made the phony attempts on James. Glamis was capable of such humor.

Calvin Burleigh loathed Glamis; or rather, found Glamis' behavior and attitudes loathsome. Yes, he would be capable of killing the man then praying for his soul. And Burleigh might have known that James was going to study the Rosetta stone book that night, and would not go to the lab to examine the box.

Anyone could have purloined Shirley's imitation Vaec box, and Burleigh would have had time to make the substitution before Glamis got to the lab. Shirley, however, didn't fit into that category. Had she gone to the lab after supper and the meeting in the recreation room, she would have been seen by one of the watching Vaec.

Unless James had indicated to her, without saying what it was, that he had something of importance he was going to work on in his quarters. But that might have applied to any of the others. It was clear, however, that the substitution was made before the meeting in the recreation room. And that was the best argument for the apparent solution: that Glamis had been caught in a trap prepared for Howard James.

But the person most likely to get a hint of James' change in plans was Amelia, and Amelia hated Glamis. The misdirection made sense in her case, and somehow the ineptness of the two attempts suggested Amelia's attempts to be clever.

As to James himself, there was motive, although it did not seem to be strong enough for murder. There was certainly opportunity. But would James have blundered so badly? He could have arranged some other sort of accident, without any preliminaries. And the stopping of the field work hurt him far more than he presumably had to gain by Glamis' death.

Burleigh or Edholm, however, might well have wanted to put an end to the expedition, but he couldn't see Edholm doing it that way. On the other hand, the very fact that James was in no real danger from either attempt suggested a person like Burleigh, who would not harm an innocent person in order to get someone else. Not do physical harm, that is. Any psychological suffering that James underwent as a result of the abrupt frustration of his work would probably be justified in Burleigh's mind by the good he would be doing the "uncorrupted natives."

Howard James had suffered an emotional breakdown after the Marlene affair and another misfortune in his profession might bring on a second. Burleigh considered himself called to combat unrighteousness. Shirley had been afraid. Amelia hated. Did she also fear Glamis for some reason? Edholm—where did he fit?

Auckland's thoughts turned to Kenneth Glamis, whom he

had last seen alive working over the microscope in the laboratory, and jotting down notes. Then, how had Phrecle put it, "Excellent Kenneth looks up from microscope and delivers instruction to self. Then puts microscope away and takes out camera." Glamis was in the habit of muttering to himself while working.

Somewhere in this maze of conjectures and evidence there was a pattern, Auckland thought, as he felt the sand around his neck. And now the pieces were beginning to fall into shape. His thoughts raced even more swiftly as the sands crept up his face and they all confirmed the suspicion he was holding when he had last spoken to Ekem-ve. Yes, yes, he was sure he knew who was out there, watching him go down. But the case was still incomplete, the clinching details missing. He ought to see it, ought to see it all now.

The thought of his own blindness was bitter in Auckland's heart as the sands touched his nostrils. He drew in a deep breath and felt them rise over his head.

## CHAPTER THIRTEEN

THERE WAS an instant of suffocation, then the giddy feeling again, and Roy Auckland was lying on something. He took a deep breath cautiously. There was air, pure air around him. Then a wave of exhaustion swept over him.

When he opened his eyes again, darkness was complete, but his mind was clear and the paralysis was gone. And now he knew where he was; he was back at headquarters, lying on his own bunk. He sent out a thought of thanks for the rescue, hoping that the Vaec would pick it up.

It was clear enough what had happened: they had teleported him to safety—a short distance when needles were being fired at him, then the much longer distance to his own quarters as he sank beneath the quicksand. What of the paralysis? He could only assume that the Vaec were also capable of control over him; a control they had declined to use upon Earthmen except in this one instance. Why?

It was most obvious: so that the culprit would see Roy Auckland sink beneath the quicksand and consider him finished. "Thanks," he thought to his potential listeners. "Will you do one more thing? Will you come to headquarters if I find I need your help in trapping the murderer? Just Ekem-ve and Hcent?"

There was no answer, which could mean that he hadn't been heard, or that the Vaec could not transmit their thoughts to him. He looked at his watch. It was nearing 10:00 P.M. according to the adjustments they had made to make the Carolinian day seem roughly equal to that of Earth. He had started back to headquarters around 7:00.

He arose and changed, wishing he had time to take a shower. There was a knock on the door. He opened it to see Shirley Mason. "Oh," she said. "I didn't think you'd come back yet, but Dr. James asked me to see, anyway." She gripped his arm. "Roy, something has happened and we're all stunned. Amelia killed herself."

Her words were a blow to his mental solar plexus. "Amelia…"

He saw now that she looked weary and frightened. There was no suggestion of surprise that he had returned. "They're all sitting around in the rec-room," she said, then added, "No one is blaming you."

"Wait," he whispered as he shut the door behind him.

"Did you examine the needle in the box?"

"Yes. It was *dodlig* mixed with tree gum to make it adhere. You couldn't smell the stuff though, any more than you could when it was in the doctor's soup."

And this, he thought, required a knowledge of chemistry.

One had to know how to extract the essence of *dodlig* from

other plants. He looked at Shirley Mason and wondered if anyone else in the expedition knew chemistry. But one more thing was clear; another item on those missing pages of the report. When swallowed, *dodlig* was quick and painless; when injected or absorbed through a break in the skin, the reaction was like a sting of a virulent insect or the bite of a poisonous serpent. He followed Shirley into the recreation room.

He looked at the assembly, who returned his glance in stony silence, then turned to Howard James who was slumped in a chair. "I'm sorry," he said. It was a totally inadequate statement, but anything further would have been meaningless. "I've failed all around."

James lifted a hand slightly. "No, Roy," he said tiredly. "You couldn't have prevented it had you been here."

"How did it happen?"

"She wanted to die, Roy," said Burleigh, "though only God knows the full reason why. All we know is that she was determined to end her life. She doped us all so that we couldn't prevent her, or find her in time."

At Auckland's puzzled frown, Edholm said, "We had just finished supper when I suddenly felt terribly sleepy. I tried to get out of my chair, and the next thing I knew Calvin here was shaking me and it was hours later. We'd all been asleep around the table, except Amelia. She wasn't there. She'd gone to her room and taken a lethal dose of sleeping pills. We found the empty bottle and an empty glass on the stand beside her bed."

"We were knocked out for about three hours or so," Shirley put in. "Amelia served the coffee at supper tonight, and she obviously put half a pill into each cup except hers. As you know, drinking them with anything hot makes them react almost immediately. Whether she took her own dose hot or cold I don't know. In either case, she'd have gone to sleep in no less than half an hour and after another hour nothing could be done for her."

"Where is she?"

"We left her where we found her."

Auckland rose. "I'll be back in a few moments," he said.

Shirley arose also and followed him out of the room.

It was hard to think of Amelia James as dead, Auckland thought, as he looked at the peaceful features of the dark-haired woman. And harder still to believe that she had killed herself. Somehow, it didn't fit with what he knew of her character. A passionate woman, yearning for life, might possibly kill herself over rejection by someone she wanted. But Amelia wasn't that sort.

"Did she leave any kind of note?" he asked Shirley.

The blonde shook her head. "And she hadn't been acting strangely, either, Roy."

"You don't think it was suicide, Shirl?"

"I—I..." Suddenly her shoulders were shaking violently, her head was buried against his chest, her arms around him convulsively. "I didn't want her to die! I didn't want anyone to die! I hated them both but I didn't want them to die!"

Auckland held her close, making comforting noises, and found himself looking toward the doorway. "Ekem-ve . . ." he started to say, then stopped as he realized no one was there. This was the second time he'd been sure a Vaec was present when none was around. What was it?

His nostrils dilated suddenly and he realized what it was: something he smelled. The faint but somewhat pleasing aroma of the Vaec, like a very discreet perfume. .

Perfume! He released Shirley gently and said, "I think I have it," and picked up the glass beside the bed. He sniffed. Yes, it was there. And that had been what he smelled on the needle in the box. It had all fallen into place now. He looked at the girl and said quietly, "We'd better join the others. It's time for the last act in this devilish little drama."

His heart felt icy as they left the room because he realized now that the case he had might be exactly what the culprit wanted him to have.

As they entered the room, Dr. James was saying, "…so you see the worst about us, Ekem-ve. Dr. Burleigh here thinks that we are not fit to associate with you and I'm beginning to wonder if he isn't right."

Ekem-ve and Hcent were standing over near the door, their single hairs straight up and unmoving. Ekem-ve said, "Excellent Earthmen not perfect. Vaec not perfect either. Like Earthman, Vaec seek help of Creator in following path to perfection. Often fail."

Auckland sent a mental "Thanks for coming" to the Vaec and said, "Much harm has been done by a most imperfect Earth person, and you can help us discover that one so we can see that harm stops."

He did not offer them seats, as the two were playing the part of natives again, who would not sit down in the presence of their superiors.

"Someone," Auckland said, "was surprised when I came into the room tonight. But that someone is a good actor. I'm referring to the person who tried to prevent me from returning at all; the person who first tried to shoot me with a poisoned needle and then lured me into quicksand and left me to sink." He nodded at the Vaec. "Thanks to my friends, I got back safely."

"No mirth in murder, excellent Roy," said Hcent.

"No mirth in finding a murderer either," Auckland said.

"One of you will not be surprised, either, when I tell you that Amelia James did not commit suicide." He paused and looked around. Shirley was breathing harder. Edholm blinked rapidly. Burleigh leaned forward, a puzzled but intent look on his face. James sat like one sunk in apathy.

"Ekem-ve," Auckland went on, "did Dr. Glamis obtain a sample of perfume from the Vaec?"

"Yes, excellent Roy. Excellent Kenneth desire it for study. Say that it may bring mirth to many Earth females if can be analyzed, reproduced by Earthmen and brought back to home planet."

"I was puzzled for a long time," Auckland went on, "about the way the *dodlig* was put into Dr. James' thermos bottle. It suggested that whoever did it must have an excellent knowledge of chemistry. Then I remembered that Phrecle had said something about *dodlig* losing its pleasing aroma when mixed with the soup.

"It seemed to me then that *dodlig*, which smells so distasteful to us, must have a pleasing odor to Vaec. I had never smelled it on any of them, but that could be explained by the fact that they knew we disliked it and were careful not to come into our presence bearing the scent.

"But if this were the case, then I should have smelled some *dodlig* in the village, and I didn't." He smiled wryly. "But minute quantities of the plant, refined, might be used in making a perfume which did indeed have a pleasing aroma. Am I right, Hcent? Is your perfume made with a *dodlig* base?"

"Excellent Roy speaks wisdom," replied the Vaec.

"So," Auckland continued, "you will all please remain where you are while Hcent searches our rooms for some sort of container of Vaec perfume. Someone obtained Dr. Glamis' sample, or part of it, to commit two murders—there was a trace of perfume in Amelia's glass."

"But I never smelled any perfume," objected Edholm.

"It isn't strong," Auckland said, "and the Vaec are nearly always wearing it. That's why I thought Ekem-ve was around twice when he wasn't; I smelled perfume without realizing it."

"But why would anyone want to kill Amelia?" asked James bewilderedly, as Hcent went out.

"Maybe she discovered something dangerous to the culprit," suggested Burleigh. "Do you think Hcent will be able to find the perfume if it's there?"

"Phrecle smelled a trace of it in the thermos bottle," Auckland answered. "But I don't think it will be concealed. There was no reason to conceal it since the killer was confident that its meaning would not be suspected and could always say that it had been obtained from Glamis, or might even admit snitching some from him."

Hcent came back a moment later, holding a test tube and two sheets of paper, which they recognized as the missing pages from the report. Auckland shot a thought at her, then asked, "Where was it, Hcent?"

"In cabinet in kitchen, excellent Roy." She held up the tube. "Much perfume here, call to seeker with clear voice. Not have to search."

"Well," sighed Edholm, "we have it, for all the help that finding it does us."

"But what were those papers doing with it?" James asked.

He looked at Burleigh. "Calvin, you took them from the report a week or so ago. I saw you taking them out and didn't think anything of it at the time." His eyes widened. "My God, you're the one, Calvin," he whispered.

He looked around him wildly, then continued. "So many things fall into place when the key is found. Your quarrels with Glamis. I always thought they were because you objected to his religious views and his behavior with Amelia. But, of course, you were jealous of him. You wanted her yourself, and he was always belittling you in her eyes. You killed him! And then, when you found that she still would have none of you, you killed her!"

"You forget I was drugged this evening," replied Burleigh.

"One person was not drugged," said Auckland. "One person had to get Amelia to her room, revive her, and induce her to drink poison. One person had to be awake and alert to try to prevent me from returning.

"That person knew that there would be time for both projects, and to get back to the table and feign unconsciousness before the others revived."

"You and Glamis were having an argument about Amelia last week, Burleigh," Edholm said. "I wasn't eavesdropping, but I heard your voices when I went by and couldn't help but catch part of the drift."

Burleigh nodded. "That much is true...the rest is false."

"Hcent," Auckland said, "now is the time for truth." He looked about the room. "I arranged with the Vaec to say the perfume and missing pages had been found in the kitchen, just as I arranged for them to say that the imitation box had been found in the shrubbery outside the building. I ask you now to tell us truthfully where all these things were found."

Hcent blinked. "All found in excellent Calvin's room."

Burleigh said nothing for a moment, then muttered softly, "The Vaec do not lie when asked to speak the truth. Then these things were found in my room. But I did not put them there. And the pages from the report—it's true that I borrowed some, but it wasn't those pages, and I put them back."

Auckland stood up. "This killer overlooked many things, and made many stupid moves. One of the things overlooked was that the Vaec perfume is quite penetrating. Ekem-ve, Hcent, who here is wearing Vaec perfume?"

The two Carolinians pointed at Shirley Mason. "Very faint," Ekem-ve said. "Excellent Shirley dilutes much."

Shirley opened her mouth, a look of horror on her face, then buried her face in her hands. "No," gasped James. He turned to Burleigh. "I—I can't believe it. Then I was wrong, about you. I—I told Auckland that I was sure that Glamis was blackmailing someone, though I didn't know who it was.

I thought it was Amelia…but it must have been Shirley."

He shook his head. "He must have made life unbearable for you. But you didn't have to be afraid. No one is executed for murder any more. The treatment is painless. You had good reason for killing him, but…"

"He forced me to come on this expedition," she sobbed. "I can't tell you the things he made me do. I wanted him to die. I hoped he'd get stung some night when he took me out without his protective suit. But nothing ever happened to him. Only…I didn't kill him."

"Miss Mason," said Edholm, "it will be much easier if you confess now. Examination under the detectors is very unpleasant. Not physical torture, but worse. You will have to tell everything you know about any question asked. You will try desperately to hold back things that really are not relevant, but hurt terribly to tell. If you confess of your own free will, then you will be asked only if you have told the truth, and nothing else will go on the public record."

"Just a minute," objected Burleigh. "I've just been on the hook myself, and it looked pretty black against me. Now it looks black against her, but maybe we're not at the truth yet."

"My fault," said Auckland, chiding himself for forgetting that the Vaec were playing the 'simple native' roles again, and thus answering what was literally asked rather than what was meant. He looked at James for a moment, then said, "Doctor, I'm stumped."

"You've done good work, Roy," James said. "It was you who thought of the right question to ask them. I'm sorry it had to be this answer."

"Oh, that isn't what has me baffled, Howard. I've been sure of the truth for some time now. But the motive, the motive, hasn't come out yet. I've been unable to deduce you see, so I shall have to ask you to tell us exactly why you killed Kenneth Glamis and your wife."

"Roy! You're out of your mind!"

"On the contrary. You missed something that Ekem-ve just said. He said that Shirley was wearing the perfume and that she dilutes it. But the perfume that was used to kill was undiluted, and the person who handled it evinces traces of it in full strength. What I should have asked was: Who here has traces of the perfume in full strength on his clothing, such as the inside of a pocket?"

The fingers now pointed at Dr. Howard James. "Inside pocket of jacket declares perfume," said Hcent.

"But I didn't put on my jacket until after we found Amelia," protested James. "Anyone could have put a drop of perfume there."

"But no one could have tampered with your drink, Doctor," said Auckland. He picked up the glass and held it out to Ekem-ve.

"Yes, excellent Roy," the Carolinian said.

"I've been watching you, you see, and I saw you pass your hand over the glass a little while ago. Yes, there's a vitamin capsule dissolving in it. A capsule which you no doubt opened and dosed with perfume."

James closed his eyes and murmured, "Amelia," softly.

## CHAPTER FOURTEEN

DR. HOWARD JAMES opened his eyes and sighed deeply. "Yes, I killed him," he said. "An affair was one thing. That I could tolerate. But she was going to divorce me and marry him. That I could not endure." He shook his head. "How she found out, I'll never know, but she did. And then when I found she was going to denounce me…"

He looked at Burleigh. "I was jealous of you, too. It seemed to me that her dislike of you was too pointed; I didn't believe it. And once she was ready to leave me, I wanted to kill every other man she had anything to do with."

Auckland took out his notebook. "That was an interesting confession, Doctor," he said to James. "I wondered if you wouldn't say something like that when you were confronted."

"What put you on to him, Roy?" asked Burleigh.

Auckland brushed off a few grains of sand on the cover.

"You know," he said to Edholm, "I don't think it will be necessary to make that test about the concussive force of a pellet exploded in the basement of the villa."

"The pellets have been tested," said James. "If a flying block had hit me, it would have killed me, or crippled me seriously. Had it been out iii the open, the concussion would have been fatal. It was a damned dangerous joke for him to pull on me. I could have been so absorbed that I didn't hear the timer ticking."

"It's quite a loud tick," Edholm said, "but as you say..." There was relief in the air now, relief and a certain measure of sympathy, tempered with caution. Retributive justice, they all knew, was a thing of the past. James would be neither executed nor tortured for his crimes; he would be treated. But that treatment, while restoring him to sanity, would leave him with an inescapable horror at himself, something which only a strong belief in divine mercy could alleviate. In either case, the rest of his life would be spent in atonement.

But he hadn't been treated yet. The madness that had expressed itself in murder was still on him. He must be prevented from adding to his offenses, for his own sake as well as that of those who stood to suffer from them.

Roy Auckland looked at him, and at the glass that had been put on the table beside Edholm. "You asked me how I got on to the truth." He smiled wryly. "I lied to you a moment ago, Doctor, when I said I was unable to deduce your motive. The fact is, I had deduced it. But I wasn't positive of it until just now. When you tried to commit suicide, you made your final and fatal error so far as your objectives are concerned.

"Huh?" asked Burleigh.

James looked up pleadingly. "You're wrong, Roy. It was Amelia. Just Amelia. I was made to kill her."

Shirley Mason gasped. "Of course! It's so simple. If he died, his confession couldn't be checked on. We could never be sure that the motive he confessed to was the true one."

"Right. So long as the true motive was not known, there was always a chance that you could reap the benefit from your crimes, even though you did not live to see it. And that is why the full truth must come out now. When you came to see me, you referred to your solution of the problem of the Vaec here on Carolus.

"I put it to you that you had already delivered a partial report on it, and that you have been working up a full report of what we will call the James hypothesis—one which would give you considerable fame among archaeologists if it were accepted—and the chances seemed very good.

"You never got over the loss of reputation you suffered through innocent involvement in the Marlene hoax. Reputable standing in science has been your obsession ever since. You could not endure to have your hypothesis questioned. That was the basis of your antagonism toward Kenneth Glamis, not his affair with your wife."

"You mean he killed Glamis because Glamis was heckling him?" Edholm sounded incredulous.

"Much more than that." He turned to the Carolinians.

"Ekem-ve, it is true, is it not, that Kenneth Glamis passed the tests you have been putting us all to, and was told the true nature of the Vaec?"

"Yes, excellent Roy, this is true. Excellent Kenneth became special friend of Vaec and learn many things hidden to others who do not understand. Prepare long joke on foolish colleague."

"And that was the beginning of the tragedy. Glamis was now vastly amused by the James hypothesis, but the joke he planned was a cruel one. He made a full report on tape, that I am sure he planned to make public *after* Dr. James had staked his reputation on errors—errors that he could not be greatly blamed for making. But Glamis couldn't keep it to himself completely. He threw hints to Amelia James—hints that she, as a loyal wife, despite her philandering, told her husband.

"That was when you decided to put an end to the expedition, Doctor, and to kill Glamis. You wanted to make sure that no one else would learn anything from the Vaec which would make your hypothesis suspect. At the same time, you would make it appear as if someone was trying to kill you, so that Glamis' death would appear to be accidental, as if he got something intended for you. And I was to solve the case the way you rigged it.

"It was clear to me from the first that the most likely explanation of the two inept attempts was that you had arranged them yourself, particularly when I found that we had noiseless timers with me. Just the poison in the soup might have worked; in fact, I think it would have deceived me, because anyone might not have known that Phrecle could smell perfume in it. How did you know about Glamis?"

"I knew he was against me," James said. "I knew he had something up his sleeve. The way he went to his room one night with a smirk on his face. I looked through the window —he didn't always have the shutters closed tightly—and saw him talking into the tape-maker."

"Then you contrived to go to his room later, when he was out, and listen to it. And I assume that, among other things, he mentioned that the Vaec perfume was made from a *dodlig* base." He turned to Shirley. "Are the methods of finding out the amount of *dodlig* in the perfume difficult?"

She shook her head. "No, if you know what test to run, it's very simple." She frowned. "And the instructions are on file here. I think anyone of us could follow them."

"You also learned about the Vaec boxes and the pet bees, although not quite enough. You didn't know they were incapable of stinging. And you knew about the imitation box that Shirley and Glamis had made. So you asked Ekem-ve to bring you a Vaec box for study. Ekem-ve, did the doctor also ask for a pet bee, too?"

"Yes, excellent Roy. Ask us not to say anything about bee. Say he plan harmless joke."

"And, of course, since the bee could not sting, it seemed harmless enough. But there were two things that made me sure it was James who was trying to frame someone— Burleigh, most likely—rather than someone else using the phony murder attempts as misdirection.

"On the night of the murder, Ekem-ve, Phrecle, Syeltan, and Hcent were watching all of us. Phrecle reported that, after the meeting in the rec-room, when we all were looking at the Rosetta stone book, Glamis came out of Dr. James' room, and went to his own.

"Syeltan, who was watching that part of the building, reported that Glamis was hunting for something in his room, very hurriedly. It was growing dark gradually, and Glamis closed the shutters on his window completely, and turned on the lights. I asked if they were sure it was Glamis, and they said he was wearing the protective suit. And of course, he was the only one of us they've ever seen wearing one.

"We all have suits, but look at this more carefully. First, Glamis was not seen *going* to James' room, suit or no suit, and he could not have gone there from the rec-room without stepping outside the building. However, this alone might just indicate that he went there before Phrecle came on watch, or Phrecle wasn't looking in the right direction at the moment.

"But why should Glamis be wearing a protective suit after sundown in the first place? We know that he didn't like wearing them. We know that when he went out on evenings, he didn't wear them. Why should he put on a suit either to go to James' room, or put on one there, just to walk back to his own room? Still more, Glamis was careless about the shutters in his room. A good part of the time, they weren't closed at all, or only partly closed. It all fits very well though when we see that a figure in a protective suit in partial darkness might be assumed to be Kenneth Glamis, but in full light, one could see clearly who was wearing the suit.

"James found the tape, took it and went through the building to Burleigh's room, probably taking off the suit and putting it in the rec-room closet, and picking up a book on the way. He was seen leaving Burleigh's room carrying a book. The tape was behind it. I assume you erased it or destroyed it, Doctor."

"I expunged those malicious lies," said James heatedly. "He poisoned you all against me. He wasn't fit to live!"

"Now," said Auckland, "we come to the most curious part of the evening. Ekem-ve had left a Vaec box in the lab, which James was presumed to examine that night. Glamis went out with Shirley for awhile, then went to the lab where Phrecle reports, he was doing some microscope work. Then, after a while, he stopped." He leafed through the pages of the notebook. " 'Excellent Kenneth looks up from microscope and delivers instruction to self. Then puts microscope away and takes out camera. Puts box on table and starts to take pictures of box. Excellent Howard unshutters window.'

"Glamis had not closed the shutters on the lab window. Why should he? James called Amelia to the window beside him and they both watched Glamis photographing the box, then Glamis looked up and saw them, and waved to them.

Thereupon both parties drew the shutters on their windows.

"But this was not the box that Ekem-ve had delivered! This was the imitation box that Glamis and Shirley had made. Now, why would Glamis suddenly stop work on his own project to take photographs of a box he recognized as an imitation? I refer you to that phrase, 'delivers instruction to self.' Phrecle could see that he was talking, but could not hear; he knew as we all knew that Glamis did talk to himself while he was working.

"The answer is simple: Glamis wasn't talking to himself.

He was talking to someone on the intercom, someone who asked him to photograph the box and close the shutters of the window while he was doing it. If anyone but James had asked this, Glamis would have said, 'This isn't a Vaec box, it's an imitation.' But for a laugh on Howard James, he'd go through the motions."

"But how is it Amelia didn't hear him?" asked Shirley.

"She was there in the room."

"Perhaps he asked her not to say anything about that, because it would cast suspicion on him. But more likely, she was asleep or dozing. Phrecle said she came to the window slowly and looked annoyed. Why? Perhaps because she had been awakened for what didn't seem to be a good reason."

"She was dozing," said James.

"The phony box with its death trap was substituted between the time we got back from the villa and supper. The shutters had to be closed, otherwise Glamis' death might have been witnessed. In the morning, James stepped into the lab and substituted the boxes again, concealing the imitation in Burleigh's room."

Auckland sighed. "I thought the watch could be taken off by dawn. That was a foolish mistake on my part. James had set intercoms through the building at open and listened in to everything I said to Ekem-ve. He knew then that he would be free to move without observation between daylight and rising time for the rest of us. I did not foresee Glamis' death. What I expected was another rigged attempt on James himself and hoped to catch him at it.

"Then James killed the pet bee and put it on the floor himself."

"He wasn't content to make it look like an accident," sighed Burleigh. "He wanted to saddle me with the whole plot. Then, I suppose, he'd arrange for me to commit suicide, so I couldn't be examined and my innocence proved."

"Exactly. Later, he learned through listening in with my conversation with you, that I was going to see Ekem-ve. What he did that night is what he accused you of doing: doping everyone, poisoning Amelia, then going out to take care of me."

Howard James' hand had slipped down into a corner of his chair. Now he lifted it, and they saw that he was holding a needlegun. He rose quickly.

"You're all against me," he said petulantly. "You're all letting yourselves be taken in by these jokers, whose one ambition in life seems to be to have a good laugh at someone's expense. I hoped I could make you see reason, but you're ready to sacrifice science for the sake of a worthless clown and his native stooges. And to listen to an amateur Sherlock Holmes.

"I hoped this wouldn't be necessary. I didn't want to kill her, either, but you forced me to it. Now I'm leaving and I advise you not to try to find me. You didn't think I was so stupid as not to have another plan ready in case of accidents, did you, Roy? You'll all be dead soon, anyway, and this time I have a foolproof explanation worked out. But first, we'll take care of these stooges."

Shirley screamed as he turned the gun toward Ekem-ve and Hcent, but the two Vaec showed no signs of alarm.

James' finger tightened and then a look of horror crossed his face and the gun fell from his fingers. It all happened even while Auckland was leaping toward the man, and he didn't see what the doctor and the others, who were following his gaze, were staring at: a little pile of needles which had suddenly appeared on top of the file cabinet several feet away.

An instant later, Auckland had hit the doctor, and the two were rolling on the floor. James was up first. He reached the door and was outside…

No! He was sitting in the chair again, his mouth open.

"I've gone mad," Burleigh whispered. "I'm seeing things!"

"No you're not, Cal," said Auckland, picking himself up and drawing Shirley, who was running to him, into his arms. "Ekem-ve, you've got to tell them now. I leave it to your wisdom as to how much. But they've got to know the meaning of it."

"You are right, Roy," said Ekem-ve, blinking rapidly. "Excellent Earthmen, two foolish natives have much to tell you, and much to ask your forgiveness for."

The two Vaec stood there, the single hairs on their heads flat down and backward, as Ekem-ve finished, saying, "but we, too, have become trapped in pride, for we rashly assumed that we understood you, Earthmen, and were confident that our tests would bring you no harm."

Burleigh shook his head. "And I, and others, were worried about our corrupting you. You are far ahead of us in so many ways. If our own pride was of as little moment…"

"The Creator has given us certain powers which seem great to you—such as what you call teleporting, as we did with the needles in Dr. James' gun, and returning him here when he tried to flee. Or what you would call hypnotic control, which makes it impossible for him to move, now, although he can see and hear us. But you, too, were given far more powers than you realize, and when you learn them, it may be that the Vaec will be simple natives in comparison."

He looked at James. "You were right about one thing, Doctor, and if you had only been content to accept the book which we left for you, and let the rest of your theory give way to truth, surely other Earthmen would have honored you. We are indeed that other culture which those whom you call the Old Martians knew.

"But we are not natives of this planet, nor colonists, nor the descendants of colonists. Our lives are very long, and we see now that this alone makes it harmful to be in contact with you, so long as yours are so short by comparison. This one thing alone would make you feel frustrated, envious, hating. It would stand in the way of your own development as an almost impassable barrier."

"You mean," asked Edholm, "man has the capacity to be long-lived, without things like the rejuvenation treatments?"

"The Creator did not intend humans to live but a day, Captain. When you learn to live as you were created to live, this and many other things now hidden from you will be yours. If we could teach you how to help yourselves, we would gladly do it. But we cannot. So we must depart."

"Amazing," said Burleigh. "That magnificent structure in the desert—all part of a joke, which was really a test of our ability to understand." He smiled at Auckland. "But some of us passed it, at least."

"Perhaps we all would have in time," said Shirley, "if this hadn't happened."

"Don't feel bitter about might-have-beens, Shirl," said Auckland. "It might have been much worse in the long run. But, Ekem-ve, just what are the Vaec doing here on Carolus? If it's something that's safe for us to know," he added.

"We are what you might call vacationists, Roy, This is one; of the Vaec's vacation planets. Now it is time for us all to return to our vocations." He looked around the group. "We shall miss this planet, which, as you have seen, is very beautiful. But we give it to you gladly and hope that you will find true mirth here."

"Then we won't see you any more?" asked Burleigh.

"When Earthmen and Vaec can meet again without harm, you will find us easily. Until then, you will never find us, however diligently you search. I hope that no Earthmen, will disbelieve us and beat against futility. Farewell."

The two Vaec wiggled their fingers and turned toward the door. There was an instant of silence. Auckland, Shirley, Edholm, and Burleigh stepped to the window, to see them walking away slowly. Then the two were gone. They turned as a gasping moan came from James' chair.

"The capsules. The vitamin capsules," he gasped. "Don't take any. I poisoned them…"

He tried to get up out of the chair, then fell back and slumped forward. Edholm bent over him. "He's in a state of shock. Psychosomatic, I'd guess, though it's only a guess." He passed a hand across his brow. "The supply ship is due in a few days, and three of us can return to Earth with it. Two will have to remain until its next trip, or a special ship is sent. He'll be one of the three to go, of course."

Shirley's hand stole into Auckland's and squeezed. He squeezed back.

In the morning, they drove the crawler to the village and found it deserted, the artifacts left behind. There would be much Vaec material here to study. He wondered if the doors in the villa would still open, and if the lights would still go on. On the way back, Auckland was bitten by an ant-like insect that they had never seen before. It stung like fire, but was apparently harmless otherwise.

"Now that the spurious aspects of this puzzle planet have been cleared up," he said, "we can get to the real problems. There may be deadly insect and animal life here, no longer kept away from us by the Vaec. Sure you want to stay?"

She indicated beyond any possible shadow of doubt that she was sure. When they arrived back, Burleigh met them, his face grave. "Howard had another poisoned capsule on him," he said. "He must have come to during the night and taken it, may he rest in peace.

"There'll be three graves here to tend now. And to be a reminder, I hope." He added, "I wouldn't mind staying on alone, if you two want to return to Earth."

He smiled faintly as he said it, knowing that they would not take him up on the offer. "Very well, then, you colonists are detailed to accompany me with shovels. Pioneers have to get practice in digging."

## THE END